ALSO BY GEORGE M. _____.

Mainly Fair Throughout The Kingdom

For Ainslie
Our lovely and loving daughter

CONTENTS

RADICAL ROADS

This story follows on from the novel *Mainly Fair Throughout the Kingdom.*

As the Kingdom of Nepal entered the year 2057 on the Bikram Sambat calendar, it was 2001 on the Gregorian calendar in Europe. Nepal is also fifteen minutes ahead of India on the international timeline despite sharing the same north/south border. Time can be selective as well as relative.

PROLOGUE

I find a shoe box in my mother's attic with loose papers and an old draft of dad's book on Hatha Yoga. The manuscript is typed, with quotes highlighted, both famous and obscure. Beside each one, dad has written an alternative meaning in pencil. Next to a guru's instruction never to feel guilty, dad writes, 'there is a need for guilt in self correction. Guilt is not a negative state when it forces one to change for the better.'

These are written clues. A time capsule from before I was born. Among a pile of loose papers, a first wedding anniversary card from my father to my mother. Inside, a poem.

Figure This

Figure is... shape,
Form
And content.
A figure of speech
Is
Of interest
Popular

Passed on.
Influencing opinions
More than fact.
Each recommendation
A jest
Rather than an instruction.
Drawing attention
Discovering
A figure of speech
Helps to be persuaded.
Repeating one
The easiest way
To influence.
Until with one stroke
The user turns
From philosopher to bigot
From poet to insurgent.
Until art marries industry
Go figure.

— J. MUNRO

In pencil dad has scribbled the following, as an afterthought, typical of his thinking process.

Take a fact
Give it a turn of speech
And screw it into
A browsing brain.
It will be adored

Imagine for a moment, I think, being married to a man like that.

PART ONE: A LAND LESS CLEMENT

1

FRIDAY 1ST JUNE 2001 ON THE GREGORIAN CALENDAR

I t's late night in Nepal and afternoon in Edinburgh. I return to our New Town flat from a short run and find a message on our answering machine. It's from Thapa Rai at the Nepal Culture Centre in Kathmandu and it's only a few moments old.

I listen to a faint voice, asking me to call him back immediately. Since I agreed to contribute to his new project *Perspectives on Nepalese Culture*, 'A Foreigner's Findings', these urgent requests are always about writing deadlines I've missed.

I take a shower, thinking this deadline is still some weeks off. I have plenty time. All that's left is for me to incorporate a passage about the King of Nepal as a living example of Nepali culture. He is, after all, the international face of the country. That jewel of tranquillity set in the Himalaya, or 'zone of peace' as King Birendra calls it, is universally popular with world travellers. Wherever the King visits, he is welcomed by leaders from a politically diverse group of countries. He can travel into India as one of their own.

Sita returns from her afternoon yoga class. She is with our teenage son, Ram. She tells me our twin four-year-old daughters have gone off to Peebles for the weekend, to stay with my mum.

Ram seems upset and I hear Sita telling him not to worry.

'People use minor setbacks as practice for coping. Teenagers even make up drama in their lives as a rehearsal.'

'That makes perfect sense, mum,' says Ram, with a slap of sarcasm.

Sita's gems of yogic wisdom can be badly timed these days.

'It's hard finding friends at a new school.' Ram sulks.

'Tell your dad what happened, while I make some Dhal Bhat.'

'He'll say, find someone to laugh it off with, and I'll discover a friend.'

Our boy knows us well.

IT'S OVER TWELVE YEARS SINCE THE THREE OF US ARRIVED IN SCOTLAND AS a family. The culmination of my three-year stay in Nepal, was to return with a wife and child. I'd gone off in search of my father's Nepali guru, the Moni Baba, but that's another story

As I towel dry my hair, I dig out my laptop. I tell Sita Thapa is hounding me on a deadline, and I will have to find my draft to review it. I pour myself a glass of Ribena, making it froth from the pressure of the tap. Ram joins us in the kitchen.

'So how *was* school today?'

I see our boy's face flinch at the mention of school. He's only recently moved school, losing close friends from the old, and is in limbo to assess new ones. I hear the phone ring and Sita goes off to answer it in the living room.

I continue discussing petty prejudices with Ram until I glimpse Sita coming back into view. She stops and supports herself in the door frame. She stays frozen, as if another step is physically impossible. I see vacant grief on her face. As I approach her, Ram joins me to hold her up.

My mind searches for an explanation. Ram asks what's wrong. Sita looks straight through him. I see her eyes roll and I begin to fear whatever she might say next. She looks at me.

'Swami Y called from Kathmandu.'

'What's happened?'

'There's terrible news from Nepal.'

Dread spills into my throat. I fear news of my dad or one of our friends.

'Speak, Sita.'

'There's been a killing... at the Royal Palace.'

'What?'

'King Birendra and Queen Aishwarya and most of the royal family, have all been murdered.'

Her words sting, but it's not the agony I readied myself for. I feel confusion and a guilty shiver of relief. It's a near miss for personal grief.

'What happened?'

'They were all shot and are dead.' Sita looks completely devastated.

'When did it happen, who did it? Was it the Maoists?'

After a moment, Sita controls herself.

'No, it happened only a few hours ago. Swami Y says that the Palace are telling the public that the royal family have ascended. But he's heard news coming out of India that Crown Prince Dipendra did this terrible deed. The prince shot his whole family.'

'The crown prince... my god, what a thing to happen.'

At news of the prince's actions, Ram begins to cry too.

As the potential consequences of this event sink in, I sense how personal this loss is for Sita and all our friends in Nepal. I hear Sita begin to chant in a whisper and rock while she holds Ram in her arms. Her condition releases an empathic wave of pain over me, too. I hold her tightly: it's not an emotional near miss, it's a delayed direct hit. We both hold Ram close as Sita sobs and wails.

A core pillar of Nepal's belief system has just been destroyed. Sita's god has been murdered. In Nepal, there will now be thirteen days of mourning and much uncertainty about the future. Sita, Ram and I hug while time disappears around us.

SITA RARELY TALKS ABOUT HER EARLY LIFE IN NEPAL. SHE HAD AN extraordinary childhood there, but much is still her secret. I have never sought all the details simply because she's moved confidently forward with her yogic approach to life here. She's always treated the past as something unchangeable, crudely defined by memories. It's standard eastern philosophy. Our future is something we are largely ignorant of, and human happiness is strongly related to that ignorance.

Sita's birthname is Momika Shakya and from the age of four she was a Kumari, one of Nepal's living goddesses in the Kathmandu Valley. Both Buddhist and Hindus revere the Kumari. She is chosen from a family clan, the Shakya. It's the clan from which the Buddha originally came.

Her monarch King Birendra, the one who's just been shot, visited her regularly when she was a child. She was raised in a Newar tradition that stretches back centuries and she was brought up on the myths and stories from Nepal's rich and varied culture. That tradition later cast her out when she reached puberty, to be replaced by another young living goddess.

Unlike her predecessors, Sita was adopted as a teenager by one of Nepal's most eminent yogis, the Moni Baba. She then lived her adolescent life in rural villages where the Baba travelled and instructed her in hatha yoga. The name Sita was given as a term of affection, then later in recognition of her accomplishments. Many former Kumaris have lived out their life uneducated and in poverty after the religious spotlight was switched off at puberty. They remained unmarried because of a perceived death curse on those who might marry them. A superstition I suppress daily.

I first met Sita Kumari because the Moni Baba was also the guru my father followed in the 1970s. He was the man I left Scotland to seek out, only to discover that my father, whom I believed dead, was in fact living as a recluse named Avadhoot in rural Nepal.

Our relationship has mended somewhat since.

I HUNGER FOR MORE INFORMATION AND DIAL NEPAL. AFTER MY FIFTH TRY, I finally get through to Thapa.

'Hello Thapaji, this is James Munro. You called me earlier, I've just heard the news.'

'Hello Jamesji. Yes.' His voice is anxious. He's frightened. 'I wanted to tell you personally.'

My heart tightens, sensing his grief.

'Here in Kathmandu, the people...' Rai breaks down crying. He tries to speak, deliberately and slowly through sobs. 'It's the curse of the Shahs being fulfilled.'

'What do you mean, curse?'

'Sita will tell you, it's our history. People are now in the streets; they are being left to speculate on what has happened. Our government is failing us. There is no news here... only street talk of the King's ascension. People are hearing from relatives in India the story of a massacre, it is being broadcast there but not here. It's such a terrible thing, both the King and Queen,' he pauses, 'and most of the royal family, killed by their son. Parricide, matricide, fratricide and sororicide all in one night. Jamesji in your knowledge of brutal history, have you ever heard of such a thing happening before?'

'Never... except maybe from biblical times.'

There is silence.

'It's true then? It was the Crown Prince who did it?'

'That's what people are saying. Yes, he went berserk and shot his whole family.'

'Any idea why?'

'Some close to the palace are saying there was a flare-up in a long-running family argument. The King and Queen have been against the prince marrying the woman of his choosing. A few have heard he was drunk or on drugs. They say he got angry, left the family gathering and returned in his army fatigues with an assault weapon and other guns. First, he shot the King; then his brother and sister and relatives; then chased after his mother. They say nine people are dead. He just walked around the palace shooting.'

'My goodness, is he trying to take control of the country?'

'No, no, the prince then shot himself.'

'God.'

'But there's more... the gods have spared his life, he's still alive... and in our tradition... he is now the King.'

'Fuck me... what a thing to happen. Sorry Thapa, I'm just outraged.'

'I have to go James, there are people at my door, there is much to do here. This news will travel around the world quickly but here it will take time for it to creep into the villages in the hills. Arrangements must be made and it's a time of great uncertainty. No one knows what will happen next. The military are rumoured to be entering the town centre, people are in shock. As is our tradition, tomorrow the funeral ghats will be prepared at Pashupati. The King and Queen and their family will be cremated in public to complete their ascension. Pray for us. Om shanti.'

'Sure Sir, I'm very sorry. Stay safe.'

I hang up and find Sita and Ram where I left them. Sita is sitting on the floor with Ram, covered in a blanket, and is still chanting. I update her with this latest information. It seems to compound her sorrow.

I know by heart the talk Sita gives to people with troubled minds, so I repeat it to her. I tell her to breathe deep, to remember nothing physically has changed within her working body. Her heart still pumps, her lungs still breathe. Her god is still alive in the life that's in her. I encourage her to keep focused on us and state that together we can weather the storm. I stop there. There is no connection. Something in her has been severed. Sita who first introduced me to sharing life's difficult encounters, is on her own.

I tell Ram to stay with his mother. I walk back to the kitchen where Sita had started cooking and turn off the gas. Our two salt and pepper figurines of Nepal's King and Queen sit there on the side of the cooker. The king lies on his side, like a chess game that's finished. His dark glasses now have a tragic look. What is this curse of the Shah's Royal dynasty that Thapa mentioned? I wonder if Mahesh knows.

Mahesh. I realise more immediate consequences of these events for us in Edinburgh and call the yoga studio to cancel Sita's evening class. The receptionist asks why, and I tell her only that something has come up. She asks if Sita is OK.

I consider my response carefully, because our Nepali friend, Mahesh, is likely to be waiting for her yoga class and may not know of the events in Nepal. He would certainly have been in touch if he'd heard. I ask if Mahesh has arrived and I'm told he is already there talking to people.

I suddenly fear for Mahesh hearing this news. I tell the receptionist to announce that the class is cancelled but to keep Mahesh there. To tell him I'm on my way with some important information for him.

I hang up the phone and Sita tells me to go quickly.

'Take him somewhere private,' she says, 'and be gentle.'

IT'S ONLY AN HOUR SINCE MY HEARING THE NEWS FROM NEPAL, BUT already it seems an eternity. I enter the studio to see a few of Sita's disappointed class members still talking to each other in the reception area. I see Mahesh gesturing and laughing. I fix my gaze on him. He is chatting to a small group of men at his side. I hear him say it must be something serious to keep Sita away. He's never known her to miss a class.

I am about to tell him the incarnation of Vishnu, his King, has just been killed. Not only that, but his new King is a mass murderer.

He reads my face as I walk towards him.

2

———————————

Sita relies on her traditional rituals to help her cope. After a sleepless night, I find her in the morning with her head completely shaven and doing the same to Ram. It's unusual for Sita to follow this tradition but she is no ordinary woman. As she ceremoniously shaves Ram's head, she tells me Ram requested this procedure. I'm relieved that our daughters are staying with my mum during this crisis. The trauma of hair loss to them would be greater than the news at their age. Sita is wearing the white cotton dress that was once a trademark of her time with the Moni Baba. She explains it's also a symbol of mourning in Nepal.

As funeral processions begin in Nepal, messages of condolence begin to arrive at our house by the hour, from students who have heard why the studio's yoga classes are cancelled. Some call and others drop by. I tell callers that Sita is currently in a state of 'contemplative respect'.

Although I'm uncertain what is going on in Sita's mind, I'm sure she is not meditating. Her brain is far too busy processing information. She is facing a world in which the god-like presence of her one-time patron is no longer here. If that doesn't put a spiritual mind into overdrive, nothing will.

In my efforts to console her, I join Sita in the physical rituals she's following. I too shave my head. I walk with her through the gardens behind our house listening to her chants and her prayers. I give offerings at the makeshift shrine she has created in our empty fireplace for the deceased royal family. I begin to fast and follow her healing routines to show her she has someone standing alongside her.

I channel her, as I remember her, because she is my definition of what support should be. On all the occasions that she was the rock and I dealt with a raging sea of emotion, she showed strength through her detachment.

Sita was taught the gods are flawless and it's not up to us to understand their purpose. If we choose to have heroes and make them seem god-like, it does not affect their state, only ours. My suspicion is that Sita feels despair mostly for the Queen. In those dying seconds, a mother lost her life to her son.

LATER, I ASK SITA ABOUT THE CURSE ON THE SHAH DYNASTY. SHE TELLS ME only that it is a legend, and that she doesn't believe in curses for many reasons, me included.

'A simple explanation would help me visualise what's going through the minds of people in Nepal right now,' I suggest.

'It was a prediction given to the first Shah King of Nepal. He was told by a holy man that there would only be as many Shah Kings as the number of toes on his feet. Birendra was the tenth King of Nepal.'

'When was the curse given?'

'Around 1770, your calendar.'

'We had problems with a few cursed kings around that time, too.'

'We must not give conversation to curses,' Sita says. 'They are vile superstitions passed on at random across Nepal. But beliefs are not all curses.'

'I know.'

'Beliefs are retained in the body, like the goodness from food, while curses are the waste that must be expelled.'

· · ·

Mahesh spends hours on our telephone with his father, who is a senior Gurkha officer in Kathmandu. He gives updates on events and the reactions of ordinary Nepalis as the shockwave continues to move through the country.

More stories of the royal rivalries and petty quarrels emerge. There are some who think the Maoists have secretly done it and framed the prince. The military were behind it, or it was the King's brother who conspired with his son, since he was conveniently out of the city on the night. There is apparently great hostility towards Prime Minister Koirala over his handling of the affair, despite there being no historic precedent for managing such carnage.

Mahesh makes plans to fly home but is told by his father to stay in Scotland. There is little he can do in Nepal except grieve. News of the King's death is slowly spreading though remote parts of the country, like the aftershocks, all with equal measure on the Richter scale of grief.

Mum insists I look after Sita very carefully. She tells me I should remember the feelings of grief I went through after losing my father as a child. As if I could forget. She says Sita has lost more than a father figure. I remember all the months of appealing to every god in existence, to change things and bring my dad back. I also recall the lack of grief in my mum back then. It took me an incredible journey to find out why.

My dad finally calls me from Kathmandu. He tells me he was in Pokhara when the news broke, and so made the bus trip overnight to attend the funerals. The bus was packed with dignitaries sitting on the roof and the whole country is in shock and disbelief. He confirms that the state-run radio initially announced that the King had passed away in an 'unanticipated incident'.

This news was followed by the usual weather forecast for Nepal, that things would be mainly fair throughout the kingdom.

'I've never seen anything like it. This much-loved King, his Queen and family, all cremated together outside the temple of Shiva the destroyer. The sight was too much for many. People were overcome with grief. I saw one group burn an effigy of Prime Minister Koirala. People were shouting he should resign or leave the country.'

'Why?'

'Apparently his deputy minister gave out the news to the Indian press that it was the Crown Prince who acted alone. Meanwhile the King's brother was made regent to the new King. He's the one who officially stated the royal family were injured in an accidental discharge from an automatic weapon! People have been left to speculate... were the royal family assassinated in a sinister political plot... or was the King just a victim of his son's insanity?'

Dad asks how Sita is coping and I tell him she is deeply affected. He reminds me she is resilient and has had previous experience facing death of those dear to her.

'She's certainly no stranger to death,' I say, 'but the Moni Baba died peacefully, not shot.'

Dad tells me that many religious leaders are gathering to offer support to the remaining members of the royal family. He adds that people will likely get in touch with Sita and to watch her carefully, as if he knows something about her that I don't.

'There will be no end to the speculation here for months to come. It's even doubtful Nepal will survive this event, as a kingdom.'

'Are you suggesting the weather forecast might no longer be mainly fair throughout the kingdom?'

'I think even the Moni Baba would see a climate change here. At the moment, it's a land less clement.'

THE NEPALESE ROYAL FAMILY'S TRAGEDY RECEIVES THE WORLD'S SPOTLIGHT with the speed and duration of a flashbulb. The young prince's patricide is relegated below yet another bloody day in the Middle East and just above a pregnancy in the lower ranks of our own royal family. In most local newspapers, there is no mention of it at all.

Less than two days after he shot himself, the Crown Prince dies of his self-inflicted wounds, leaving the King's brother as the next in line to the throne. Seldom has a country suffered the death of two heads of state in such quick succession. Rarely has a mass murderer been treated with such a respectful burial by those he most offended.

. . .

MAHESH TAKES IT UPON HIMSELF TO EXPLAIN THE LEVEL OF GRIEF AND THE scale this calamity is for us. He suggests this tragedy for Nepalis is ten times more serious than the death of Princess Diana in the UK.

'Why do you say ten times worse?' I ask.

'Because there were ten times more deaths to Nepal's royal lineage than there was to your royal family here.'

As news filters through to Sita's students, they create a small shrine in the yoga studio and people drop by to leave bunches of flowers. By the end of the thirteenth day of mourning, the offerings have reached all the way along the corridor to the studio entrance.

At the appropriate astrological time, Mahesh arranges a small group of friends to carry the withered flowers in baskets down to the Water of Leith. His intention is to cast them onto the water as many would have done on the Bagmati River. Two locals accuse him of fly-tipping and threaten to call the police. The group then bring the dead flowers back to our house where we light a bonfire in the backyard. Sita organises an impromptu puja and conducts these rituals, sans-sacrifices, at our personal funeral ghat. Mahesh respectfully places the flowers into the flames in batches.

Sita mentions our spiritual links with the masses in Kathmandu. Then she questions why such a well-loved and worthy ruler would meet such an end to his life. If you've been brought up to believe in karma, these are the sort of questions that run through your mind at times like these.

3

For a full three weeks Sita acts not as I know her, but as a living goddess, mourning and in exile. Along with my mum, Mahesh, and the twins, Ram and I give her all the support we can.

I should have known there would be a cultural tradition to end the mourning. And as it turns out, after the appointed day, Sita snaps out of her gloom, immediately making phone contact with our friends in Nepal.

Sita speaks to Swami Y and he tells her that Tilak and Maya have been trying to reach her. They are in Kathmandu after paying their respects. Swami Y organises a time when we can all speak together.

The call is mostly spoken in Nepali and for the first time I hear Sita say she has been considering coming to Nepal. I hear Tilak tell her something at length in Nepali, but he is speaking so fast I don't understand. Whatever Tilak tells Sita, she seems to take it to heart, and not in a helpful way.

Tilak and I have a moment of conversation at the end of the call. When I ask him what he said to Sita, he tells me that despite all the upheaval, the community leaders are going ahead with the appointment of a new Kumari. Another living goddess will be chosen soon. He also says there are plans for a summit of spiritual leaders in the capital. Tilak says that Swamy Y has already suggested to the organisers that Sita comes to Nepal to attend. She's been named as a representative for the teachings of the Moni Baba.

Tilak shares more of the popular conspiracy theories. The son of the new King is of special concern. He was of similar age to the Crown Prince and in the eyes of many a bad influence on him. He has become the new heir to the throne. He was miraculously out of town on the fateful night of the shooting, so the conspiracy gossip is fuelled with claims of curses and karma.

Maoist rebels are another factor, and no one can predict how they'll respond in the aftermath of this tragedy. They have been calling for an end to the monarchy since the beginning of their struggle. Just how they might take advantage of this situation is anyone's guess.

THAT NIGHT, AFTER HER LONG CALL WITH TILAK, SITA ENTERS THE LIVING room with an expression I have rarely seen. It's a forced smile. She looks exhausted and is still wearing the white cotton dress she's inhabited for two weeks. It's now washed clean and pristine. Her hair has begun to grow back and as I sit on our sofa, she slides over beside me. Her hand sweeps around my shoulder and I feel a distinct shudder of doom. 'There's a meeting of spiritual leaders taking place in Kathmandu.'

'I know. Tilak mentioned it.'

'Did he tell you when?'

'No... but this is good thing, no?'

'The meeting is taking place in three weeks' time. Tilak said Swamy Y will send me an invitation. They would like me to speak about the legacy of the Moni Baba.'

'It's fine, we can cope for a few days. Mahesh and I can keep the studio going while you're away.'

'I want to stay for longer than the meeting. I want to do other things too. I heard they are about to choose a new Kumari and I think officials may now be open to some changes. There are efforts at political healing because there is currently so much confusion.'

'Things just wither and fall off the body politic, they rarely heal. Sorry, that's a bad allegory. It's the nature of politics to face eternal opposition.'

'I've talked this trip through.'

'With whom?'

'With Ram. I thought it might be interesting for him to come and spend some time in Nepal and get in touch with his roots too.'

I look for an expression of humour in her eyes, but there is none. 'Ram has other things on his mind.'

'But he's also curious about Nepal.'

'I don't believe he's interested in the Nepal of the moment. He should definitely visit, but only when things settle more.'

'I feel the need to go back to Nepal now. I have a chance to contribute something.'

'And what if Ram wants to stay and finish this year's education? Have you even asked him? And how do I fit into the plans?'

'I'm hoping you will let me go. I also considered that you should come too. But I think you don't want to leave your home here.'

'Sita, it's *our* home. This is what we've built together.'

'I know but I want to go for this meeting at least.'

'OK, just answer me one question.'

Sita looks relieved. 'What is your question?'

'How can we afford this?'

Sita gets up and walks out of the room. She returns with a little Nepali silk pouch I've seen occasionally, among her few possessions. She carried it here from Nepal. She asks me to open the palms of my hand.

As I do so, she pours out a number of large gold coins.

'My god... where did you get these?'

'They were given to me.'

'When?' I examine the coins carefully. They each have a Nepali inscription on them and what looks like a date.

'Did the Moni Baba give these to you?'

'No... King Birendra.'

'The King! For what?'

'Each time the King visits a young Kumari, he gives her a coin in gratitude. It's a reward for her providing good luck during his reign.'

'My god, it's like living in a fairy-tale with you. Is this a dream?'

'These twelve coins represent the time I served the King as a living goddess. I've made up my mind, James... and we *can* afford it.'

She accepts my silence as approval, and I hide my fears.

4

With all her yogic cylinders firing again, I try to figure out what I can do to support Sita. The more thought I give to her challenges, the more I see everything we've created here at risk. I see a chasm opening between where we are now and where Sita is taking us. I'm certain staying here is best for Ram's immediate future, and thankfully he agrees. The twins have been brought up to believe Kathmandu is just south of Peebles so are content to hear mummy will bring them back presents from her trip. I sense Sita is vulnerable for the first time and therefore unpredictable. I'm concerned she may be trying to fix something that's beyond her.

When Sita first began to learn English, she became fascinated by the international use of acronyms. When I told her people could suffer from PTSD after facing severe trauma, she became interested to the point of obsession and in doing so found a whole new undiscovered vocabulary. Post Traumatic Stress was something she instinctively understood, but she wanted to know the difference between a disorder, a syndrome, and a disease.

'How do you know it's a disorder?' she asked.

Her English was still basic back then, and I explained that illness was broken into different categories. A disease was something for which the cause, the treatment and the cure were known. A syndrome on the other hand was an illness which had multiple causes. For centuries we have sucked up cultures and words from other languages and made them our own in the English language. Those discovering a cure for ailments usually gave them their names.

'All ethnic groups have discovered illness and given them names, haven't they?'

'Yes, of course.'

'And in our culture, the cure is very often the repetition of a god's name.' These words, she thought, were infused with the same powers of explanation we allocated to made-up acronyms.

'But the naming of a disease is not a cure... it's only an indication that a cure exists. Anything that was supposedly cured by a god, nowadays in the West, people would call a placebo,' I said. 'It's a Latin word which scientists use to describe a positive belief. When something appears to cure people without medicine.'

'Exactly. And if it works, what's the difference between calling it a placebo or crediting it to Laxmi, Ganesh or Kali?'

As these early language lessons progressed, I could feel the cogs of understanding speed up in Sita's brain. She would laugh at the idea of an acronym because they were unpronounceable to her. Saying someone suffered from PTSD would just confuse the gods. At least in a chant to the gods, you would not need a full sentence of explanation.

The words *placebo* and *nocebo* became of particular interest to her. She saw in them the same all-embracing god-like explanation she found in her own languages. She believed that the core values of yoga could be explained using these words. That yoga gave us the ability to summon at will... the power of placebo.

Before we left Nepal, Sita told me she had discovered a new ailment and that she wanted to name it.

I asked her what the symptoms of this ailment were.

'It's when people fall out of love with a place, or someone.'

'Is it a disease or a syndrome?' I asked.

'I've seen it several times in people. When they are about to leave home, they will begin to find faults to help them justify their move away.'

She explained, if a person decides to leave somewhere that they love, it is common to find them suddenly mentioning all the things they dislike. She'd even observed this in herself, with her life in Kathmandu. She'd already begun to see things she could easily leave behind, things she disliked, in a place she had formerly loved.

I asked what name she had for this syndrome.

She said she'd made up an acronym. She called it FOOLS. Falling Out Of Love Syndrome... which can be cured by separation.

'If it's curable, it must be a disease.'

'It's not always curable and deserves the S of syndrome,' she insisted, 'if only to become a memorable acronym?'

'I LEAVE NEXT WEEKEND. MAHESH MADE ALL THE TRAVEL ARRANGEMENTS. I gave him four gold coins and in return he gave me enough money to make the trip. He says the coins are more valuable than the gold they contain, since they were handled by the King. I can buy them back later if I want to. I've taken nothing from the studio savings.'

'Have you told my dad you're coming?'

I see a tear form in Sita's eye, the only clue that this is challenging her too.

'The Avadhoot will meet me at Tribhuvan airport. He has also been invited to the summit.'

'Did you tell my mum this?'

'I'm leaving that to you.'

'Thanks for that.'

'Don't be sad.'

'I'm not sad about us, Sita. I'm sad about Nepal and how you will find it. I can only imagine the changes. This has all been so rushed... it hasn't felt like a joint decision.'

'I did not have the strength to argue with you, James.'

'The children will be just fine; they don't really need a mother.'

Sita smiles sadly and we hug.

SITA IS WEARING A HIGH COLLARED SILK SHIRT UNDER A TWEED JACKET with matching waistcoat and blue jeans. She carries only hand luggage with a few light clothes including her simple white dress. She's packed a fresh copy of my dad's yoga book, that he requested, and some gifts for friends. She looks stylish and confident in a way that's very different from when we both first arrived at this airport.

She is about to board a plane for the second time in her life to go back to the place where she was born and raised. This time she's flying alone. No longer hesitant in the English language or unfamiliar with the wider world, she is on her own individual quest.

Before she boards, Ram is particularly quiet. He holds onto my hand with a strong teenage grip. He hasn't done this since he was a child. The girls are at an age when they have a vague understanding of purpose but not of time. They are easily diverted. They run off together, when one of them spots a Thomas the Tank Engine children's ride. We follow them and I pop in coins so they can sit together on a shaking plastic seat for Sita's last few minutes.

Sita turns to hug Ram, and I hear her whispering something in Nepali into his ear. Then she turns to me and gives me a kiss square on the lips. She clasps our hands together in a mutual Namaste sign and she walks off through the door. No farewells are spoken.

AFTER SITA LEAVES, I TAKE RAM AND THE TWINS DOWN TO SEE MY MUM. She acts like she's been expecting us.

'I'm sorry, James. Get over it. Tough it out for the next few weeks and she'll be back here, and the world will move on.'

'It's strange, how things have unfolded in this way.'

'What do you mean?'

'Just when I think I can really support Sita, she chooses to leave.'

'Sita will not see this as leaving anything, she'll see it as her duty.'

'I know her, it's not duty. That's something she once said can dissolve conscious love. I hope it's not duty.'

'Where will she stay, once she gets to Kathmandu?'

'With Swami Y until the summit and then she'll hang out a little longer to see some of our friends. There are plenty of people who'll look after her. She has celebrity status.'

'I hope that doesn't bring her problems with the Reds. The Moni Baba is old-school now, just like your dad is. Politically irrelevant. Mahesh told me he thinks there may be trouble from Maoists at this meeting.'

'He didn't say anything to me.'

'He doesn't want you to worry.'

'Her father-in-law will help her.'

'Your dad?' I hear in mum's tone change.

'Your husband.'

'There was a time I wouldn't have trusted him to look after a hamster without meditating it to death. But he seems to have changed.'

'How do you meditate something to death?'

'You ignore it completely; treat it as if it doesn't exist.'

'This summit is supposed to provide answers to a crisis, not become the crisis.'

'Ram and the twins need their mother. Your dad doesn't have a good track-record looking after anyone but himself. But I'm sure he'll look out for Sita, and she knows this.'

'She's known him all her life... dad was like an uncle to her before she met me.'

'We need to feel proud of Sita. As a woman at this event, it'll be quite an honour.'

'I know.'

'What date does she come back?'

'She has an open ticket, but I hope she'll be back in three or four weeks.'

'Open ticket?' she asks, staring at me.

I swallow as my throat dries. Mum never misses a chance to prod me.

Should I have insisted that we all go as a family? Have I read this all the wrong way?

'She hasn't said anything to you about FOOLS love, has she?'

'What the hell's fools' love?'

'Just a family acronym.'

I calm myself, cuddle my mum and hope our living goddess arrives back safely in a few weeks' time. I prepare to step up my parenting game.

5

Children are like new limbs you grow onto your existing physical body. As they grow, you realise how attached and responsible you are. At first there is little appreciation of their true association until they begin to move around independently. And just when they are mobile, you appreciate you have never utilised such limbs before. You marvel at their speed, their skills, their ignorance, and their potential fearlessness. Then at the time of most wonderment, your oldest child begins to morph like a butterfly into a separate being. Just when you've become familiar with what they were.

Ram is already approaching his morph stage by entering his teenage years. Soon after Sita leaves, he takes off to spend more time with friends. He doesn't talk about Sita. He seems determined to make her absence of little relevance to his new lifestyle. He loves his mum, but I can tell he's beginning to imagine his future without either of us.

The twins, however, present those now familiar challenges of their age group. A few days after Sita leaves, I walk into their bedroom and find Meena sitting on the floor surrounded by her hair. She has cut it off to the bone with the kitchen scissors. She looks at me with a sad look, saying Maya won't let her finish. As I turn towards Maya's bed, I see she has buried herself in covers with a pillow over her head. As I lift the pillow, I'm relieved to see that she still has hair.

'She wanted to do it herself,' says Meena.

'Good girl Maya,' I say, 'you don't have to do everything Meena does.'

'But she tried, daddy. She just gave up.'

'What do you mean she gave up?'

Maya then sits up showing me the half bald side of her head, cut as short as Meena's.

'What to do, daddy?' Maya says.

I can't help but laugh. There is no blood involved, so it's innocent and not self-harming. Why worry. One has not sheared the other, which might have happened a year ago. They have managed to do this to themselves. We have clearly entered a new phase. Sita has been trying to tame wild Meena, while at the same time encourage shy Maya. I'll have some good news to give her. In solidarity with their mother, they have decided to cut all their hair off.

After I finish the job and properly shave their heads, I tell them both it will grow back quickly, just like their mother's. They both help me to tidy up the hairdressing salon.

At the end of Sita's first week of absence, Ram organises a sibling assessment of my parenting skills. I'm told I don't make food as nicely, nor do I play games with the twins as much as their mum does. They tell me they miss their mother but like it when I play songs to them on my guitar. I decide to do this more often. It's something that brings me peace, too.

I introduce an occasional talent show with songs and dances on nights I don't feel like bedtime stories. Meena wants to become an astronaut-princess while Maya's ambition is to look after extinct animals. She has a special interest in unicorns and dinosaurs but appreciates they will have to be kept apart.

One night after I play a sad song by Radiohead, Meena snuggles up to me.

'Hi daddy, I could be mummy while she's away,' she tells me.

'That would be nice,' I say.

'Until she comes back... then she can be mummy again.'

She runs off to tell her sister that she is taking mummy's place until she comes back. I then hear her imitate Sita's voice, telling Maya to go brush her teeth.

I find myself having wild dreams, waking regularly at night and hardly getting any sleep. I'll dream of catching a falling child or losing one in the street.

Finally, after ten days, Sita calls me and apologises for the delay. The date of the summit has been twice postponed. She's seen both my dad and Swamy Y but she's not met Tilak or our friend Maya yet. She asks how her girls are doing and if Ram is coping. I tell her about the hair cutting and Ram's coping mechanisms, hanging out with new friends.

Sita says she's been moved by all the cultural events in Kathmandu.

'Many of our ceremonies are beautiful and wonderful,' she says. 'I love them, despite what I now think some of the consequences are. The spectacle of these traditions is worth keeping.'

'And what are the consequences?'

'Kumaris who experience PTSD for the rest of their lives.'

Sita then tells me Kathmandu is full to the brim of clean shaven and well-groomed young men.

'Royal patricide will do that.'

'Show respect, James, there is a population of crew-cut youth on every street corner, taking things very seriously.'

'And here too in our children's bedroom.'

'Did you keep our daughters' hair, after it was cut off?' Sita asks.

'No, I didn't keep the hair.'

'No matter, it's not a tradition that's relevant anymore.'

I struggle to think what tradition she is talking about.

'Was I supposed to keep the hair of twins, to mix with the toenails of frogs?'

'Frogs don't have toenails; everyone knows that.'

There is a moment of silence.

'The freshly cut hair of twins,' she says, 'is always mixed with the saliva of a yeti. All faith-healing Jankharis use it to prevent the spread of sarcasm.'

Hearing the cogs of Sita's brain rewinding into her Scottish comeback mode gives me hope for the future.

THERE SEEMS LITTLE AN INDIVIDUAL CAN DO TO STOP NEPAL SLIDING INTO A period of political uncertainty and perhaps chaos. The process was set in motion by the bullets from a Crown Prince's gun, yet many still believe this fate was set long ago by the Shah family's decision to worship the deity, Kali. What chance do any spiritual leaders have to sort out the new dynamics of social change in Nepal? They may chant mantras to kingdom come and encourage people to cope, but this latest breed of Maoists has their own ideas of power and a new social order.

I call my mum while the children are asleep one night. She tells me not to worry and not to pick any arguments with Sita, because it will risk destroying Sita's imaginary world.

'Why do you say that?'

'Because she is a strong woman with some very mixed cultural baggage. And you are a large part of that baggage in her world.'

'Whenever she takes something on, she feels a deep conviction towards it and that's when I fear for her.'

'You must allow her to move on.'

This is guru-speak from mum. It's hard enough having a dad who projects his guru-ship and a wife who can easily outdo both of my parents.

'Don't destroy her belief that you are here for her as her loving husband, her partner in whatever she does.'

'What if *she* changes that belief?'

'That would be fatal to your relationship.'

Next day I call Sita and get through to her briefly at the Summit Hotel where she's staying. She keeps the conversation very formal. She tells me Nepal is cautiously moving forward. People are trying to act normally. Tourism has been affected by both the disturbances and the tragedy, but things are now slowly returning to normal. There is a hard-core climbing community, who make Nepal their destination irrespective of what's going on politically. They have come back in numbers. There are summits to climb, Sherpas to be paid, dreams to be fulfilled, despite any local misfortune. There are even some tourists arriving on pre-booked trips who don't know the country is in crisis.

I give my update on the state of play with the children and inform her of their recent talent contests.

She tells me to look out for a letter she has just sent me.

'A letter?'

'I've sent you a letter. I wanted to explain the other reason I came back to Nepal.'

'Sita,' I say, 'what other reason?'

'I'm sorry James, I should have talked it through with you but I could not find the words to speak, so I wrote them down. I hope you will forgive me.' Sita, obviously upset, hangs up.

I sit down, confused. Letters... fucking letters. The emotional assassin's weapon of choice.

To understand the future is different from predicting it. The first takes time, the second takes far less patience, and is much more popular.

PART TWO: TWELVE YEARS EARLIER

6

ARRIVAL IN SCOTLAND

Our plane banks to the left as we approach Edinburgh airport over the Firth of Forth. Sita presses her forehead against the window and looks down at the road and rail bridges that span the river. One more new visual experience for Sita Munro, on a day of firsts.

'Is that a rollercoaster, next to that bridge?' she asks.

'Both are bridges,' I explain.

Sita has never flown before, nor seen a river so wide. Until ten hours ago, she had never set foot outside the landlocked boundaries of her homeland Nepal.

'Such large bridges,' she states.

She lifts Ram, our two-year-old son, across her lap and points to the red structure.

'See the bridges. They connect these two pieces of land,' she says in Nepali, and he nods his head. Our two-year old is unimpressed. His head turns towards the more interesting wing of the aircraft and the roar of its engines.

'The Ganges must look like this from the air,' Sita says.

'Yes,' I laugh, 'but with funeral ghats instead of Fife's industrial flares.'

With a screech of tyres and a roar of engines, our third long-haul flight of the day comes to an end. I see relief on Sita's face. I change my watch back to local time, hoping my mind can adjust as easily.

At immigration we are waved through with remarkable speed, and enter baggage claim. The familiarity of Edinburgh begins to kick in after three years in hibernation. I notice a group of elderly couples pacing the arrivals hall from Majorca, in their summer clothes, with their booty of wine. There's also a gang of young women arriving for, or from a hen party, complete with bunny ears and tutus. People are fighting with their wheely suitcases, as if it is the suitcase's fault to have rolled over on one wheel and twisted their arm. There are returning golfers carrying clubs past people in uniforms. So many uniforms, for airline staff and sports teams, and service staff. The travellers seem extraordinarily well dressed, and most are staring at us.

I'm wearing a faded white t-shirt with dusty cut-off trousers, sandals, and a blanket over my shoulders. Sita has on a red silk skirt with a Nepali bodice and a shawl. Our belongings are stuffed into two canvas bags. At the baggage claim, I pick up a roll of my dad's paintings and my guitar. A roaming family, from suspicious origins, looking for refuge.

The airport buses appear cleaner than I remember. They are also more regular and with shorter queues. Our meagre luggage loaded, we head off towards Edinburgh. Each car in the city seems brand new. Sita is fascinated by the number of chimneys and stone houses. She sees the castle and the Scott Monument for the first time and seems captivated by the grandeur of the city centre. As we depart the bus at Waverley Bridge, the locals thank the bus driver, a custom well preserved in Edinburgh. A couple of American tourists ask the driver if there's a ski-lift to the fort.

We make the short walk to St Andrew Square and board a bus to my mum's home in Peebles.

SITA'S RESPONSE TO *TERRA FIRMA* IS THAT SHE DOZES OFF FOR THE FIRST time in ten hours. I listen to the banter of locals around us. Their accents seem thicker, somehow. Sita may struggle to understand people here, despite her two years of listening to me. My accent has been tidied up, purely to become understood. A few rows in front of us a man tells his children to behave themselves. I hear him shout this instruction, to make his point clear. 'Behave yourselves!' It's my first shouting-man experience in over three years. I look at Sita and whisper in her ear, unheard, that there is a place for yoga here.

The last leg of our journey is a half-mile trek along the idyllic River Tweed. Sita carries Ram and I struggle like a porter with all that we own. The walk is as peaceful as you can find anywhere. It's almost midday when we reach mum's cottage gate and my heart skips a cautionary beat. The urge to forgive is at risk.

We find mum watering hydrangeas. She's on her knees, wearing a large, buckled straw hat. She takes it off. I see her once unruly Debbie Harry hair has turned greyer.

She stands smiling then walks forward to embrace Sita and Ram. She takes me in a long hug, whispering, 'Welcome home son.' She pushes me back to arm's length but flinches when our eyes meet.

'You've made a granny of me,' she says.

'Ram's deceitful nan.' I can't resist first blood.

Sita immediately interrupts, talking to me in Nepali. She asks that I please bring this issue up later. I answer her in Nepali. My words come spitting out in obvious anger. I tell her I need to sort this out sooner rather than later.

'*Huncha*,' mum answers.

I'd forgotten mum understands Nepali. She turns and agrees at length with Sita, then looking straight at me, continues in English. 'You tell him, Sita,' she says, 'we can talk about this later. How was your journey? Come in and have some lunch. If I remember correctly, airline food is never *ramro ko lagi*.'

The confrontation I've rehearsed for days is abandoned. Mum pushes me indoors and whispers quietly, 'bide your time, son.'

Our bags are put into the spare room and Sita and Ram are offered a tour of the house, which quickly becomes a classic clash of cultures.

'Why is it called a spare room?' Sita asks.

'It's kept empty for friends or family.'

'But it's not empty?'

'It's a storeroom, that she lets people stay in when visiting,' I elaborate.

While Sita is shown the kitchen, she asks if she can use the latrine. Mum opens the bathroom door for her. Sita rushes in and proceeds to relieve herself, leaving the door wide open for us to see and hear all. I gently close door.

'Some things still to learn?' mum asks.

'Yes. But this is the desperation of a phenomenally controlled bladder.'

Sita re-emerges and the tour continues. Mum leads her into the living room. Sita looks at me, miming the words 'living room'. I guess she's considering what might not be alive, in other rooms.

'The garden outside is my mum's real living room,' I say. 'All her real responsibilities are out there.'

'How Nepali,' says Sita.

7

In my years away, mum's put a lot of work into her cottage and garden. Ivy is everywhere it can grow, creeping up garden walls, blending with the masonry on the house. Her garden is full of colour schemes, a palette of plants and fauna, all experiments for her business.

For the next few days, Sita walks around the lawns while mum gives her a commentary on her most prized bushes, shrubs and flowers. Sita learns to wear wellington boots and is shown how a clothes pole works for drying clothes. It's an ingenious idea Sita thinks would work well in the hills of Nepal.

'I use this garden as my landscaping sketchbook.'

'Do you grow anything to eat?' Sita asks.

'I'm a gardener, not a farmer. I like beautiful colour combinations.'

'And yet... there's nothing more beautiful than a field of rice,' I say, taking Sita's side.

Mum remains quiet, just for a moment.

'I must take Sita to the local shops, to show her where she can buy food, and get some clothing and essentials.' Mum steps back and looks at me from head to toe.

Our sparring of words makes me realise how scruffy we must look to mum and how financially dependant we are on her just now. It's a realisation that takes some of the sting out of my exchange, but not all.

'I may have to borrow money from you.'

'That's OK... your resettlement grant for shopping is on me, until you can find a way to pay your way,' she says with a new authority in her voice. 'We'll go to the charity shop. There's a wide selection of clothes for Sita there.'

'Why a charity shop, mum? Because of where Sita's from?'

'No, son! So she can look like she's been here for a long time.'

Late into the evenings I sit outside with Sita on metal chairs with the smell of Earl Grey mingling with the scent of mum's night-scented phlox. Mum seems committed to spending most of her time with Sita and instructing her on the workings of a Western home. She obviously sees the need to bring her daughter-in-law affectionately up to speed. I see it is a tactic to avoid me. While we are this dependant on her hospitality, it's difficult to confront her in the way I wish to.

I plan to find employment once more in the Public Health sector. If I'd come back to the UK alone, I'd probably have gone straight to London to find a research project needing help. I'd likely also be meeting regularly in a pub with friends, discussing my gap years in Nepal. I tell Sita this.

It is my lifestyle, not the place, that is different. I have a wife instead of a succession of girlfriends. There is Ram, a growing boy, as demanding as anything that's ever entered my life. My mother, free of the secret she's kept all these years, is trying with invention to win back my trust. I've resisted contacting old friends because I fully embrace these changes in my life. I want to help Sita learn more language skills. Scot's English will be a challenge for her, but she's keen to learn. So far in her life, she's mastered Newari, Hindi, Tibetan, Nepali and its several dialects. Scots should be a doddle. She asks me what UK means. I tell her it's an acronym for United Kingdom. She asks what an acronym is.

.   .   .

After returning from a shopping trip Sita announces that Western women are different here, from those she's met in Nepal.

'*Tapa iko matalaba ke ho?*' I ask her in Nepali what she means.

'Here they're well dressed and clean.'

'I guess... compared to hippy travellers and trekkers.'

'They are, how you say, confident also, more critical too,' she says.

'That sounds like a description of my mum, not Western women,' I say.

'They are not afraid to speak their minds.'

I realise Sita is now winding me up, with uncharacteristic generalisations.

'And the men here,' I say, 'they can't be easily fooled either.'

'Now you know what you sounded like, describing Nepali people to me in Kathmandu,' she teases.

Sita is fascinated by the long daylight hours. We'll sit out late before she feels the nocturnal urge to sleep. In the mornings we take Ram for short walks around the village to exhaust him as much as possible. Sita has many conversations in Nepali with my mum and instructs me not to speak ill of her. She tells me that mum is very cautious of me, that she never mentions my dad, and that she adores her grandson.

Ram's inquisitive nature seems to have amplified into full display. Mum encourages it. Despite the risks to her garden, she emboldens him. She gently reprimands him when he runs down the pathway pulling chrysanthemum heads. She stops him and talks to her plants and flowers, encouraging him to do the same. Exploration even if it includes destruction seems Ram's prime purpose, and he seems fearless of falls when climbing.

Mum often makes Ram sit down on the path, giving him stones to play with and watching carefully that he doesn't eat them.

'You'll love the gardens in Edinburgh,' mum tells Sita, 'if you move up there.' I sense she's tiring of us.

'I'm looking forward to seeing the city and its people,' Sita replies.

'Aye, the people,' mum looks at me, then says, 'with the prickly thistle as their national emblem.'

I decide it's time. The jibing and false pleasantries have continued long enough.

'Mum, we need to talk.'

She nods and I follow her, alone, into the kitchen.

'I was not sure your dad was still alive.' Mum pre-empts my question.

'Why let me believe a lie all these years?'

'Because... he has been as good as dead to us both. And this information still needs to be kept secret.'

I stare at her, seeking more.

'Secrets easily become lies. They take on their own ego. They live and grow inside you. Their sole purpose is to protect themselves from being revealed. '

She fills a kettle of water from the tap, opens a lid on the AGA and slaps it on. The eternal heat of the cooker hisses away the drips.

'It was your dad who first came up with the idea of an insurance scam. It was crazy, but we were desperate for money. I'd never heard of anyone who had ever tried such a scheme. You can hardly believe it now, that he thought of this as a solution to our problems. It was our wild young minds, subjected to complete poverty. It didn't even occur to me it was a criminal act or that it would go on so long unresolved. It was pure survival of our family at the time. We'd travelled to Nepal, run out of money and couldn't support ourselves any longer. Your dad thought faking his death, disappearing for a bit and claiming insurance money was a better option than borrowing from friends and family at home. Once you and I returned to Scotland, he was going to join us later.'

'So, you both decided to tell me he was dead?'

'I know, a moment of madness. He convinced me to keep you ignorant until the right time. What other way was there? As soon as he disappeared, I questioned his motives. I brought you home by borrowing money from my dad. It all became daft. I accepted the insurance money because it was offered, and I paid my dad back. Since then, your dad made it very easy to believe he was dead. The truth would have meant jail for him and perhaps me. I don't fully understand it all myself.'

'You should know that I've forgiven him, and I think you should too.

I'm very glad I met him and spent time with him in Nepal. He's now part of my life again.'

'If you can forgive him... why all this drama with me?'

'Because I thought we were close and yet you maintained this deceit. And because you can't seem to forgive him now.'

'Well.'

'He didn't speak unkindly of you at all, he—'

'That's his way,' mum cuts me off in a more aggressive tone, 'ever since he began to read those yoga manuscripts, he will not badmouth anyone. Thinks he's only here to talk godly words and that he'll lose karmic points if he insults anyone. You may not understand my perspective just now... but you will as you watch Ram grow. At some point, you'll realise how much children need and respond to a father. Children force you to re-invent yourself. You helped me change into a better person. Your father has just remained the same – a cocky bastard.'

'I realise what I've missed, but...'

'It's only when you take responsibility for your own child,' mum interrupts again, 'that you see all the little things that influence their life and how it turns them into adults. And you realise what made you who you are.'

'I still want to be influenced by both you and dad,' I interrupt her, 'and yes, I'm still in the process of becoming a parent.'

'Let me finish. Your father simply escaped the need to change, and he called it enlightenment. He has other children. You know about them, you told me on the phone.'

'Yes.'

'You say yes, but he is not a father to them either. They all have real fathers; he was just the seed donor. Don't get me wrong, I love your dad, it's just I know him too well. I used to read all the books he was interested in. I practiced yoga every day. I even taught a few classes. But it was being a parent that taught me to be unselfish and if you never take on any responsibility for your children... well, enough said!'

'It's strange you say unselfish because that's how people describe dad. You should talk to Sita about him. She's known him more than half her life. You should hear what he's been doing for some of the poorest people in Nepal.'

Mum looks surprised, but then lashes out again. 'I'm not interested in what he's been doing there. It's what he hasn't done for us, especially you, that's always been the concern for me.'

'He's sent you some of his paintings. He's put much of his life into creating them and he wants to give something back to you. Do you know how good they are?'

'He's not giving anything back to me... he'd be the first to say he didn't take anything from me, except himself. A painting is not much of a repayment.'

'Mother, there are forty paintings, and they are worth lots of money.'

'As much as a life-insurance policy?'

'More.'

'Sounds like you've been completely taken in by the Avadhoot, that's what he calls himself nowadays isn't it? We should talk more about this, but don't go around talking about him as your dad. If people hear he's alive it won't be long till the long arm of the law gets involved.'

'That's highly unlikely.'

'Remember your dad has to remain dead. Otherwise he's a criminal and so am I.'

'OK, but we should talk more.'

'And you should take an interest in what's happening here and get an honest job. I didn't educate you to follow in your dad's footsteps.'

'Well, I shall try. Things have changed in public health. It'll take a little time getting up to speed.'

'I'll help you however I can.'

'Thanks. What's been happening while I've been away?'

'A shipyard worker, of all people, is now the leader of Poland. There's a career path your dad missed. People are all using personal computers. Someone's invented a World Wide Web for communication. It's a fad.'

8

Whenever there's the chance, I take Sita on hill walks around Peebles or drive her around in mum's 'flower van' through the Scottish Borders. As the summer sets in, mum suggests I help with her landscape business. While I look for a real job, I should still earn my keep. Both Sita and I begin to travel with her to help on a few landscaping contracts. It's a great introduction for Ram and Sita to spend time seeing the countryside and meeting the variety of characters my mum has as clients.

Ironically, one of the first places she takes us is a Tibetan Centre that exists in a local country house near Eskdalemuir, only a few miles away. For the past few years she has traded flower seeds with the gardeners there. It was founded by three Tibetan monks in the sixties. They were part of a group of over three hundred monks who fled Tibet over the Himalaya when the Chinese invaded in 1950. Only fourteen survived the nine-month trek through the mountains to Assam. After finding asylum in Scotland they began to construct an elaborate monastic building, naming it Samye Ling after the first monastery in Tibet.

At one stage, the monks couldn't get planning permission for the structure of their monastery because the proposed building would be seen from the road. Nearby residents objected, saying the building would not fit the local scenery.

Mum explains they'd begun the structure with volunteer help and were well into digging the foundations. In a stroke of Buddhist wisdom, the monks stopped work on the building and turned their volunteer help to building a large hill between their building and the road. Once the hill was complete, the new building could not be seen from the road.

Sita is fascinated by this story and talks at length to some of the visiting monks. Mum tells her that the Tibetans arrived here with one basic life skill.

'They came here with an ability to teach compassion,' she says, 'to a country that had never considered such a thing could be taught.'

Sita enjoys visiting the Samye Ling shrine room because it gives her a feeling of home. She is cautious, however, not to become too associated with the Buddhist monks. Her yogini instincts bristle at the exclusivity of every religion's doctrine and the potential for differences they breed.

MUM'S ADMINISTRATIVE SKILLS ARE MEDIEVAL AND WOULD BE CONSIDERED out of date in Nepal. She stores her receipts in the garden shed, on a shelf with stones on top to keep them from blowing away. When the shelf is full, they are moved to office drawers and then lastly into a metal cabinet containing all receipts since her business began. I convince her to upgrade her business model to at least Victorian book-keeping standards. Mum still believes she needs to physically feel receipts and payment vouchers for them to be remembered. I suggest she mulches her cabinet of receipts as compost to feed to her plants. Then as the plants grow older, they will be able to tell her who's paid and been paid, and what's pending.

This year, mum's main assignment is the landscaping of Kindare House, a nursing home on the outskirts of Peebles. The home inherited a substantial donation after the death of one of its residents and management have decided to renovate both the buildings and its sizeable gardens.

In the early design stage, mum had concerns over how to treat a large sloping field which sits in front of the main building. She shared this challenge with us and out of the blue, Sita suggested terracing the hill. Mum immediately became enthusiastic and shared Sita's idea in her proposal. The building of a few miniature terraces, just like those in Nepal, have now been approved. They are to be made of peat and heather.

Sita and mum spend hours together in the field, working manually on their creative arrangements of dirt and rocks.

I take time to photograph dad's paintings and distribute images by mail to local art dealers in Edinburgh and Glasgow. I also send off a letter to my former lecturers at the LSHTM, the London School of Hygiene and Tropical Medicine.

KINDARE HOUSE SITS FACING A VALLEY OF PINE TREES WITH RICH GRASS AND crop-covered slopes. A row of pylons sweeps past the home like a cable car into the horizon. Sheep speckle the hillside like dandruff on a green moleskin jacket.

As part of the ground renovation, the approach road to the home is newly surfaced with tarmacadam. One day there is a serious dispute among a group of old men at the entrance. Parked randomly near the gate are five mobility scooters. The old men are taking issue with a fence builder because their access to a path has been blocked.

At first my sympathies are with the five old residents, until I hear the quality of abuse they are piling on the poor labourer. Like a geriatric gang of Hells Angels, they harass the young man until he walks away. He obviously can't finish or let them through until his fence is complete, so he goes on strike and sits. They continue cursing him as they rev up their engines and drive back in formation to the nursing home. When they park near where I'm standing, they shout at me that the fence-post man has ruined their biker-gang outing.

When Sita hears the commotion, she steps forward to try to calm things down. I'm surprised how quickly she succeeds, until I realise she is claiming responsibility for the roadworks. The bikers' response to Sita is overwhelmingly good-humoured.

The path is being repaired because of a minor landslide from one of Sita's terraces. She apologises, and I watch each of the old men mellow and show sympathy towards her. Sita's years of experience caring for the aged Moni Baba has come in handy.

In the following weeks, Sita encounters more dramas among residents around the home and is often requested as a peacekeeper. She talks and befriends several older women, and so begins Sita's first real insight into the minds of the elderly Scot.

The women, she tells me, are far more verbal than the men. They tell her the care home is divided into two groups. The condemned and the as yet un-condemned. Those condemned have already been told what they will die of, and the others have not yet been diagnosed with a fatal illness. There're still multiple-choice options for the un-condemned.

During her conversations with the residents, Sita holds many a hand and rubs many a foot. It is such an unusual thing to do, and yet it seems the physical interaction is genuinely welcomed.

'God forbid people touching each other in our society,' mum tells Sita. 'Aside from a handshake, any other physical contact is regarded as inappropriate.'

Sita gives residents a level of attention they don't get from carers or even family members. I notice some begin to dress noticeably smarter for her visits and she is obviously charmed by this response.

Between the hard labour in the garden, we often fit in a break in the cafeteria talking and listening to stories from residents. Sita struggles to understand the stronger accents but has a knack of getting them to talk slower with her line of questions. In doing so, she uncovers a wealth of information about their early memories and at night she'll often tell me.

Elsie MacGilvery is the home's oldest resident at ninety-eight years old. One day her carer shows Sita Elsie's family photographs, some from as far back as 1910. In one faded shot the women are carrying heavy loads in their bare feet in the Highlands. Sita is surprised by the similarity to her life in Nepal and impressed that Elsie still remembers this lifestyle in some detail. She tells Sita when she was a young woman, she was once the Ludo champion of the Commonwealth. A skill she developed when her folks moved to a cottage in the Borders. As she looks through the photos, she points to faces and says, 'That's thingmi and that's thingmi. Oh an there's thingmi too.' Her mind recognises but can't remember names.

Other residents also tell Sita of their life and hardships. Everyone learned to read and write at primary school but only a few attended secondary school beyond their thirteenth birthday. Old Bill Lennox recalls how as a teenager his father passed on his pair of football boots to him and his brother. They had to share the one pair between them. Bill was left footed and his brother right footed. On big games, Bill would wear one boot with his plimsol on the other. His brother the same. Both played in the village football championship. They got beat in the cup final because the defenders in the other team all had two boots. In those days, crowds cheered more for the tackles than the goals.

Maisy Macdonald is another of Sita's new friends. An outspoken eighty-three-year-old, very much in control of conversations, despite having reduced physical capabilities, she's from a long line of Highland folk who lived out the later part of their life in Leith after the war. She has an older brother Tam and a wee sister Isa, also serving out their time at the nursing home.

'If ye git Tam, Isa an me on yer side, you'll get onathing done here. They cry us, the Macdonald mafia.'

Soon, everyone within hearing distance joins in to help with translations for Sita.

On one occasion Maisy tries to repeat something she's said to Sita by shouting so loud, her false teeth fly out of her mouth and across the cafeteria floor.

'Ha ha!' her wee sister yells. 'Yer teeth went skating across the flair, like a curling stane. If ah had ma broom, a could ave made them go further.'

The hilarity draws more attention and people are laughing so loud it attracts the attention of staff. Maisy gets on her hands and knees looking for her dentures. Others ask if she's lost a contact lens.

'No, it's ma teeth,' she shouts in near hysterics.

'Let me help,' Sita says, folding herself into a yoga posture, to see under a chair.

'Here they are.' Sita smiles, holding them outwards and upwards towards Maisy.

'They'll no bite ye hen, withoot ma gums roon them,' Maisy says.

Maisy and her sister become lost in their own cloud of merriment.

'Aucht, yer gums shrink when yi get old,' she says. 'Ma teeth jiggle aroond, like Spanish castanets, in ma mooth.'

Maisy thanks Sita for finding her teeth. And amid the chorus of laughter, Maisy says, 'isn't she a gorgeous wee Pocahontas?'

Sita looks confused, and no one tries to translate for her.

9

Sita and my mum work so hard on their terraces for the whole of June and July, I can see a physical change in Sita. She manages to fashion a selection of stones in Andy Goldsworthy-like walls, to support mum's elegant flowerbeds.

Ram uses his time to grow in height and make friends with a three-legged sheep dog called Skipper. Each day he'll scamper through the grounds with the dog hopping behind him, in any weather. He's always under the watchful eye of the dog's owner, Auld Jock. Whenever it's time for Ram to return, we inform Jock who then obliges with three whistles and Ram is herded back to us, like a lost lamb.

Despite the good spirits in the nursing home, there are plenty of fragile residents in the condemned group who are struggling with the finality of old age. Maisy says that the end of life can be fun, but she expects the very end really sucks. Sita is surprised by the level of knowledge each have of their illness. Many can describe in detail what's wrong with them, knowing all the medical names of their ailments and treatments. Some have gifted their savings to charities dealing with their affliction, hoping they'll be spared the end they currently know in so much detail. For others that are too far advanced to care for cures, it is as if someone has announced that life's long party is over, and they now just want to go home.

Bob the bookie is perhaps the most isolated and morbid resident. The ex-bookmaker no longer cares whether it is day or night. He chooses to live alone in his room with his curtains drawn. He will get up to dress and eat whenever he wants. He'll then wander around the home, watch TV, eat a sandwich then go back to bed when he's tired. He says there are now fourteen days in a week for him... but then again, some weeks there are only five. He hasn't used his clock since the battery ran out a few weeks ago, or maybe it was a year. He can't be bothered with other residents or carers since all they seem to want is to know his business. He makes do with calling inmates on the internal phone whenever he feels like it and giving them tips on the horses. Most have no interest in horse racing and believe he's either making up the horse names or using names from a far distant past. It's not unusual for residents to get calls at four in the morning. 'Black Whisky for the 3 o'clock at Cheltenham.'

In a rare conversation with Sita he tells her he's got every illness in the alphabet, from Angina to Xenophobia. 'It's a gambler's nightmare,' he says, 'guessing what will finally take you. All the people I relied on have died, vanished like money on a bad bet.'

Maisy has a fake fire and mantelpiece in her room. Although the care home has central heating, they have allowed a few of the very elderly residents to have a magi-coal fire, because they were brought up sitting in front of real coal fires.

One day Sita asks Maisy what she keeps in the large vase on her mantelpiece. It's covered in tinfoil, and she asks what's in it. Maisy tells her it's her family.

Sita looks confused, so Maisy explains slowly and I translate.

'That's ma mother and fathur's ashes, along wi Bill my husband, his folks and our belove'd wee dog.'

Sita ask why she keeps all the ashes in the same vase.

'A used tae have six separate vases on the mantelpiece. Ah just thought that ah wid hae nae mare room fur ma sister or brother if they go before me. A canny make the mantelpiece ony bigger, so ah just poured awe the ashes intae the one vase and shook it like a jar o muesli. Some o them in there didnae get on sae well in life, but now they get on jist fine taegether. An a've now got room on the mantel for my specs an ma telly's remote control.'

In the middle of this conversation, Sita takes Maisy's hand and holds it. There are tears in Maisy's eyes. Then she turns to me, 'ah always try tae tell Sita something new, whenever a remember it.'

'Good for you, Maisy.'

'A recently got a letter fur Bill addressed to the auld hoose, asking if he wanted to change his motor insurance. He'd never driven a car in his life,' she says. 'A also git awe these letters promising me money when I reach seventy-five. I'm now eighty-three! Insurance folk... they're awe just eidjits! Nae wonder people try tae scam them.'

WHEN MUM FINISHES HER WORK AT KINDARE HOUSE, THE NEWLY landscaped gardens are opened with a grand party. Tables and snacks are prepared outside. Bunting is hung, like prayer flags, with flapping Kindare logos towards the gods. The residents all line up for cucumber sandwiches topped with a leaf of mint. It's an emotional day for Sita, saying farewell to a new set of friends, some of whom she may never see again.

'Congratulations,' I say, on our drive home. 'You certainly won the Kindare popularity award today.'

'It's so strange.'

'What is?'

'Creating a home for old people. Bringing them together in one place to spend their final days together. Especially when they've all had such varied lives.'

'I think for most, it's their choice.'

'Old people in Nepal interact with every age group in the community until the day they die. They are not left alone in their age groups.'

'We herd them through old age together for their own safe-keeping, because the rest of us are all too busy.'

'They seem to talk a lot among themselves, about the things they have loved and lost and what worries them.'

'It's our cultural practice, it's called moaning.'

'It's very different.'

'Isn't it called chanting in Nepal?'

'What I'm saying is that words can hurt as well as heal. I'm still not sure of people's intent when they speak English to me. I'm used to older people giving me their experiences of life... to help heal the fears of the young.'

Sita begins to talk in Nepali to make herself better understood. It flows from her as fluidly as guru-speak.

'Think of people in rural Nepal. People live far apart, days of walking from each other. Miles from any health post, with no one to care for them except their family. It's a lifestyle that everyone has no choice but to cope with across the hill country. You can walk for days to find a neighbour yet when you arrive, they are doing the same as you would in your home. In Scotland, your neighbours all have different jobs, different experiences, different worries and therefore different lives.'

'Are you saying people here have more worries because they have more experiences in life?'

'No, of course not, our mind is the problem solver until the very end, and like life itself, it's ever fearful of failure. Wherever and whatever age you are, the mind will find problems to solve.'

'So what are you saying?'

'That there's more, how do you say, complexity, about living in the West than I thought there'd be.'

I START TO THINK MORE BROADLY IN MY JOB SEARCH AND BY CHANCE HEAR that my old Professor will be visiting Edinburgh for a conference. He would like to informally meet with me, to discuss the letters I've written to him.

Most all the Victorian hotels sprinkled around Edinburgh's city centre still retain the feeling of smoke-filled rooms, abandoned the night before. Professor Clark chooses to meet me in one of the most iconic lounges in the North British Hotel. This large square block of stone towers emerges above Waverley station on Princes Street. The wind whistles around the elegant building from every angle and we meet for afternoon tea. Professor Clark rushes in to join me at a table he's reserved. He's on a deadline, of course. With his tweed jacket, corduroy trousers and tassel of white hair, all that's missing is a pipe in his mouth.

'No one's interested in studying public health these days, most want to study medicine,' Professor Clark says, by way of greeting. 'Remind me what years you studied in London?'

'The mid-eighties.'

'So why do you want to research public health?'

'Perhaps I can find a research niche in public health, that lets me capitalise on my experiences from Nepal.'

'And what exactly can we learn from a country like Nepal? You have five minutes.'

'Western health systems clearly make a valuable contribution at the delivery end of medicine. The investment that goes into the front-line work is famous for extending the final weeks and months of life.'

'You only have five minutes. Be precise. What can any developing country offer industrial nations?'

'Much,' I state confidently. 'Resilience for one and how diet and activities can affect mental health as much as social conditions.'

'What do you mean?'

'Here medicine believes it also has a role to play in the complex area of mental health. Over in Nepal, medical research has discovered that dietary issues such as worms among children, iodine deficiency in adults are the main causes of mental illness. People here face an accumulation of more mental-health issues every year, but never look at their diet as a source of the cause. It's regularly viewed that outside forces such as stress from society or relationships cause mental-health issues here. Yet people over there cope with far more hardships, without having access to medical help.'

'So, you think we are all woosies here, pampered by the nanny state's health service?'

'Not at all. I just think there's a bias in research here, swayed by people selling things and not necessarily looking closely at what's happening.'

'That's very grand. So what do *you* offer this country now?'

'Instead of being looked at as out of the loop because I spent time in Nepal, perhaps I can reframe my experiences as a new loop to provide work for myself here. People here can be informed better before reaching the stage of accepting a life of free pharmaceutical drugs or treatment from mental-health professionals.'

'You want to reduce this protection they receive?'

'It's where this protection comes from that should be the issue. Many a hill farmer in Nepal has never taken a pharmaceutical drug or seen a doctor in their life. Here this situation would be thought of as a deprivation. The common perception that people in developing countries die before they reach forty is also an illusion created by statistics. It's because so many children die before their fifth birthday, that's what brings down the average life expectancy. If you survive your first five years of life, it's likely you can live to a ripe old age. I'm not suggesting we ignore medical advances in public health, especially those that save children, but we can also learn from those who survive long relatively good healthy lives without any medical attention.'

'All this comes from your time in Nepal?'

'Not all... a few ideas come from a recent stint working at a Peebles care home.'

'Interesting. I've given you ten minutes. Professor Barclay told me you might be worth meeting. Must rush. I'll be in touch.'

It's not exactly the job interview I'd hoped for, but it's more than a cup of tea with an old professor. If Bark-loudly, my old communication lecturer, told him about me, I may have a chance. But I have absolutely no idea what will happen next.

When I arrive home, Sita asks how my meeting went and I tell her that nothing definite has come out of it.

I then rant on to Sita with new thoughts I wish I'd shared with Professor Clark. How our health systems may only survive if other parts of society contribute more to highlighting prevention. All supply systems whether electricity or a phoneline are most under threat when we all use it at the same time. When it comes to maintaining health, any preventive measures that help to slow people's slippage into the major care categories should be welcomed. That's what I think could become a niche area for further study in health-care provision.

I tell Sita that Professor Clark himself is getting old and therefore it's difficult to gauge or understand what his intentions are. He's lived his life in academia. All that he knows about places like Nepal is from books. Something might come out of it, but I don't know when.

Sita tells me in Nepali that old people understand best the effects of their own lifestyle. That's what their minds live with in old age.

'Adding more beds to a care home is not a sign of improving health, it is a sign of the spread of poor health,' she says.

Sita will often say the most obvious things in a way that makes it sound like you've just understood it. I tell her this, and I dig out some paper to note her observations down. I encourage her to continue talking to me in English or simple Nepali.

'Who is to blame if young people go out into the forest, get lost and eat poison berries?' Sita asks me.

'The wicked witch who gives them the poison?'

'Old people who are prevented from telling the young about poison berries in the forest can't be blamed if it happens. Those preventing this conversation are to blame. There is just one life, for each of us. It's eternally linked from young to old by what we do in it. How the young behave affects how they age. If they get lost at any time without knowledge, the berries may kill them.'

10

I tell mum of my grand idea for health communication and how I might be given some work from Professor Clark. She brings me back to earth with a crash and a financial awakening. Having finished her work season, she's now low on work herself but has found me an immediate job opportunity.

'It'll settle my mind and be helpful if you contribute a little for your keep over the next few months.'

Mum says this as she bashes clay pots into small chippings with a hammer, to lay as a foundation in some larger clay pots.

'What's this job?'

'It's at the local church. They're looking for an assistant to help with youth sports training. It's temporary and involves youth fitness training. Some twenty boys and girls, all between twelve and sixteen... the randy years.'

'And my qualifications are?'

'You want work, don't you?'

'Yes... but?'

'It'll be a start for you. I've no more big landscape jobs this year, only small gardening plots.'

'You still need my bookkeeping skills, don't you?'

'Bookkeeping is easy if there's nothing in the way of money coming in. If you were hired as my bookkeeper, you'd be the first to fire yourself.'

'The family curse... always running out of money.'

'Well, let me know if you want this job or not. You'll meet some children who are far worse off than you've ever been. Some have suffered serious abuse or come from broken homes. The local minister is looking for a life-skills coach.'

'Full-time?'

'Three days a week. You'll be perfect. I've already spoken to the minister about you.'

'I never intended to stay and work in Peebles.'

'Consider this a short-term opportunity.'

I wander over to the garden shed and take a more serious look at dad's artwork. In the right gallery, these could be worth thousands of pounds to a collector. I take some more photos including close-up images of the more traditional work, to mix up his existing portfolio.

One particular painting unrolls to eight feet by four. It shows in fine detail a hillside much like the traditional landscapes of Nepal, but in the heavenly spaces usually reserved for gods, he's painted astronauts. On the ground, hill people in villages are seated in front of TVs. The astronaut figures, unlike traditional Bodhisattvas on clouds, are walking through space. Some are tied to space capsules or marching through barren landscapes on strange planets. At first it looks like a naïve painter has been fooling with traditions, but it's so well painted it carries a potent surrealist meaning. It shows an industrious heaven, and on earth people are wearing protective clothing painted in environments that resemble a biblical hell from old Dutch paintings.

I find another large masterpiece, full of detail. It too challenges the notion that the heavens are an inviting place to ascend to. In the centre where the Buddha normally appears, dad has illustrated an equally inhospitable molten lava environment, below the earth's surface. This single band of lifegiving earth circles the middle of the painting, showing a blue ribbon of air and water, our essentials for existence. It's a Surrealist interpretation, because from a distance the painting could be mistaken for a Buddhist wheel of life. He's rendered it in exquisite detail, showing human forms trapped by what surrounds us.

I send these new photos out to another bunch of art dealers across the country and almost immediately receive a reply from Leith. A gallery in my dad's old neighbourhood, specialising in Oriental Art. I ask mum if I can borrow the flower van and head back to dad's birthplace with a roll of his paintings.

THE 'ORIENTAL ART' THAT'S ON DISPLAY IN THE WINDOW OF THE LEITH Yard-stick Gallery has a selection of small painted scenes with Chinese mountains and Japanese blossoms. There are two crude paintings of the Buddha, the type that tourists buy in the marketplace in Kathmandu for the price of a soft drink. On the far wall, other international paintings are on display. There's a black silhouette of the Eiffel Tower on white paper and a selection of bull-fighting images, all likely bought at an equivalent marketplace stall in France and Spain.

I ring the doorbell and, after a moment, the door buzzes open.

An elderly woman wearing an apron strides confidently towards me.

'Hi sweety, how can I help you today?'

'Hi, I'm James Munro. I called earlier about some artwork from Nepal, that I want to sell.'

'Oh aye. I'm Barbara, folks call me Babs,' she giggles. 'Jim told me you'd be coming. He's ma husband, and the owner and the buyer. Let me get him, he's through the back framing. Take a wee look around. He's been all over the world collecting.'

'So I see.' I try to conjure up fake enthusiasm, fearing this could be a complete waste of time.

Babs disappears through a beaded curtain, and I hear her shout at the top of her voice. 'Hi Jimmy – the tanka-man's here!'

I hear a buzz saw fall silent and a voice shouting back. 'Gimme a minute.' The buzz saw starts up again, full throttle, and after an aggressive burst, the noise cuts off.

Jim's gallery is painted entirely in white and has been sectioned into three areas. One contains a small collection of international work, the other a display of craftwork, sculpture, paintings of pets, Highland cows and landscape scenes. Basically, all things tourist-popular in Scotland. The third and largest area is dedicated to a single artist. As I walk into this space, I try to imagine dad's work hanging here.

Jim walks through the beads, wipes his hands on his apron, takes it off then shakes my hand.

'Hello... James? I'm Jim Miller, we spoke on the phone.'

'Hi.'

'Let's look at what you've brought in.'

I begin to unroll dad's paintings and Jim seems to sense my reluctance. I ask him a question to break the mood.

'I see you have display space for exhibitions of individual artists. Do you get many people coming to your exhibition openings?'

'Aye, quite a few.'

'Do other dealers come?'

Jim suddenly seems cautious. He looks hard at me.

'It all depends on the artist,' he says.

'How many people usually come?'

'Well... we had a full house for the Picasso originals last month.'

He laughs... longer than he needs to, at his own joke.

'Where are you from, lad?'

'Leith originally,' I say, smiling.

'OK. Where in Leith?'

'My parents lived in Fort Street.'

'You must be related to the Munros from Fort Street... are you?'

'Yes,' I swallow, startled by where this could lead, 'did you know my parents?'

'No, I just put the name Munro together with your street and made a guess. Bit of a detective, eh? Follow me, these look bigger than I thought. Let's see what you've brought to show me.'

Jim leads me through the beads into a much larger workspace and clears away old brochures from a central table.

'Don't judge this place from what you see on the gallery walls. As it says in the yellow pages, I'm an art dealer, not so much an exhibitor.

What I deal in, doesn't stay long in my possession. This is a just a grand sized place for storage.'

'Where are your buyers from?'

'I trade some with Hong Kong, New York, but mostly London and from what you said on the phone you have some fine pieces to show me.'

I open my package and take three of the smaller tankas out and unroll them across the worktable. Jim switches on more of the gallery lights and dad's paintings are suddenly illuminated. Jim inhales deeply, as if he too is affected by the detail and ambiance of the paintings. They look far more radiant than in mum's shed. I think back to first seeing these in dad's underground bunker in Dhoti.

'This is some fine artwork, son.'

'So, what do you think? What are they worth?'

'To whom... is the question. It's a matter of who is likely to be interested in owning pieces of this quality.'

'Do you know of anyone?'

'If you can authenticate the work, perhaps I do.'

'What do you mean authenticate?'

'Dealers pay big money for artwork, only when they know the full story of the artist. Is he dead or alive, is there more to come, what's he done of note? Do you have any documentation to show that you own it? Can you tell me anything about the artist?'

'The artist is alive, and his name is the Avadhoot. He lives in Nepal, and I know he's sold some work to dealers in the USA.'

'Excellent. If you have the documents that prove these sales, that's a big step forward. Also, if you have any photos of the work he's sold, preferably in situ, that could prove their worth. Even photos of the artist working on them can help.'

'Well, that may be a problem. He's a bit of a recluse.'

'A recluse, meaning he could be a con artist?'

'What makes you say that?'

'Forgive my directness. The recluse artist is the oldest con in the book. Someone who never makes appearances, only works on his own. I've had it up to here with the inner self-expression of artists who magically turns out hundreds of paintings into the marketplace, once his price is right. It's a scam, they have an army of wee craftsmen turning out mass-production work. It's very easy to build an audience using a fake reputation these days. People seem to sell almost anything in terms of content, but it's very risky for dealers like me.'

'It's not like that. I've met the man, he's real and he does live like a recluse.'

'OK, fine, I believe you. Just get me some documentation and I'll try to help. I have contacts in New York that might be interested in paying good money for this quality, but they'll need proof of life.'

'Alright.'

'Failing that, I could exhibit them here – hung next to my Highland cow collection.'

'You're still taking the piss?'

'Not really. I could get the Leith elite interested. That's another route you might make some pocket money from.'

'What sort of money do you think I'm after?'

'This work deserves a price tag of between ten to fifteen thousand pounds per canvas. I doubt there is anywhere outside the main art dealing centres in London, New York or Hong Kong that would successfully sell it for that price.'

'OK, that's interesting. Thanks for your time, Jim. I'll see what I can do about authentication and ownership.'

'Can I interest you in an oil painting of Edinburgh Castle done in the style of Van Gogh – yours for fifty quid?'

'Maybe next time.'

'Do your folks still live in Fort Street?'

'No, my mother lives in Peebles.'

'And your father?'

I pause, then answer.

'He's dead.'

'Sorry to hear that son, good luck and keep in touch.'

I wrap up dad's paintings and leave the shop. For the first time since knowing the truth, I've publicly stated my dad's dead. I too am perpetuating the family lie.

11

Mum's waiting on my return home. 'Any success?'

'No, not really. The dealer thinks dad's work is valuable, but that he's an unknown artist. I didn't even try to sell the abstract hybrids. That's a different market altogether.'

'How many have you shown them to now?'

'I've sent photos around the country to galleries, some in Glasgow and Edinburgh.'

'And?'

'Most haven't responded.'

'So basically, the paintings are worthless?'

'Only until I find the right art dealer. I think the hybrids have the most potential.'

'What hybrids are you talking about?'

'The ones where dad's added non-traditional characters, like superheroes from comic books or Greek and Roman legends. It's the sort of work that could provoke interest from the Surreal art world.'

'The whole art world is surreal.'

'I'm searching for ways to support my wife and family, mum, remember?'

'I know. Is there nothing from your university contacts?'

'Not yet.'

'Have you thought about Sita teaching yoga?'

'I'm not sure that's what she wants to do.'

'It's one way for her to get to know the natives better.'

'Yes, but she's still a little hesitant with language.'

'She'll pick it up pretty quickly. Whatever she chooses, she'll do it well, that lass will.'

'I know.'

'Let me get in touch with some of my contacts in Edinburgh and see if any have information that'll help. These days they pay good money for an experienced yoga teacher.'

'Oh god, I hadn't even thought about that.'

'What?'

'Sita is not likely to charge anyone for her teaching yoga to them. She thinks yoginis who teach for money become *bhoginis*. It's a cultural thing. She believes money influences your motives to teach. The need to keep increasing one's income forces you to become repetitive and therefore less likely to help an individual when they need it most. She believes there is actually very little that people really need to know to get them started with yoga, and once it's begun the need for a teacher disappears. Spontaneity is a key part of sharing what she knows. That's when it's most valuable.'

'Then you'll have to teach the lassie about capitalism, son. The work ethic over the beg ethic.'

'Capitalist ethics, that's a subject we Munros are very qualified at teaching.'

I agree to meet the Minister John McRae on a park bench for a real job interview, at the side of the River Tweed. He's in his sixties, wears his black vest and dog-collar under a herringbone jacket. He has thick rimmed glasses with one eye glazed and a black patch underneath. His teeth smile yellow, framed by a trimmed white beard.

John was an army chaplain and served in the Falklands. He lost his eye in a motorbike accident just a few years later. He tells me he returned to Peebles where he 'half sees' my mum regularly. He's chosen to live out his retirement serving the Church of Scotland.

Swans are sitting on the grass with their young cygnets in the water as we approach the bench. They flap their wings aggressively as we sit down too close to their young. The adult swans hiss at us and John hisses back. They take to the water like ships launching in the Clyde, then turn to make sure they are safe.

'They are the heaviest bird in the world that can fly,' John says. 'And they're fearless when looking after their young.'

'Has my mum put you up to this?' I ask.

'She's still looking out for you, if that's what you mean?'

'Like a mama swan?'

'Her a swan... Ah go on!' He begins to sing in a Danny Kaye voice. *There once was an ugly duckling.* I hear you have a degree in Health Care Communication,' he finishes.

'Yes.'

'We could use someone with your experience for the church's social club activities. We have two youth groups in town to deal with. And we need help – to keep them apart.'

'Not the McCapulets and the McMontagues again, is it?'

'There's one group that meets three times a week in the church hall. They do sports activity and listen to the B-52s and Kylie. The other group meets on random nights in the graveyard at the back of the church, they listen to The Prodigy and do cheap booze and drugs.'

'Drugs... in Peebles?'

'People are in denial, but yes it's a growing problem.'

'Where do the drugs come from?'

'Glasgow, Edinburgh and bigger cities in England. This idea, of using drugs, however, getting high and being trendy, I believe comes from the US of A.'

'What drugs do people take?'

'A range of what they call recreational drugs, which makes it sound harmless. Anything from weed to glue, anything they don't have to pay much for. Do you do any sport?'

'No, I'm not big on sport.'

'But you look fit.'

'I've recently done a lot of walking.'

'What's a lot?'

'Three years in the hills of Nepal.'

'Really?'

'Yes.'

'Do you know anything about yoga?'

I'm so surprised by this question, I answer without thinking.

'I do a little, but my wife knows more.'

'We are considering a morning yoga class for children with special needs, but I can't find a qualified teacher. Do you think your wife would be interested in taking it?'

'I could ask her.'

'The money's not much.'

'If she agrees, she won't accept money.'

'Really. Why not?'

'Because she believes... anyway... she's like the people of Finland, they don't charge for teaching children.'

'But can she teach?'

'Yes John, she's the best yoga teacher in the whole world, a real yogini... but what about this paid job for me? What do I have to do?'

'As I said we have this teen group, they're all involved in a variety of sports. They come together at the church club for life-skills and fitness tuition. They need the sort of encouragement they're not getting at home, for whatever reason. If you can keep them on a path toward healthier ways, it's three nights a week and ten pound an hour. There'll be as many snacks and as much Irn-Bru as you'd like. We have it donated by local shops.'

'Well, there's a starting point.'

'What do you mean?'

'Life-skill numero one... wean teenagers off addiction to sugary drinks and junk food.'

'So, you'll give it a try?'

'I suppose. Do any of the group play musical instruments?'

'We have one lassie from the choir who likes singing folk stuff and there's Bob Harper's son Kenny who plays the guitar. But he's a difficult one. His dad played in a failed rock band and died of an overdose when Kenny was eight years old. He's now become what I'd call a potential problem... moving regularly between the church hall to the graveyard, like a teenage virus.'

'That's a bit strong.'

'I'm forever praying that he's taking positive things from the church to the grave-stoners, but I'm in fear he's bringing temptation into the church. I'm always on the lookout... to protect the flock.'

'That's an interesting figure of speech, John. Protecting the flock, the mindless sheep.'

'So, you'll ask your wife about this yoga class?'

'Yes.'

'There, that was easy... two Munros for the price of one. I'll throw in free fish suppers for your wife if she doesn't take coin. Let me know if she's interested.'

12

I tell mum and Sita about my meeting with Minister McRae, and my new salary. Sita seems excited about teaching yoga to children. 'It could help you develop your language skills and be a source of friends for Ram,' I say.

Sita asks what 'special' children means and once she understands, she is even more enthusiastic. Mum seems pleased.

'That minister knows more about our family than you let on,' I prod.

'He was a help, when you left.'

'He sings Danny Kaye, mum. Isn't that a bit old, even for you?'

'When are you starting work?'

'Next week my biggest challenge, according to Minister John, is to keep a virus boy, the son of Bob, from introducing drugs to the church group.'

'He told you about Kenny?'

'You know him?'

'John thinks he's the devil incarnate. Poor soul, he's had a hard young life.'

'He told me he'd be difficult, not that he was pure evil.'

'His father died of a drug overdose and Kenny tracked down the suppliers. He now seems to have joined up with them in an unholy alliance. John thinks he only attends the church youth group because he fancies Fiona, the folk-singing lassie.'

'Well maybe I can help them form a duo and they can sing The Prodigy in a folky style.'

'It's hardly the job your degree deserves, so keep looking for other options too.'

'I know. It's Peebles, mum,' I say. 'It's the Barabase of Scotland.'

MINISTER JOHN ASKS ME PRIVATELY WHO IS LIABLE WITH HEALTH AND Safety insurance rules, if people follow instructions from a qualified teacher who is not being paid. I tell him I don't know.

On day one, Minister John introduces both parents and students to Sita and tells them to follow her instructions very carefully He doesn't want anyone to hurt themselves. He reminds parents that they are all here of their own free will and that he doesn't expect any lawsuits. I swallow hard. Sita doesn't actually have any official yoga teaching qualifications from this country.

Sita has taught children with physical and mental difficulties before but never more than one at a time. She immediately discovers that a full class is extremely difficult to supervise safely. She loses her voice during the first session and comes home exhausted. She has never had to talk instructions repeatedly before. It is especially important for the balancing exercises so children with mental coordination problems can try something new and become familiar with the postures. She tells me she must take over their physical guidance by talking through each posture. She can only hold their attention by carefully explaining each step. When they try, she must be by their side, so they do not overbalance or go beyond their capacity to hold a posture. She finds the only way to keep their attention is to constantly talk out loud and try to keep an eye on each one. By week three she is more confident, and she invites me along to see her progress. I stand and watch her move among the children like a gunnery sergeant on the training field, carefully drilling troops. Only Sita is talking gently and encouraging them to perform and keep focused.

'Mary – hold that position longer, hold, hold, hold it, there that's good, you're doing well, more that's it, more. Watch it, Anne you too, hold it you are doing well, a bit more, a bit more – you can do this,' Sita instructs with her now creaking voice.

The girls are slowly becoming more adept and attentive on the most basic of postures. I see how exhausting it must be.

Minister McRae tells me my group all come from parents who are Christian but hold little interest in religion. He feeds me more random facts in the hope that I can develop an appropriate programme for the group. One child's parent recently died; another's parents are divorced; one has punched his brother, damaging his sibling in an assault and is under caution. Hardly the research I'm usually given before a health-care assignment, but I'll give the job a try.

In Minister John's world this is the age where hormones and testosterone kick in, as a dangerous mix. Nothing can distract these youngsters from their passionate search for recognition, friendship, and new relationships. Any skill taught to this age group is only accepted if they relate it to future employment or how to score a sexual partner. Coming of age, to Minister John, is that sudden irresistible urge to define what you want to work at, or who you want to screw. In his words, it's the age where teenagers become emotional entrepreneurs. If you allow testosterone-fuelled oligarchs to mix with liberal libidos, all hell will break loose.

I question Minister McRae on his persistently negative view of youth, reminding him that I fitted his criteria to join this group when I was a teen.

'I'm not negative,' he says, 'I'm pragmatic. I come from a military background – practice for fighting a war, even if it's an emotional war, can give some order to young minds.'

'I thought you came from a spiritual background.'

'I do but no one in your group is likely to choose religion as a career path.'

'Not everyone will go through military training either, will they?'

'Let's agree on what happens to them now, right here. Drugs and booze play an important role in their psyche because they are seen as adult activities. That in turn helps to loosen inhibitions over sex. For some, they also peddle drugs as a source of income. Where parents might recognise their teens as being vulnerable, I accept they are all potentially lethal to others too.'

Minister John calls teenage male angst the single most destructive force in the universe, because at this age a certain type of man is made. The traits of abuse, violence, crime, and most of society's ills can be germinated during this time. Kenny embodies this threat locally and it seems Kenny comes with the job.

My group is held on alternate nights to Sita's yoga class, in the same hall. There are fourteen children, and they act as if everyone is highly suspicious of attention. I never thought that attention could be so required in one class like Sita's and so unwanted in another like mine. When I first walk in to take my session the full assemble do not even gather around, and already look bored. There is no sign of evil incarnate being present

I spend my first week walking around the various groups offering to lift weights, handing out biscuits and ruminating on what might be possible to do with this group. Minister John appears twice to see how I'm doing. He accepts he has a role to play in the community's social cohesion, but he'd rather not have this weekly responsibility himself, so he's officially handed it over to me. He expects me to come up with anything in the way of learning sessions that keeps them occupied or makes them feel wanted.

'And if you have any trouble thinking up lessons, there's always the Bible,' he says. 'Keep the good seeds watered and bad seeds weeded.'

In week two, Kenny walks straight towards me through a shaft of light from a stained-glass window. He stares down into my face as I sit on a bench. All that's missing is a minor organ chord to announce his arrival. His gaze is unflinching as he asks, 'Are you James?' in a voice that is not quite fully broken.

'Yes, you must be Kenny,' I say. 'Sit here and join us.' I stand to offer my seat.

'How did you know I was Kenny?' he asks in the higher of his two voices.

'Because you're carrying a guitar case. Minister McRae told me you played.'

'Do you play?'

'Yes.'

Suddenly there is silence in the room. I'm aware that others are showing interest in this exchange.

'Can I borrow your guitar for a moment?'

Kenny reluctantly hands me his guitar case. He's wearing a Nirvana t-shirt. He's joined by a young red-headed girl I assume is Fiona and they both look at me with curiosity. Others in the group stop chatting and gather round. I take out Kenny's guitar and check it's in tune.

'Thank you all for coming tonight,' I say and strum a chord to match my words. 'If you come to these sessions three times a week... perhaps we can work out the life that you seek.' I strum another chord.

I stop for a moment, then play a few chords in the style of Metallica. 'The Lord's my Shepherd,' I begin to scream.

I see the shock on everyone's faces, so I continue.

'In pasture's green, there are things unseen – don't go to the graveyard or you'll be seen—' I repeat it faster and again. I then change the end to 'the graveyard's obscene,' most all are laughing.

I finish with one line spoken, 'Although I've been walking in death's dark vale,' then sing '—yeah yeah yeah... yeah,' with a guitar flourish from the Book of ancient Beatles.

The ice finally seems broken.

SITA'S CLASSES COME TO AN END AFTER FIVE INTENSIVE WEEKS. SHE HAS never taught such a difficult class before, nor seen such rewards in only a few weeks. Everyone who attends is surprised at the changes in the physical condition of their children in just over a month. Parents tell Sita that their children have begun to practice at home, and it is helping them. Two children with the most complicated physical challenges understand their limitations but remember and repeat Sita's classes at home. For these very brief moments in her class, Sita helps those with mental problems develop their coordination to new levels. By stepping into the role of controller over their physical movements, she has them trying things they have never done before, with bends and balancing.

For the last weeks of Sita's classes, I join her, while mum looks after Ram. Minister McRae also makes visits, encouraged by parents and impressed at the results. By enlisting more volunteers to help her watch over each child she spreads the work, and all confess to returning home exhausted.

Sita demonstrates that any willing outsider can step into the role of overseer by taking responsibility and supervising movements, even with children who have limited skills or no interest in exploring their own physical capabilities.

One girl in her teens manages a summersault on a floor mat for the first time in her life. Another can balance on one leg repeatedly, the rewards of simple practice. The parents of these children tell Sita of many changes they have noticed at home. Even during this brief period, the improved physical conditioning and coordination of the children has brought a sense of accomplishment. Sita has clearly made the children feel happy attending her classes and added an additional quality to their life, reducing their chances of accidental falls.

When Minister McRae thanks Sita for her hard work, she tells him it was the Moni Baba's principles of conscious love that worked and is the main reason these children have responded positively.

'Whenever they show no interest, you have to become their route towards interest,' she says.

Minister McRae tells Sita he'd be interested to hear more about this Baba. 'The children have definitely fallen in love with you.'

'Yes, that seems very true,' I say.

'It's not me they love... it's the attention that's being given to them.' Sita looks at me as if I should know better.

13

As my group continues, the sporting sect ask me questions while they pump iron and drink Irn-Bru.

No one has any idea on a map where Nepal is, but one boy has heard of the Gurkhas from seeing them perform at Edinburgh's Military Tattoo.

I'm shocked to discover that no one in the whole group has ever walked to any of the surrounding hilltops around their home.

'Why,' they ask, 'would anyone do that? There's absolutely nothing up there.'

The others seem permanently in their own world, bristling with protective comebacks whenever I bring up a topic for conversation. I would much rather infiltrate their lives through my statistics and influence them from a distance. A special skill, like Sita has, is necessary to draw people towards you. Most of us, it seems, just wander through life, chasing a few things and friends and making up fantasies to live by.

Those who are into sports seem to manage themselves well. I spend some time chatting to them, but mostly I walk around demonstrating ways of tidying up snack wrappers or wiping down sweaty weights and equipment.

The sporty group tell me there are very few opportunities for them to take their interests to a professional level. The young men who play football are the ones who travel most, and they see this as a way of visiting places beyond where they live. Those who have difficult times at home seem the quietest. I'm aware it will take time for me to get to know all of them better.

I decide to follow up on Kenny's interest in music. I ask the whole group if they know what Nirvana means. They say it's the name of a pop group and I tell them, it's also a state of mind. I suggest that I bring along someone who knows more about the Nirvana state of mind, one night. No one objects.

Things seem to go well for the next couple of meetings and in between I learn a few Nirvana songs to play at the start of the sessions. I take along my guitar and play some duets with Kenny. I discover that Kenny likes Jeff Buckley and that he hates jazz, especially Kenny G's brand of smooth sounds. This tells me more about the boy than he realises. I tell him that I loved listening and playing Tim Buckley's song when I was his age, but I've not heard much of his son Jeff Buckley. Kenny tells me Jeff would have been the biggest thing in pop, had Nirvana and Grunge music not come along to take over the charts.

Kenny seems different to how Minister McRae described him. He tells me how he felt when he lost his father to drugs. He gives me an honest and emotional explanation. His father taught him to play the guitar, when he was very young he says. I tell him my mother taught me, and that I also lost my dad when I was a boy.

I gauge a growing bond with Kenny, so I ask him outright why Minister John suspects him of being involved with drugs.

'He thinks he kens everything in this dump.'

'He seems to know those who sell drugs. He's told me they're the people responsible for your father's death.'

'Ma dad's the one responsible, no them. And I dinnae take drugs,' he says. 'I'm friends with them folks cause they were the only ones who could tell me a side of ma dad I didnae know.'

'Are you talking about the people who meet up in the graveyard?'

'I don't want to talk about them.'

'Why?'

'If I talk to you, they'll hear aboot it, an they'll think I'm a snitch for Monster McRae.'

As we talk more, I find out that Fiona is the love of Kenny's life. A fiery red-headed who's fourteen but looks twenty, she comes from a strict Christian family. She and Kenny have begun to record a few songs together on a Fostex four-track recorder. I have no idea what a Fostex is, so when Kenny leaves early as he always does, I find Fiona alone and talk to her.

'The Fostex was a Christmas gift from my parents,' Fiona tells me. 'They thought it'd help me in my choir practice because I can record my voice harmonising on different tracks. Like a one-woman choir.'

'That sounds fantastic. What a great gift.'

'Yeh, but since I started coming here and singing with Kenny, they think it's the worst gift ever. My dad's been dropping me off and collecting me after every meeting because he doesn't like Kenny.'

Fiona tells me she has no brothers or sisters, and just enjoys singing. She's moved on to the church folk group, because the choir only perform hymns, but now she also likes the Spice Girls. She says she's really begun to enjoy this after-hours group, because people are different, not all from the church.

As the next few weeks pass there are more group discussions and music jamming sessions. We don't talk politics or anything social, but the group delights in bringing along new music they have heard and like from the radio or on tape.

I discover the graveyard group also like sharing music. They have quite a high success rate in welcoming people into their circle. I'm told it's because they offer genuine concern to anyone who's in trouble. They also offer potent and dangerous drugs. The appeal of being welcomed is more popular than the appeal of being corrected.

I ask Fiona if I can hear some of the recordings she's made with Kenny, and after she speaks to him, they play their tape for me. I listen on Kenny's headphones. No one else in the hall can hear. I'm very impressed indeed, both with their singing and this technology. The Fostex four-track cassette tape recorder is a wonder of portable recording equipment. And I am only now discovering it.

Fiona shows me how to work the Fostex and plays more of their recordings. On one track she sings in beautiful harmony on a song Kenny wrote himself. After Kenny leaves, I ask if she'll let me borrow the Fostex until the next session.

AT HOME ON TRACKS THREE AND FOUR, I ADD A SIMPLE BASS AND A LEAD guitar to Kenny and Fiona's song. After a few experimental takes, I play the newly mixed song to my mum and Sita.

'Have you played this to Minister John?' mum asks. 'He'll give you a raise. Some extra crisps, maybe. It's such a nice song.'

'How cool is this tape-deck, it's like a home studio. I believe I'm making some headway with Kenny.'

'Don't get too cocky,' mum says. 'Minister John sees these sessions as recreational support, not preparations for pop careers.'

UNUSUALLY, AT THE NEXT MEETING, KENNY DOESN'T SHOW. WE GO through the evening much as normal. Towards the end I give Fiona her tape back with my additions to Kenny's song, along with her magnificent multi-track machine.

As she leaves, I meet her father who has come to pick her up. I spontaneously praise Fiona's singing talents on her duet with Kenny. At the mention of his name, I see her father immediately looking around the room. From the expression on his face, I see why the boy always leaves early.

On the Tuesday of week ten, the last season of this group, Sita is booked to talk about the true meaning of the word Nirvana. We are all settled in and waiting for Kenny and Fiona to arrive. It's unusual that they are both late.

Suddenly, the hall door is pushed open, and I instantly recognise danger. Kenny walks aggressively towards me, his movements and facial expressions etched with anger.

'Hey Munro,' he shouts. He's carrying a hammer.

The boy marches straight towards me, shouting at the top of his voice, 'You bastard... only got this job because Minister McRae is fucking your mother.'

'Hey, hold on,' I stammer.

He turns sideways and slams the hammer down onto a wooden chair. The hammer goes straight through the seat and when he can't pull it out, he leaves it there and continues towards me.

'What right have you to give my song tae Fiona's fucking dad? That cunt has stopped her from seeing me. He's a fucking...' His last words choke while leaving his mouth. He then turns towards Sita.

'Kenny-ji,' Sita says gently.

'Kenny G...' he shouts from his anger cloud. 'What's he got to do with this? Don't call me Kenny G!'

Sita says his name again. 'Kenny, calm yourself.' She reaches out her hand.

'Fuck off, Indian bitch, what's this got to do with you anyway?'

The words spray from his mouth, like bullets.

'Go back to where you fucking came from,' he shouts at Sita.

I lunge at Kenny, but I'm held back by the footballers who have rushed around us. A chorus of concerns are shouted from all around the hall.

'Hi Ken; get a grip, man.'

'Out of order, pal.'

'Don't be a prick, Kenny.'

There are several loud 'Kenny!' shouts from the lassies, too.

'You can all go fuck yourselves,' Kenny screams. 'You're all conniving bastards, the lot of you.'

Before I can confront him, he storms out, slamming the church door so loud I hear the bell vibrate in the steeple.

I try to reach out to Fiona's parents to explain and make peace. Kenny has already been round to their house, with some mates from the graveyard, and threatened her dad. Her parents refuse to see me.

Sita fully understands what Kenny said to her. She says she's witnessed many a young man in need of emotional help. She would never give up on such a person, but I do. In such circumstances, I believe I'm no longer able to help him.

In the past I may have responded differently to such a physical confrontation, but now I can't ignore the middle age in me. When Kenny walked out of the church door I felt relief, not just that he'd left, but also because I saw my old self leave with him.

Mum says Minister McRae is already fixing things to get some help for the boy.

I tell mum it's now my wish to leave Peebles, to get out of her grey hair and move to either Glasgow or Edinburgh. I tell her I want to give Sita and Ram a chance to expand their horizons in a city environment.

'It was a watershed moment, mum. Quite scary really, to watch Sita be confronted with such aggression.'

'I believe she's been through worse. She told me it was like being in Pipelands in Nepal, when Ram's wee friend was killed.'

'Yes... that was traumatic. You don't forget that type of confrontation easily.'

'Imagine dealing with that sort of aggression thirty times a week.'

'What do you mean?'

'John McRae told me he knows a policeman in Glasgow who will arrest on average thirty people over the weekend for being aggressively drunk, drugged or disorderly.'

'I'm not going to become a policeman, mum.'

'No, but if you go live in a city centre, it's an environment with higher risks than here.'

I then ask mum if she has been in a relationship with Minister McRae. She covers one eye with her hand and smiles. 'That man has had one eye on me since he moved here. But don't you believe Kenny. John McRae was just a good friend to me when you left for Nepal.'

Time-keepers believe planning is required for events to take place. Life, in turn, offers the time to take opportunities when they arise.

PART THREE: EDINBURGH – MORE THAN A CASTLE

1

A month after my confrontation with Kenny, mum tells me she's found an opportunity for us in the city, where a flat is available from a former client.

Bill Baxter is a retired property investor. His wife Jenny taught at one of Edinburgh's leading private secondary schools. They have a ground-floor flat in Ainslie Place, in the New Town. It one of those properties that does not match the description of available floor space and value in other cities. Although it's officially a ground floor at the front, it drops down two more floors at the back with access to its own garden and the larger private gardens lining the historic crescent. A gem of a place, so my mother tells me. She worked on landscaping the garden.

The Baxters' only daughter is married to an Aussie, and now lives in Australia. They intend to join her for the birth of their first grandchild. They're looking forward to becoming grandparents. We can house-sit their place for free whilst they're away, but Bill asks if we might be prepared to pay a small rental fee if they extend their stay longer. It's a deal which seems mutually beneficial, giving us at least half a year to sort out our financial situation. Sita asks if they have a living room. They say they have three bedrooms and a gym in the basement, with a living room, lounge and kitchen on the ground floor. There's also a second basement where the Baxters plan to store their belongings. We can live in every other room.

My mum invites the Baxters down to Peebles to meet us. They immediately take to Sita and tell her how much she will like the private garden running between Dean Village and Stockbridge, alongside the Water of Leith. We thank them for their generosity and accept the Baxters' terms.

After they leave, Sita jokes, 'they didn't say if they had a toilet.'

'I assure you, Sita, there will be at least two bathrooms with toilets, if not more,' mum says.

'With doors, I hope,' Sita quips.

WE FIT EVERYTHING INTO MUM'S MINI AND HEAD TOWARDS AULD REEKIE the day the Baxters leave.

Sita stands on the doorstep, in awe of the stone-built terrace around us, and is handed the keys by Mrs Baxter. We are quickly shown around the house and then mum leaves, taking the Baxters to the airport. We are left with Ram in our extraordinary new home in what Edinburgh calls its New Town.

I tell Sita the crescent was built in 1822, while Nepal's most brutal King Rajendra Shah was in power.

'Are the Baxters rich?' Sita asks.

'Not super rich, but pretty well-off... like a Dixit... not quite a Rana.'

'Did they inherit this home from their family?'

'I doubt it. Both the Baxters had good jobs and probably bought this when they were younger. He worked in the property markets so he would recognise a good buy. They may still be paying their mortgage.'

'What's a mortgage?'

'It's money that a bank will lend you, but only if you fulfil certain conditions. I'll explain later.'

'OK,' Sita says, using her new favourite word, which she first thought was an acronym.

Although Sita has visited royal palaces and grand government buildings in Nepal, she's struck by the fact these homes in Edinburgh are for ordinary people. To see so many stone buildings all lined up together, street after street, rows of front doors, not for government, royalty or tourist crowds, surprises her.

'The front of most all these houses in the New Town look out over communal gardens,' I say. 'There's also a larger garden at the back and that's how my mum met the Baxters, when she was hired to landscape it.'

'Do we have to look after the gardens?'

'No. But I have to find a paying job or in six months we will have to leave.'

'It seems a pity, perhaps we could terrace the back garden into rice paddies, sell the rice, and offer to buy this place from them.'

'Or if Mrs Munro were to charge for yoga classes?'

We both hug each other in a space that suddenly embraces both of us. Our need to set a goal for ourselves over the next six months sinks in as a priority. I believe in this moment we have found a place we could happily remain.

THE BAXTERS' FLAT IS DECORATED IN A MODERN WAY AND IS OF COURSE fully furnished. Our belongings fit into the hall cupboard. Sita learns two more room names. The laundry room and the home gym, complete with exercise bike, rowing and running machines.

'Why do people have a machine to walk on and a bike that doesn't take them anywhere?' she asks.

'People now like to exercise at home. It's faster and convenient in case they need to go somewhere, looking fit.'

'Machines which go nowhere, take them there faster?'

'Yes, and people feel so good after they've exercised, they enjoy a good rest after exhausting themselves.'

Sita begins to make lists of her observations in this new environment. It is the nearest thing to a diary that I've seen her keep and she tells me it helps with her language development. She has most difficultly with our association with negative expressions, like mentioning hardships or who we call the poor. What she sees hardly seems poor in her eyes. The fact that everyone lives in a solid stone or brick house protected from the elements with running water, a kitchen, and a toilet. She tells me she's never heard people talk as if they are grateful for these things.

'Depending on where they're from or have travelled to, I've not seen any stats, but I'd say most people here feel thankful. Some will tell you they are miserable when they see how much stuff other people have, that they can't afford.'

'That's quite a growing source of misery then?'

'Yes, listing the things you can't afford can be an unbearable source of misery here.'

MUM VISITS REGULARLY TO CHECK WE'VE SETTLED IN AND TO HELP WITH Ram. She calls it 'Educating Sita', and most of it involves teaching her how the numerous household appliances work. Sita loves the *dhobi-ghat* laundry room with its large washer and drier. She can't believe so much washing can happen in such a short time. Also, there are two large freezers for storage. The Baxters have left these stocked, with an invitation to use up whatever's left. I explain that most things like meat and fish are labelled. Sita's knowledge of animal body parts is increased after each visit to the freezer. She's fascinated that some are called game animals. What indeed is the game associated with these animals? Domesticated doesn't have an equivalent in her vocabulary.

The heating is another luxury. Sita is in awe of the speed of temperature change both in our weather and our homes. She masters the central heating thermostat very quickly. As autumn sets in, the trees shed their leaves over our cobbled street. One day, I find Sita searching for leaves big enough to make dinner plates from. It's a seasonal habit. She fails, however, to find Scottish leaves big enough.

The flat becomes our home. I write to dad, send him photos and ask if he can supply me with some provenance for his paintings. I need a backstory of the Avadhoot, as the artist. Or some receipts from his past sales in the USA and perhaps a photo of him – with his clothes on. I mention we will either have to pay rent after six months or find another place to stay if the Baxters come back.

Mum drives us to Costco for a winter shop, to buy supplies in bulk. She warns Sita the coming winter requires us to stock up as if we were living in the Arctic Circle.

Sita stands inside the entrance as people push past her with trollies the size of Land Rovers. She finds consumers buying enough food to last a village in Nepal through the monsoon season.

Ram is also overwhelmed in an aisle of toys. It is not the toys he is excited by, but the images printed on the boxes. He has never seen a pedal car before, and now he sees a life-size child sitting in their own car, on dozens of boxes piled high to the ceiling. He asks if he can have one. I tell him there's no space in the house for him to ride this little car. Sita suggests we could place it on top of the running machine, and he could peddle himself to eternity.

City life offers Sita an abundance of choices, comforts, and rules she's never had.

She loves the privacy of our arched walkway and the garden at the back. She'll wander for hours through this grey stone world, along the river leading to Stockbridge. It's in cold contrast to the warm mud, wood, and red brick of home. Only the walking part's familiar. Some days I'll take charge of Ram while she heads out into the streets at dawn and returns exhausted at dusk, as if the villager in her must maximize her time in the reducing daylight.

Sita prefers shopping in smaller stores even though the owners are not keen on her bartering for the goods on sale. She'll often take the back streets and head out food shopping after dark. The reason for this stealth is that she likes to carry her shopping bags slung over her head and doesn't really want to be seen doing it. She says she carries heavier loads this way more easily than dangling bags from each arm.

There is an Indian spice shop in Portobello she frequently visits. She thinks nothing of the walk down there and loves going through Holyrood Park.

I have an enduring vision of her walking ahead of me over the

Radical Road down towards Portobello with a shopping bag braced across her head like a Nepali porter with a bamboo *doko* basket. This circuit has become her favourite walk in the city. For a short time each week, she can be back in the hills of Nepal.

2

Edinburgh is sophisticated but a rather single-race city to be a country's capital these days. Most of the year, it's rare to see any international faces except in the student parts of town or the city centre. Only during the Edinburgh festivals are locals outnumbered by visitors.

Sita often stops and talks to Indian or Pakistani women she meets in the street or in shops.

'*Namasti,*' she'll say... to which they respond with a mix of suspicion and caution.

I explain that approaching strangers on the street is not the same custom it is in rural Nepal. Most local young Asians have their heritage in middle England or come from larger cities across Asia. They have more similarity in their upbringing with me, than with Sita.

Sita asks if it's the way she speaks English that is causing a barrier to further conversation. I tell her that here, anything too unfamiliar, even non-threatening banter, will spark suspicion in locals. She asks me to make a list of acceptable expressions she can use to greet people here. I make a list of one: 'Hiya.' I tell her to start with that, then listen to what the strangers say... most likely it will only be a 'Hiya' in return.

Sita decides that reading more will help her develop her language skills. I dig out a set of modern authors, including one of my favourites, John Fowles. Sita asks for books written by women. I mention Agatha Christie, telling Sita she is the world's most successful writer and has sold more books than any man.

'And when you feel ready, you must read Isabel Allende.'

SITA FINDS A COLLECTION OF TOURIST BROCHURES AND MAPS IN THE Baxters' living room shelves. There is also a collection of books by Scottish authors and a complete shelf of Audrey Hepburn VHS tapes.

The brochures provide Sita with several maps of our neighbourhood and insights into some of the writing gurus of Edinburgh. In one small booklet on Sir Walter Scott, she finds several quotes that she likes and reads them out to me and to Ram. Sita's also very impressed with the temple built for Walter Scott on Princes Street, the largest anywhere in the world to honour a writer. She can't really believe that such a structure was erected for someone who made up stories.

I introduce Sita to the Central Public Library on George IV Bridge, walking her over to where dad first found writings about the Moni Baba, BKS Iyengar, Swami Sivananda and Ramakrishna.

Alongside these same authors, I now find my dad's book on Hatha yoga sitting on the shelf. As I reach out to touch it, Sita puts her hand on mine and I feel a faint wave of nostalgia wash through me. I think my destiny and Sita's started with just such a movement, of my dad's hand towards a book on this spot.

Sita seems overwhelmed by the magnitude of the library. We find more books written by our set of local authors, artists, and inventors, all of whom Sita now knows lived within walking distance of our flat.

Sita borrows another book by Sir Walter Scott. She has taken to his writing like a Victorian debutante. This new field of study also provides her with some interesting comebacks in our conversations.

'I'm interested why they called this period the Scottish Enlightenment.'

'Much of Scott's writing is now antiquated, Sita.'

'For whom,' she asks, 'is it antiquated?'

'Attitudes towards relationships between men and women have changed since these books were written.'

'Are you saying there's no such thing as timeless wisdom?'

'Surely wisdom is continually subject to change?'

Sita takes a moment to flip through her notes. '*Where I choose to take noble risks, you make mean observations of paltry decorum.* Isn't that a timeless observation?'

'I suppose,' I say, agreeing so as not to sound paltry.

I believe Sita's love of the Scott novels is based on her unique set of comparisons. She can easily imagine life in the hills of Nepal in the stories Scott tells. When I tell her of Walter Scott's involvement in creating the Radical Road, she begins to see the handprints of the unemployed weavers who once made her favourite stone-lined path. She looks into the reasons for its name and finds a time of transition in Scottish history much like her own country is going through.

I tell Sita there are some more famous observations made on the cliff face that runs beside the Radical Road. I read her the story of John Hutton, who became the godfather of geology by chipping away samples of the rocks there. He challenged the religious leaders of his time who claimed the earth was made by God and even fixed the date of its creation. Hutton showed how much older layers of rock formed, in a geological timescale.

That people could walk among rocks and see more than just rock is a major revelation to Sita. She knows the quality of knowledge people of Nepal have gained in their long history of living and working across mountainous lands. But the idea that someone could walk into a village in Nepal, lift a rock and ask villagers, do you know how old this is? They would think the question a form of madness.

The idea that you can see fossil and foliage forms in rocks or even in photographs, that you can tell a stone's age, spot elements, find samples of extinct animals, just by looking closely, opens her mind. Her yogini training has moved her on from believing in religious dogma in her own country. Her yoga provides her an understanding of the value and necessity of faith... but now I believe she sees some limitations to faith alone.

I remind her that when I walked into Nepali villages not knowing anything about the language, culture or the people, I could spot a child dying from diarrhoea-related illness. The dehydrated child had a visible dent in the top of its skull, as if someone had chipped out a piece, from a smooth rock.

SITA IS FASCINATED WITH THE QUALITY OF SOUND FROM THE BAXTERS' expensive hi-fi system. She keeps it permanently tuned to Radio Three, the classical station, not for the music but for the way in which people talk about the music. She is fascinated by the strange sequences of classical music and baffled by the descriptions. Some pieces 'wallow in tonal sweetness' while others are 'bathed in luscious originality'. She asks me one day what a commentator means by saying a certain piece of piano music 'offers robust naivety'. I tell her it's another figure of speech; a poetic interpretation that could be applied to her own enquiries into the English language.

Sita begins to read to Ram at night. Robert Louis Stevenson regularly puts him to sleep. On crisp winter days, I also take Ram on adventures around the gardens of the New Town. I show him the nooks and crannies that inspired Stevenson to write his tales of pirates. We walk the streets where Arthur Conan Doyle once strode before writing his Sherlock Holmes detective stories. I add explanations for Ram, whose English is now vastly improved.

'The man who invented the telephone was born in that house there,' I tell him, walking up South Charlotte Street.

'What was his name?'

'Alexander Graham Bell.'

'Bell?'

'Yes.'

'Ha, ha that's funny.'

'Why's that funny?'

'His name, Bell. Will he answer if we ring him?'

'No Ram, he's dead now.'

'How did he die?'

'I think you should ask your mum that.'

That evening Sita puts Ram to bed with a story she's researched at his request: How Alexander Bell Moved to Canada and the USA and Made Lots of Money. Ram asks when we can go there.

Sita tells me she likes Walter's social commentary and Robert's imagination, but she has little interest in Arthur or indeed in Agatha. She says she sees the value in writing about exploration, adventure and love, but that she has no time for crime stories.

'Why is that?'

'Because writing about bad behaviour inspires readers to copy such behaviour.'

For Sita, it's neither helpful or worth reading or doing anything, if it inspires bad habits or as she now calls it, unbecoming behaviour.

I mention that crime fiction is one of the world's largest categories of book sales and that it's usually the behaviour of the detective to seek out and punish bad criminals that people like reading about. I point out that most popular movies are also full of tragic experiences, murders and crimes.

She smiles back, as if to her, this explains why we have so many of these horrible things happening here.

By Ram's fourth birthday we have spent a year in Scotland, and we enrol him in a community playgroup in Stockbridge. It's another old church hall. He's become a miniature likeness of Sita. He has her yogic agility on climbing frames, her concentration when given a toy and has a Gurkha's stubbornness when asked to do something he doesn't want to do. The only trait he picks up from his new playgroup, is that he now shout-talks to his pals, like a football fan.

We hear the good news from the Baxters in Australia. The new granddaughter has been born and is coincidently the cutest child alive. Our spell of house-sitting can be extended if we are willing to pay a little rent. The Baxters have decided to stay longer with their daughter. We negotiate a one-year rental agreement for the flat, telling them we are interested in staying.

It's a relief for me. We love this flat and my worries over finding new accommodation begin to subside. I also begin some part-time proof-reading work in Public Health given to me by Professor Clark. Perhaps he can find some more consultancy work if I do this well.

3

The long dark nights of winter are hardest for Sita to adjust to. In Nepal, at any time of year one can easily walk downhill towards heat, or uphill to cool air, and the hours of night and day hardly change. Here our seasons still dictate much of our physical behaviour, much of which now seems indoors.

After Ram is asleep, Sita expands her knowledge of Western ways by watching old movies on TV. The Baxters' VHS collection has become a treasure trove of discovery.

Her favourite movie is 'Big Country'. Here is Jean Simmons using a water pump, just as Sita used to, but she rides a horse and says things like, 'A farm you can walk around is not much of a homestead out here,' while Gregory Peck replies, 'you'll need a hundred miles of fence.'

Sita is exposed to the notion of mass farm-land management, another concept she has never encountered before. She also watches Audrey Hepburn movies, not so much for the dialogue but for the clothes. Mum is the one who encourages Sita to wear Western clothes and Audrey is the first movie star that Sita thinks looks Nepali.

My mum arrives one day telling us that she's finally received the last payment on the landscaping job for Kindare nursing home. She presents a large cash bonus for Sita, because of the labour and work she put into the job. She suggests it will help us get through the winter until I find a full-time job. I remind her I'm still doing her books and to be careful with cash payments. Mum also delivers a package from my dad, sent before he heard we had moved into town. It contains letters from Swami Y, Tilak and Maya.

When mum leaves, I take the letters into our living room and read them aloud to Sita. Tilak and Maya are well, their daughters enjoying school and the mill is still prospering.

Dad's letter offers some insight into the changing politics and Maoist activities in the hills of Nepal. He is concerned that there is growing support to Maoists movement from India and tactical indifference from China. Ironically, he says, in the home of Maoism the Chinese are slowly moving towards the socialist version of capitalism. Dad also includes a type-written provenance document, outlining the career and past commissions of the artist known as the Avadhoot.

Swamy Y sends a separate message for Sita, begging her to return and teach yoga in Kathmandu. Thankfully, even through the darkest months of her first winter in Scotland, Sita's eyes are firmly fixed on her life and family here.

Next day Sita takes some of mum's bonus money and finds a local tailoring shop. It's run by a Moldovan family, and she takes along some cheap blouses, tweed waistcoats and large skirts obtained from charity shops and has them Hepburnised to her waistline. Sita creates an assortment of theatrical costumes, as modest as Nepali dress and as stylish as Sabrina in Paris.

As daylight grows longer and the temperature rises again, I borrow mum's Mini for a long weekend and take Sita and Ram up to the Highlands. I have this notion that showing Sita some mountains, and a croft, and introducing her to the coast will complete her familiarisation process.

We spend our first night in a small cottage near Aviemore and the next day take the ski-lift to the top of the Cairngorms. We then hike a short distance to the top of the nearest peak. We look to the east and west where we can see the faint outline of both coasts of Scotland.

I'd forgotten how desolate and beautiful the Cairngorms are. We see deer stroll across a distant hill and I begin to view our surroundings through Sita's eyes.

'I'd say it's a three day walk to the east coast and about the same to the west,' she tells me confidently.

She almost seems ready to walk to Aberdeen, and in a burst of enthusiasm we hike a little more. Ram runs alongside us, until I have to carry him. I notice Sita is wearing the thin flat sandals she has worn since our arrival. These are the same shoes she wore to cross high-altitude passes in the Himal. Suddenly I regret not having warned her of the terrain here. The soles of her feet have less of the leathery protection than when she arrived, and the heather and thick grasses have begun to slash her ankles and lower legs. Sita quickly learns why ramblers here wear boots.

It's a comparatively short trek. As we descend on the ski-lift, Sita asks how many days walk it would be to London. I calculate such a walk would take five weeks at Nepali pace from Edinburgh. Sita suggests I bring her more often to the Highlands. Then maybe one day we could trek south to London.

We drive home through Glen Coe, while the spring light is special. The sky seems to hold back the sunset longer, making the place even more inspirational. I point out the ancient rockfaces and mention the massacre that took place here 1692.

'How many people died?' she asks.

'Thirty to forty, including some women and children.'

'Not so many,' she says.

'I guess not, but people are still talking about it today.'

'Nepal's first Shah king cut the noses and lips off all men in Kirtipur. It was a punishment usually given to unfaithful wives.'

'Wow, spare their lives, but let's take off their noses and lips.'

'Who wrote the story of this Glen Coe massacre, those who were wronged or those who carried it out?'

'There are many stories. No one was ever brought to justice for it.'

'So, the punishment has been left out of this story?'

When we return the Mini to mum, she inspects the damage to Sita's ankles and scolds her. She has already introduced her to the wellington boot. These are preventable wounds, she tells Sita.

Mum also gifts Sita with her first swimming costume. The next trip, mum suggests, should be to Portobello where she can go onto the beach and bathe in the healing waters. I warn Sita the water will be as cold as the public tap at Thyangboche, near Everest.

Despite the passage of time, Sita's observations about her new homeland are still formative. She likes nothing better than to discuss them with me in private. She never talks about her experiences to my mum or in the street because she says it would force her to stick to her opinions before they're ready. She prefers to have our discussions, and in time, she says her attitudes will then fully form. She tells me she enjoys collecting new experiences and that her social silence, in the meantime, is her chosen coping strategy.

It's fascinating to watch Sita's process of learning. She'll protect herself from jumping onto bandwagons of thought or forming stereotypical ideas. It's these intimate conversations with her I love most. To be close to someone who looks with new eyes at what you have taken for granted all your life, must be one of the most mind-expanding experiences one can ever have.

We spend hours talking about an encounter or an event in her day that most couples would accommodate quickly or ignore. I look forward to these times not just because they take me out of my own world, but because Sita has this remarkable ability to transcend uncomfortable experiences, no matter how hard it is for me to witness them at the time. I'm curious how she expands her horizons and continues to grow in confidence, with an enthusiasm for life that regularly infects both Ram and me.

· · ·

AT PORTOBELLO BEACH, MUM IS THE FIRST TO STRIP OFF AND RUN IN, KNEE deep. Sita hands Ram over to me, takes off her dress and stands at the water's edge. She seems apprehensive and turns to look at me, wading backwards into the sea. She has never faced nor backed into such a large-scale body of water. She splashes through the small waves as they roll onto the shallow beach. She takes another couple of steps back, then squats in a few feet of water to her shoulders. She splashes the water over her head. A symbolic baptism. I know how much she appreciates the rare gift of water, much more than any local here could possibly imagine. She keeps her gaze towards land and feels the texture of the water. I take Ram's clothes off and roll up my trousers. Bare-footed I carry him into the water, dipping him in next to Sita. He screams and shouts that the water is too cold.

'Maybe this is where shouting started,' Sita says, looking at me. She smiles, taking Ram into her arms and quietening him.

A group of teenage lads walk past, along the beach. They turn and look at Sita as she splashes with Ram in the water. I hear one shout aloud to the others. 'Looks like a happy Paki.' The insult rolls off his tongue with thoughtless ease.

My old self and new unite in a rush of anger. Sita smiles at the boys, ignorant of their hurtful intent. This casual racism fuels a cruel purpose in me. My head is boiling as much as my feet are freezing. Mum gives the boys the finger as they laugh. One responds with the much more aggressive fist thrust under his arm ... and they all laugh. I use all my yogic control to avoid giving the lad a Glasgow kiss.

I TELL SITA I FIND IT FRUSTRATING TO WITNESS FLASHES OF PREJUDICE against her or our boy. It's the frequency rather than individual insults that annoy me. I've encountered bigotries on my travels. Nothing here really compares to the scale of a repugnant caste system, particularly in certain parts of India and Nepal. But it never felt personal. This does. I feel such a deep resentment against the perpetrators, possibly because I regard this as home. I'd like to weed out these 'characters' as they are warmly referred to locally. They have been around since my youth, never moved outside their neighbourhood and have assumed an authority based on a flimsy familiarity of the place. They are the people I once laughed with and although most are harmless, some are trapped in an ignorant bigoted mindset of which they are not even aware.

Along with our beach encounter, I witness several young lads and lassies shouting mindless hurtful comment at Sita, mostly for a laugh amongst themselves. They continually make guesses at where they think she comes from. Sometimes I find myself shouting threatening things back. On such occasions, Sita looks disapprovingly at me.

I understand Sita is never invisible to locals in the way I am. When the sun is shining and people dress in light clothes, she attracts musk-like attention, as an attractive Nepali woman. She looks at home in good weather, when her outfits and physical confidence can draw compliments. On dull wintery days, her skin looks darker, and the frequency of hurtful comments seem to increase. The prejudice season seems to run from November to March, with a peak in February. It's as if bigots change mindsets seasonally. 'We'll tolerate people like you here in the summer because you make us feel we're on holiday. But if you're still here in the winter, you must be a loser.' A very special resentment is kept for foreigners who have nowhere better to go. Such is the dismal feelings some locals have on their own surroundings.

I hear impatience turn to insults when Sita innocently holds up a bus queue, not sure of the right bus number. One summer's day we pass a group of builders on their tea break, and they wolf whistle at Sita. One shouts from a scaffold, 'I've heard it's nice.' I thrust a middle finger back towards him, causing even more laughs from his builder pals. It's this 'friendly' banter that now enrages me.

When I tell Sita of my annoyances, she expresses disappointment in me. She defends the insulters. She looks into my eyes, rubs my neck, and tells me that it's impossible for anyone to fully understand what they have not experienced.

4

I hear from Jim Miller at the Leith Art Collective. He's found someone in London who deals in Fine Art and is interested in looking closer at the Avadhoot's tanka paintings. I make appointments to visit the London dealers he recommends as well as my old professor at the London School of Hygiene and Tropical Medicine.

Disappointingly, after five days racing around London, I find only one art dealer who shows any interest in the tankas. It seems any quick sale of dad's paintings is still a distant prospect.

More positive is my LSHTM professor, who gives me details of work he's compiling through a survey on mental-health issues.

I tell Sita my best chance of earning money lies in this expanding area of public-health consultancies.

'It sounds like mental health needs yoga,' Sita says.

'What?'

'Learning more control.'

'Any new branch of Mental Health will involve looking at pages of statistics without ever having to meet a sick person. That's what people in my job do before they can give advice. That's what I'm qualified to do.'

'So it's numbers and statistics that interests gurus of today – not people or their intuition?' Sita asks.

'Statistics highlight what's relevant. My professor agrees that while we spend millions trying to prevent death in the last weeks of life, facts are now pouring in to show more of the conditions we suffer from in later life are self-inflicted and preventable. He's encouraging me to study the wider quality of our life, especially as it relates to mental health. He's retiring soon and there will be more possibilities for consultancies in communication research that he'll send to me.'

On the phone, Sita seems excited. 'That's wonderful, when's your first pay-check?'

'I've told him we are pretty desperate for a regular income.'

'What does it involve?'

'Looking for gaps in the current research and interpreting the findings of some surveys already finished.'

'And travel?'

'Not in the beginning.' I hesitate, 'but travel would be required later. And the salary's good. It will cover our rent and for you to come along if you want.'

'I don't think I can, with Ram's schooling.'

'Let's see. I have to go now.'

'I've missed you.'

'I've missed you more.'

'How do you know that?'

'I've examined the data. You're a yogini and more controlled, so the odds are that I miss you more.'

My dad talks about time as the solution to problems. He refers to time as the healer. Yet the more problems you amass, the longer time is needed to clear out the backlog and regain a sense of being healed.

PART FOUR: EMPLOYMENT

14

After I return to Edinburgh, I find Sita unusually animated and excited. We have a cup of Nepali chai, while she tells me her time alone has been productive. She has made two new friends in the space of my week away.

'Two at once,' I say, 'like Edinburgh buses,' a reference she doesn't understand. She continues, telling me she may also have found paid work for herself.

'That's interesting,' I say, struggling to imagine what that might be.

'I was shopping at the supermarket, looking at spices and I was approached by a young woman who asked me where I was from. When I told her, she became very excited and friendly and asked if I knew anything about massage.'

'My goodness,' I reply, searching for words.

'It was such a coincidence,' Sita says. 'I never expected anyone here to ask me such a thing. When I said I did know about yoga massage, the woman introduced herself and told me to contact her for possible work. Her name is Cindy, and she gave me her business card.'

'How interesting.' I look at the card, which reads, 'Healing from Feeling – Sauna and Massage' with a phone number and no address. 'Was Cindy Scottish?'

'Yes I think so. We didn't talk long. She had a Scottish accent and was nicely dressed, like a movie star. It sounds interesting, doesn't it?'

'It's definitely something we need to talk more about.'

'Then walking home later,' Sita continues, seeming even more excited, 'I passed the Indian take-away at Haymarket and this young Asian man dropped his bag of food outside when he came out. I heard him curse in Nepali and so I spoke to him. He's a student studying computer science at Napier University. His name is Mahesh Guatam and he gave me his card also, with his phone number.'

'Amazing, you'll soon need a Filofax.'

'A what?'

'A diary. Amazing though to find a Nepali friend and have job offer on the same day.'

Sita smiles. '*Huncha.*'

'Please don't call Cindy just yet.'

'OK but I would like to invite Mahesh over for *Dal Bhat* and *Tarkari* soon?'

'Sure.'

The idea of having someone over for diner makes me suddenly realise how isolated we've been since we arrived here. We have both been so preoccupied with ourselves and our family survival that we haven't invited anyone except my mother to visit us. This was never our lifestyle in Kathmandu. I realise that I've been on full alert to protect Sita from any harm and have unintentionally separated us from the people and community around us. Although Cindy sounds like a no-go, Mahesh could be a godsend, and within a few days Sita invites him for dinner.

DESPITE US HAVING A DOORBELL, I HEAR THE FAINT BUT PERSISTENT SOUND of thumping on our front door. It is a noise I'm so unfamiliar with, I ignore it at first, thinking it may be workmen in the upstairs flat. The sound continues until I finally hear the brass knocker being used in unison with the thumping. I open the door, to find a young man with a huge grin and bleeding knuckles.

'You must be Mahesh?'

'Yes, you have a big house and a strong door.'

I point to the electric doorbell and see his eyes light up in much the same way as Sita's did in her days of cultural discovery.

'I'm James, Mahesh, *Tapai kasaari ho...* come in – how are you?'

'I was about to return home,' he says, holding up his damaged hand. 'We don't have bells with power in the Kathmandu Valley.'

'Yes we do,' Sita says, 'but we ring them to summon a deity. Welcome, Mahesh.'

I treat Mahesh's wounded fist like a medic. His middle knuckle is bleeding and I bathe his hand in Dettol. Sita puts a plaster on his wound. She speaks to him in floods of Nepali.

While she chats, I feel both nostalgic and refreshed. This indeed is a welcome coincidence; our first social Nepali dinner since we moved here.

Our guest seems nervous and talks quickly in a mix of Nepali and English. He arrived in Scotland only six weeks ago to study computer programming. He is twenty-three years old. He has a handsome big face with the features of a Tibetan monk. He's also just over five foot tall with the stout frame of a Gurkha.

During our evening's conversation, Mahesh slowly relaxes. He eats energetically with his fingers and tells us he is the third son of a prominent Gurkha Major, not the British Gurkhas, but the Nepalese Gurkhas. He was brought up in Gorkha province and educated in Kathmandu. He mentions his father is currently serving in Lebanon, for the United Nations Peacekeepers.

Mahesh explains how embarrassed he was to be caught swearing outside the Indian take-away by Sita.

'I said some very rude words and this woman looked at me and smiled.'

He is keen to hear the full story of how Sita and I met. When Sita mentions our links to the Moni Baba, Mahesh becomes as excited as a devotee. He tells us his father regularly met the Moni Baba and he personally saw the Baba when he was a child. He also mentions he has seen the famous Avadhoot from a distance but has never met him. We keep quiet about our family ties to the insurance-fraud Sanyassin.

Mahesh questions us long into the night, seeming reluctant to leave. Our first social dinner lasts until an hour before sunrise. When Mahesh leaves, he namastes us, walking backward, almost to the edge of Charlotte Square. It takes Sita and I a few days to recover our sleep pattern.

MAHESH QUICKLY BECOMES SUCH A REGULAR VISITOR THAT WE PREPARE A bed in our study for him to sleep over. Sita tells me she is very pleased to know that Mahesh is bi.

'It will be good for Ram,' she says.

It's then I realise that what Sita means is that Mahesh is bilingual. He quickly becomes Uncle Mahesh to Ram and plays as if he is the same age as him. Mahesh often helps by walking Ram to his new nursery school in Stockbridge. He makes Sita laugh out loud reconstructing Nepali games and telling boyhood stories from their homeland. He talks for hours in both English and Nepali, making fun and good sense by combining words from each language. A brand-new bubble of trust is made between Mahesh, Sita and I, and we make sure Ram sits in on all our discussions, so he can learn more of his mother tongue.

Mahesh also tells us the regular Nepali gossip from his relatives in Kathmandu. One evening while he cooks Badjas, he reminds me of Tilak as he talks about his father's adventures and service with the Gurkhas. I am transported back to meals in Barabase where Tilak told his own tales.

'My dad's Gurkha regiment in the UN Peacekeepers became famous in Nepal. The were part of the peacekeeping force who stood firm on a bridge in Lebanon and did not let the Israelis cross during their invasion in 1982.'

'I remember reading about that incident,' I say.

'I know nothing about it,' Sita confesses.

'My dad was stationed at a Lebanese border checkpoint, and it was the only place on the zone line of UN's peacekeeping forces that Israel did not break through. The stand-off was abandoned later, after the Israelis drove around or through all the other UN checkpoints without any difficulty. I believe the Israeli generals knew my father's troops would've resisted to a man. They were the only soldiers working for the UN that day, that did their job.'

15

It's summer and Sita is keen to go north once more. She explains to Mahesh that these are not really mountains by Nepal standards, more foothills. We agree to take Mahesh and Ram in the flower van to climb a Munro near Killin. Sita asks me to explain what a Munro is to Mahesh.

'There are more than three hundred of these hills across Scotland, all are over three thousand feet in height,' I say.

Mahesh looks suitably impressed. 'I've heard of the Scottish Highlands. So your family owns over three hundred hills?'

I realise it's my perceived ownership that's impressed Mahesh, not the height of our mountains.

'James' family don't own them Mahesh, but they are named after a man called Munro who discovered and measured them. They do that a lot here,' Sita says.

We park in a picturesque car park and pull Ram and our gear out of the back of mum's van. A set of returning hill walkers walk towards us and stop to chat. They greet us like neighbours.

'They should enjoy it,' one woman says to me, 'though the last part's a bit steep for strangers.'

The other woman turns to look at Ram then Mahesh and says, 'What a handsome wee boy, looks just like his dad.'

Mahesh nods, bewildered. Even nice country folk make guesses at reality.

Ram takes off, running up the trail, passing an older man struggling behind this group.

'Mind and keep an eye on the wee one, and keep the gates shut, there are lambs on the hills today.'

'Cheers,' I say and we all march off.

'Did these ladies think I was Ram's father?' Mahesh asks.

'Yes. You're perceptive.'

'And did that old man offer you a drink?'

'No – cheers is also a figure of speech here... meaning gratitude.'

FROM A DISTANCE, MAHESH HAS THE PHYSIQUE OF A TEENAGER, YET FEW people here would appreciate how strong he is. Early on our hill trek he lifts and carries Ram on his shoulders to the summit, without so much as a deep breath. At the top he takes in the view and chases Ram around the top cairn while Sita and I dig out our picnic sandwiches and a flask full of Nepali lassi.

Two young women arrive at the top as we sit. They politely wish us a good day and stand for a moment taking photos of each other.

'He's a Munro,' Mahesh says to them, as if I own the hill.

'Well well. And here we are Munro bagging,' comes the reply with laughter.

Mahesh then takes a drink and shouts 'cheers' to the young women.

'Cheers,' they shout back.

I explain to Mahesh that Munro bagging means the women are trying to climb all the Munros.

'In one day?' he asks.

'No.'

'How many have you bagged?' I ask the women.

'We've done one hundred and thirteen, in the past five years,' one says, smiling proudly at me.

From behind, I hear Sita shout, 'Mahesh, while we are here... would you like another lassi?'

The woman I'm talking to glares at Sita, then at me.

'It's a yoghurt drink, not you, she's offering.'

The lassies walk on, laughing while we picnic.

THE WEATHER IS MUCH BETTER THAN THE LAST TIME WE VISITED THE Highlands, and to Sita it seems a different country. Such is the mask of the seasons here. Mahesh lies on his back and tells us he has a new appreciation of Scotland.

'And why's that?' I ask.

'I think finding peace in today's world can be hard,' Mahesh philosophises.

'It's always difficult if you are searching for peace, don't you think?'

'But I think you can find it here.'

'What do you think, Sita?'

'Peace is everywhere... until it is disturbed. Mahesh's right, you can find it here, but only if you can see it in a cucumber sandwich.'

ON THE WAY DOWN, RAM DISCOVERS AN INJURED GROUSE. IT LOOKS lifeless but as he bends to examine it, one wing flaps. The other seems damaged with a pellet shot. Mahesh lifts the bird and insists on taking it home so he can help it to heal. I explain that would be illegal and try to talk him out of it. Ram, however, pleads like a monk for us to save the creature. He has a calming effect on the bird, and it does not resist his handling of it.

We end up bringing the bird back to Edinburgh. I think it's unlikely to last the night; it hardly moves on the journey home. Mahesh keeps it wrapped in his rain jacket. He teaches Ram a Nepali song which they both sing to it on the way home. Mahesh the bird-whisperer then smuggles it into his flat at the University halls of residence. I have no idea of his healing skills but a week later, he tells us the bird is still alive, doing well, and he'll bring it over to show Ram one day soon.

Ram is excited by the prospect of having a pet bird. Two of his friends in nursery class have budgies and they have talked about their pets at show and tell. Ram asks if he might be able to take his new pet grouse into his school one day and show it off to friends. Mahesh, however, has other plans.

Three weeks after sneaking the grouse into his student accommodation, Mahesh brings the fully recovered bird around to our flat. We have invited him to come for dinner to celebrate Deshain, the largest festival on Nepal's substantial list of religious celebrations. Once he arrives, Mahesh shows us how healed the bird is. The grouse struts and nods like a whisky advert across the carpet. Ram is fascinated, a little afraid and very excited. Mahesh then invites Ram to join him in the garden to see more. I wonder what more the bird can do in our backyard. Mahesh proceeds with bird in hand down our stairs towards the back garden, Ram skipping along in pursuit behind him.

Sita, who has been in the kitchen all this time, asks me where Mahesh has taken Ram. I tell her, he's taken him down with the bird into the garden.

'I suspect he's trained it to stand on his arm like a hawk. I just hope he's not going to let Ram try anything daft.'

Sita suddenly runs towards our back window to look out, over the garden. I join her and watch Mahesh and Ram both stride towards the woodpile at the end of the garden. I notice Mahesh has a rolled-up newspaper under his arm. Sita whispers something to herself in Nepali.

'What?' I ask her.

She pushes up the sash window, bends down and calls out loud in Nepali. It's a whole string of words, so fast I can only make out, *Durga* and *shakti peeths*.

She turns to me and says, 'He's going to sacrifice the bird.'

Then with her head thrust back out the window, Sita screams like a Scottish fishwife, 'No Mahesh, no!' in English, followed by another torrent of Nepali. She turns to me and says, 'Go!'

Running out the back door, I see Mahesh with his hand on the grouse's body and a kukri knife poised high above its head.

'Stop,' I shout.

He pauses when he sees me.

'What's wrong, Jamesji? It's a huntable bird, no?'

I run and lift Ram up, placing my hands over his eyes. Mahesh looks at me then up towards Sita and says with a pleading voice, 'It is our custom at Deshain.'

He seems determined to follow through with this. One arm is still poised high with the knife.

'Not here,' I call out, 'don't do it here, where the neighbours can see.' I stress anyone witnessing this might call the police.

He tells me he does not want to mess up our house. I whisk Ram back inside and Sita takes over negotiations from our window. She urges Mahesh to leave his makeshift chopping block and come back into the house.

This now infamous grouse, having been shot by man and nursed back to life with loving care, has its head ceremoniously removed in our bathtub. I'm a little shocked that Sita has let him do this, but Mahesh seems very grateful he's been allowed to complete this sacrifice.

'We have to give thought and prayer for the millions of other chickens, thousands of goats and hundreds of buffaloes, at this very moment, sacrificed for the ancient tradition at Deshain in Nepal.'

By way of putting me properly in my place, Mahesh also asks me to compare what he's doing with the Western world's celebrations during Thanksgiving or our Christmas festivals. These celebrations include much more slaughter. The only difference is ours is done on an industrial scale, out of our sight.

'Exactly,' I say, 'out of sight and there's a reason for that.'

'What we call sacrifice, you just call food preparation,' Mahesh says.

He then plucks and cooks the bird, chanting to the gods to protect us all as a family as he does so.

Sita meantime occupies Ram in his bedroom, explaining some of the gentler aspects of the festival to him. We agree not to mention that Mahesh will eat his giant pet budgie for dinner later tonight.

Mahesh says his countrymen will be following his example no matter what distance they are from home or the laws they now live with.

I tell him this is not an argument that would work with our police.

Sita tells him that the laws here should be obeyed. Some have been made by a woman.

'What do you mean?' Mahesh asks... and I too await Sita's answer.

'British people voted to be ruled by a woman – Mrs Margaret Thatcher, a woman, was once a Prime Minister here.'

'Like all fellow Nepalese, today I am giving sacrifice to the Goddess Kali.'

Thatcher and Kali, I think. One and the same.

16

As well as being a traditionalist and a scientist, Mahesh would make an excellent writer of religious stories. He is greatly influenced by the superstitions that pose as beliefs in Nepal and he tells elaborate tales of the miracles that his gods have manifested across the Himal. There is not a minute in Mahesh's day when he does not acknowledge the presence of a God in everything he does. Whether crossing a street or a bridge, boarding a bus or buying a take-away curry, he whispers prayers to the gods to cast out worry and help him through life. The pinnacle of his devotion and a guidance for much of what he wants to do with his life comes from the King of Nepal.

King Birendra is to both Mahesh and Sita the living incarnation of Vishnu and inspires daily worship by all his subjects, both in the country and across the world. Mahesh's stories remind me of all the young men I spent time discussing religion and philosophy with, in Barabase. During that time, I was impressed by the strength of their beliefs and loyalty to the King as a coping mechanism for the harsh conditions they lived in. I find it interesting to see Mahesh keep these beliefs alive here, even in the academic environment he now inhabits.

Mahesh informs us his father is now back living in Nepal and that he's heard that one of the country's most famous statues has begun 'sweating'. The statue of Lord Bhimeshor Mahadeva, in Dolakha district, some hundred and thirty kilometres east from Kathmandu, has been seen perspiring. This is a very bad sign for the country since the last time the idol sweated was in 1961 and later that year, hundreds of towns and villages were wiped out by floodwaters. The most famous sweat before that was in 1934, when an earthquake claimed almost twenty thousand lives across Nepal.

Mahesh tells us that the King has sent two he-goats to be sacrificed at the temple to stop the sweating. His father stresses that because the King has acted so quickly, things should now be alright. Mahesh tells Sita that she need not worry about the situation back home. The goats' spirits will act as a deodorant, I assume.

Sita also knows this temple and the Bhimeshor statue, having been there with the Moni Baba. She explains to Mahesh that the statue represents not just one God but three and that the statue only takes on the form of Bhimishor from four until ten in the morning. Mahesh is a little disturbed by this information.

'From ten till twelve the statue represents Lord Shiva,' Sita says, 'and all through the afternoon that same statue is worshipped as Lord Vishnu. There is no need to be concerned until one knows exactly which of the gods has been sweating.'

Sita takes Mahesh's hands in hers and for the first time in my company speaks to him as if he was her confused little bother.

'These old beliefs were abandoned by modern sages like the Moni Baba years ago. He encouraged people to evolve their beliefs,' adds Sita.

'It's not the sacrifice of goats or birds that make a difference,' she continues, hinting at Mahesh's bath-tub grouse kill. 'These were habits formed at a time when there were great hardships. Parents persuaded to offer their children as sacrifice in times of social stress. A wife instructed to throw herself onto her husband's funeral pyre. These beliefs must find their way into our stories and history books, to educate us, not be kept as a murderous practice.'

. . .

For the next few weeks, I bury myself in health research to earn my modest salary.

I find much has changed in the field of Public Health research. A flood of new information methods is currently available because of the AIDS pandemic. It is shared by universities and health institutions globally. There seems new global interest in analysing communication successes that prevents the need for drugs. At the same time, the search for new drugs and medicine goes on.

Sita is happy to see me at work and gives me the space I need. She fosters her relationship with Mahesh like an older sister to a brother. They regularly partner up for events and outings around the University. On one morning in particular, Mahesh arrives at our door very early and breathless.

'Son chai cha?' (How are you?)

I reply with a Namaste sign, my palms pressed together, still in my pyjamas.

'I came to see if you are both interested in seeing a movie this evening at the Student Union. They are showing the film 'Caravan'. It's a docu-drama shot in Mustang. It's very good, I hear, and tickets are selling fast.'

'Perhaps Sita will go with you,' I say. 'I still have much reading to do, and I need to look after Ram.'

Sita joins us in her pyjamas, and to my surprise changes into a long skirt and t-shirt in front of Mahesh. She voices interest in seeing the film. After a time is set, Mahesh sprints off to get the tickets.

Thinking of what I might be missing by not seeing this film, I take my mind back to Nepal's high valleys and the lifestyles there. It opens the floodgate on a new stream of thought for the analysis I'm writing. This perhaps is the unique perspective I can bring to the project. My practical experiences of health in Nepal. What can the Western medical knowledge, practiced by six hundred registered doctors in Nepal, do in comparison to the influences of four hundred thousand faith healers to a population of some nineteen million?

I think of the comparisons that Western health authorities make. If you are guided by averages and you only average people in the West, their lifestyles are already laced with the effects of pharmaceutical drugs, the overconsumption of food and all the many habits with side effects. In terms of influence, we may have hundreds of thousands of medically trained doctors, but in our case they are outnumbered by the massive influence of advertisers encouraging consumption.

The health averages of people here are not necessarily averages to aspire to. Surely an average should include all human ways of life and environments. That might be the petri dish I can examine further. This line of thought fits in with the limitations of mapping Western health problems as some hybrid strain, built in a world of plenty and overconsumption.

I AM STILL WORKING ON MY PROPOSAL WHEN SITA AND MAHESH RETURN from their night out, full of enthusiasm. When I ask how they enjoyed the movie, Sita says she loved it.

'*Deri ramro* – a beautiful glimpse of home,' she smiles.

Mahesh begs to differ. 'It was good,' he says, 'but they did not show enough of the hardship in the yak herdsman's life. They took a very romantic view of our tough lifestyle, filming mostly the beautiful landscape of our country.'

Sita says Mahesh is being too critical. He laughs back at her, his criticism dissolved by her positivity. Sita says that there were many couples around them and she overheard some wishing they could go and see a place such as Nepal.

'And all I could think about,' Mahesh says, 'was how many young people in Kathmandu want to visit here.'

I tell them I've been working, writing a new proposal all the time they were out.

'What are you writing about?' Mahesh asks.

'I want to suggest the Western lifestyle should not become the gold standard for health behaviour. Health insurance people here tend only to study their subscribers. It's an interesting angle, I think.'

Mahesh tells us he must leave. He has an early morning class. Sita thanks him for taking her out and she sees him to the door.

I hear the front door open, but it doesn't close. I suddenly grow curious and walk towards the hallway. I see Sita and Mahesh whispering. I hear Mahesh say in Nepali, 'You must tell him.'

Sita answers, 'I will when the time is right.'

Then to my amazement, Sita takes Mahesh's face in her hands and kisses him full on the lips. She holds it for longer than a farewell gesture. She breaks the kiss and looks into his eyes and then kisses him again, for even longer.

A familiar trauma begins to rumble through my interior. A wave of betrayal sweeps over me as a physical sensation. I feel like someone has kicked me solidly in the stomach. It's set a hive of bees off in my gut. My legs become weak and I squat. If I thought I'd made myself better protected from hurt in my time with Sita, I was wrong. Hurt jumps once more onto my back and sets off an emotional panic. Part of my brain rides headlong towards a cliff-face of disbelief.

17

M y usual defence of withdrawal kicks in. It's easy under the guise of work, but I can't write anything. I sit alone seeking explanation.

For the next few days, my pretence of being deeply occupied holds out. I wait to see if Sita says anything to me, but she doesn't. Alone, my imagination runs riot. I feel physically sick whenever I think that my trust has been shattered. I run though what it might be that Mahesh thinks Sita should tell me. I feel no change from her nor any sense of malice but the vision of what I witnessed is too real to ignore. It's that familiar camouflage of deceit.

Any type of confrontation with Sita is still too upsetting for me to consider, but Mahesh is a different matter.

When he arrives for a cup of Nepali chai, Mahesh seems completely normal. No outburst of emotion and I see no change in him since I last saw him. He tells me he's received a letter from Kathmandu. Having moved back to Nepal from UN duties, his dad's regiment has been re-assigned to the Royal Palace. He tells me there are several districts now where there's growing unrest and support for Maoist sympathies in the hills.

'This is communism which is coming from the Naxal States in India,' he says.

After his third cup of sweet chai, he's still acting like the sweet man I once knew and not the man I saw locking lips with my wife. I prepare my attack with a distraction.

'Karl Marx could never have predicted how modern technology would destroy communism in the West. Where workers once rioted against conditions, technology has eased their physical burden. Don't you think the same could be said for changing labour conditions in Nepal? A culturally diluted call for a Marxist revolution is not really going to work.'

'It's not diluting the call, Jamesji, it's answering the call. My studies show a future where even more will be done remotely. I can't explain why my countrymen in Nepal have such a sudden and late interest in a communist leadership. But my father says he is afraid there is a chance they might succeed.'

'Mahesh... I saw you kissing Sita before you left here, after your movie night.'

Mahesh's skin turns purple red.

'So that's what's been troubling you.' Sita laughs and steps forward. She holds my shoulder at arm's length.

I look at her with surprise. There's no redness or pallor, no shake in her voice and no movements in her eye contact with me. This is not the caught-you moment I expected.

'Mahesh did not kiss me. I kissed Mahesh.'

'Why?'

'Because he's thinking of asking a fellow student out and he told me he'd never kissed a woman before.'

My anger drains like a bath unplugged. I quickly try to re-boot my brain.

'You seemed to enjoy it...' comes out before the re-boot is complete.

'I did, and so did he. Didn't you, Mahesh?'

Mahesh remains silent, looking down.

Sita continues, 'I'm sure we both felt the charge of a loving kiss. I did not want him to experience the gesture of a farewell kiss. The way people do here, on the cheek.'

'So what is it that you think Sita has to tell me, Mahesh?'

Sita drops her eye contact. I'm not out of the woods yet. She looks at Mahesh and says, 'Yes, there is something I need to tell you.'

The relief I started to feel is put on hold.

'When you were in London, I found the business card of Cindy, the woman I met at the supermarket. I called her and I've had a couple of meetings with her.'

'You called... the woman offering you work in a massage parlour?'

'Yes.'

I laugh with relief. 'Why didn't you say anything?'

'I wanted to try to find work for myself. I was going to tell you if I was successful, not before.'

'So, did you find work?'

'No, not yet, but I demonstrated my yogic massage.'

'How did you do that?

'I massaged her.'

'Where?'

'On our bed.'

Suitably chastised, Mahesh takes his leave. He sheepishly declines when I offer to kiss him goodnight. Then I continue talking to Sita.

'I invited Cindy here to discuss the possibility of working part-time at her sauna.'

Sita keeps talking with enthusiasm, explaining how Cindy has told her that many of the people who come to the sauna just need to feel some love and attention. She is obviously imagining a different scenario to what I am. She tells me that Cindy was very impressed with her massage techniques.

'And what techniques did you teach her?'

'Those I learned from the Moni Baba,' she states. As if this makes the whole idea legitimate.

'Cindy has offered training on how to do more types of massage. The sauna is not far from here.'

'I'm so very relieved that this is the secret that you have finally revealed,' I laugh. 'But the thought that you are seriously considering doing massage for punters in a 'sauna' off Rose Street, has my nervous energy turning into hysterics.'

'Perhaps we can visit Cindy together?'

As the night finally ends Sita, follows me into the bedroom. Ram is sound asleep and for the first time in a while we fall into each other's arms. We are well schooled in the touches that form our ritual foreplay. It is different for me this night, bathed in relief as I am.

I have no doubt that Sita would make a wonderful masseuse. I have been the recipient of her sensitive and invigorating touch for years. She need only place a hand on me anywhere, at any time, and I feel a surge of energy. It has never occurred to me that she might like to do this to others and make a living from doing so. As we roll on our bed, I can't shake off an image of Cindy being massaged here by my wife.

18

Sita is making breakfast wearing her black Sabrina sweatpants with her Nepali chulo blouse, which exposes her bare midriff. I suddenly visualise this outfit as a potential sauna uniform and shudder at how our conversations on the subject could unfold, if handled poorly. Sita tells me to wake Ram for his porridge. I walk through to see our boy still asleep in a forward death posture. He looks longer horizontal than when he's standing. I feel ultra-protective of our family unit. I let the boy sleep longer and return to Sita.

'I want to talk more about Cindy and this sauna job, Sita.'

'I think you should hold back your fears until you meet her.'

'Do you know what men expect when they go to a sauna or a massage parlour here?'

Sita steps back, recognising a change in my tone.

'It may not be what you think it is.'

'Please, tell me what I think... swamiji.'

I pause.

'Remember our conversations with Swami Y when we first met, and he said that Western people pay for everything in their lives including water?'

'Yes.'

'Well here, people also pay for love... or sexual relief, to be more precise.'

'Yes, Cindy explained that.'

'Did she actually tell you what you might be asked to do?'

'Only that I would never be asked to do anything I did not want to do. What do you mean by sexual relief?'

I sense danger here. I know Sita is not this innocent or ignorant.

'In saunas here... not all... but in some, people pay for sex.'

'I understand.'

'We have to make sure that it is not one of those saunas that this Cindy is asking you to work in.'

There is a long silence... too long for my comfort.

'Those who pay for love are just as in need of it as those who do not. Everyone requires intimate physical contact and love. People search for it in whatever way they can. Let's go and see this place before we decide.'

I sense a risk now. If we visit a grubby loft, Sita might not see it as such. It might seem modern or nicely decorated in comparison to the ramshackle rooms she's taught yoga in.

'You treat our lovemaking as a physical itch that we need to scratch now and then,' she says.

'Are you talking about us or the global we?'

'You and I.'

'That's a bit harsh.'

I'm unsure what more to say so I go with the positive.

'It's more like a lovely itch?'

Sita laughs as if yet again I'm trying to understand something that she's already answered for me. She rests her head on my shoulder.

'One day, you'll accept something as being potentially helpful. And be less suspicious. This is my discovery on a path for a solution, not the solution.'

'So you really are considering working for Cindy?'

'If it helps with our money problems, yes.'

'I think she may be proposing that you do more than just massage men.'

'Yes... I know it's with women too. See it my way. This is your culture trying to understand the basics of tantra yoga.'

'And what's the aim of that?'

'Not to take sex too seriously... it's not a disease.'

SITA PLACES SUCH IMPORTANCE ON MEETING CINDY BECAUSE THEY MET coincidentally and that's how the gods work. I must remind myself that it's not her burning desire to become a masseuse. It's much more indicative of Sita's approach to life... going with the flow, living without a fixed plan, so that one can take advantage of coincidences. She believes they happen for a reason.

Sita realises she has limited opportunities to work, she has no educational qualifications and although I think I understand completely why Cindy has appeared in our life, I'm obliged to find out more.

One afternoon while mum watches Ram, we head off to visit Cindy's sauna.

'If this seems like an illegal business, I will tell you in Nepali and so be prepared to walk out,' I tell Sita earnestly.

'What's illegal about massage?'

'How it ends.'

We turn into one of Edinburgh's north facing, forever-dark lanes, from an already dark street.

'I'll walk away, as long as your lingam stops talking to me.'

'What do you mean?'

'James, it's as if it's not been you... in our recent conversations.'

We reach the door and I ring the buzzer.

'Bong-jour,' a recorded voice crackles from a tiny speaker.

'It's Sita and James, here to see Cindy,' I shout in my thickest accent. There is a moment of silence, and we're buzzed in.

We climb a narrow flight of stairs, half of which I believe is the original width. The left side is stone wall, the right thin hardboard. It's covered in wallpaper of trees with pink spring blossoms. At the top we enter a sparse waiting room. There's a large gold mirror reflecting a disco-ball light onto cane furniture. On a small round table is a goldfish bowl with a single goldfish swimming in circles. As I turn and look back, I see the way out is down the same staircase, split by the wallpapered hardboard down the middle. Instead of blossom trees on the way down the wallpaper has autumn leaves, presumably to make visitors feel they've been here for a whole summer. It's clearly designed so those leaving will not to be seen by those entering... and vice versa.

In a side room, two young women in robes are sitting on cane chairs talking and looking bored. Another woman walks in behind the girls.

'Welcome to Healing by Feeling,' she says.

'We're not customers,' I say.

'Ah ken,' says Cindy. 'You must be Mr Sita.'

Cindy is much younger than I thought she'd be, looking around the same age as Sita. She's slim, with dyed black hair and purple streaks. She's wearing a pair of black tracksuit bottoms with two tears slashed across each thigh. She has a sequinned tank top with a few shiny studs protruding from her shoulders and a simple black leather collar round her neck. It's a mixed look, Scottish Goth, part pet dog, part mauled by dog. Her outfit flashes whenever the disco light catches it, and she seems seriously on her guard.

She takes us on a tour of the premises, except for one room where she tells us there's a customer inside.

'They're havin the Train to Nirvana treatment,' she says.

We're shown four other rooms, each of the first three wallpapered with glossy vinyl prints to create different environments: a beach scene with blue sky and sea, a dark graveyard and a highrise office view over New York. The fourth room is empty and looks under decoration. Each also has what looks like a painters' papering table with a yoga matt and blanket on top. The place is even seedier than I expected, so I believe Sita will be suitably put off the idea of working here. As we return to reception, we walk past the Train to Nirvana room, and we can all clearly hear that someone is about to arrive at the station.

'I guess this place is exactly what you imagined it to be, Mr Sita,' Cindy says, 'so let's get straight to the point.' She lifts a spiral-bound folder from under the reception, flips through to the end, presses the page open and swivels the book around so we can see. Sita and I look at a panoramic view of the Himalaya. At the centre is *Machhapuchhare* Fish Tail mountain and on either side the Annapurna range of mountains stretch out majestically on either side.

'If Sita wants the job here we can put this onto the wall in that last room. She can feel at home and do onything she wants inside. Some people come for a massage, some a cuddle, some for a talk and some want more. They awe pay the same fee, so I don't really care what happens inside the room. My girls and a couple of freelance men control things and I look after them. But also... I never like seeing a dissatisfied customer... it's ma business policy. So, there you are.'

I ask Cindy why she thought that Sita might like to come and work here.

'I didnae think she would,' she replies. 'After she got in contact with me, ah just didnae want to lose touch wi her. I've never met onyone quite like her before. And we got along fine at your hoose.'

I suddenly glimpse an honesty in Cindy beneath her bravado, until she continues. 'She wants a job and I'd like to help her... isn't that OK with you?' Cindy moves closer to me. 'It's just business: take it or leave it.'

'We're not customers.'

'So... what is it that you do for a living, Mr Sita?'

I'm so taken aback by this question, I fire out the first thing that enters my mind.

'I'm a council Health Inspector,' I answer, as if it's a threat.

'Well, you might meet some of your council colleagues here, if you come back tonight.'

We both laugh and Sita looks puzzled.

'Can I offer you some soda or tea?'

'No thanks. We'll have to get going. Thanks for the tour and your time.'

'No problem, Mr Health Inspector. But get back to me soon,' she says. 'We always encourage inspections here.' Cindy speaks like a character time-warped into the present from a Benny Hill show.

As we leave, Sita gives Cindy a *namaste* sign with her hands clasped, and Cindy gives one in return. As we walk down the stairs, the hardboard wall rattles. Before we reach the bottom, I hear Cindy shout.

'You're welcome back anytime, Mr Sita. I owe yeh two free massages, for the two yur wife gave me... on yer very comfie bed.'

Most of the walk home is in silence but once we reach the quieter streets of the New Town, I ask Sita what she thought of the visit.

'I like Cindy,' she says, 'but I think really I need to meet more people here to find work.'

'So what sort of work would you like to do?'

'Well, I had thought to start with teaching some traditional Nepali yoga classes, so I could meet people. I thought it might be at Cindy's place but now I've seen it, it's far too small. I don't know how to find a place to teach.'

'I can explore that idea with you, but isn't teaching yoga still an earning problem for you?'

'Why's that?'

'Because of your insistence of never charging folk in case you become a *Bhogini*.'

'While you were away, I discussed this with your mum, and she suggested a solution to that issue.'

'My mum? What did she say?'

'She told me that in lots of churches here, there's an "honesty box" at the door. People put in whatever donation they can afford if they feel grateful for what they've learned.'

19

Mahesh will occasionally join us midway between our homes, in the children's playpark at the west end of Princes Street Gardens. There is a row of wooden seats facing the west side of Edinburgh Castle and at certain times of day these gardens are deserted and quiet. Sita discovered this route from new town to old town on her early shopping trips. Ram loves climbing the wooden frames and swings on ropes. It's his now well-practiced Gurkha commando circuit.

Even if you are non-religious, in Edinburgh city centre there's no getting away from churches and steeples. Many have been converted into houses or power stations, but they are still there, grand and imposing. Sitting under St Cuthbert, one still operational church, Mahesh joins me on the park bench.

'Well, did you see it?' I ask.

'Yes it's in there as you said, the Honesty Box.'

'What do you think?'

'Yogis in Nepal carry a pot, for donations.'

'But could such an idea work here?'

'You know more than I do about the tax situation, but I do have some ideas.'

Mahesh then tells me his suggestion for our business plan. He suggests we invite people to an introductory yoga class and then ask them how much salary they make. He says we can instruct them to give a percentage donation for Sita's class. Mahesh thinks only by asking what people earn, will Sita be able to estimate how much she should ask for.

'There's a flaw in this approach, Mahesh.'

'OK, tell me.'

'Everyone I've ever known in my life,' I say, 'including my relatives and close friends, would give you the same answer to such a question.'

'What's that?'

'It's too rude to tell you and we are sitting in front of a church. If you wish Sita to experience a complete wall of silence in her first yoga class, just ask people what salary they earn.'

Disappointment crosses Mahesh's face.

'There's no doubt the popularity of Hatha yoga in Edinburgh has greatly increased since my dad wrote his book.'

'Your dad wrote a book on yoga?'

Oops, I think.

'What's your girlfriend's name?' I ask Mahesh quickly.

'It's Mandy.'

'Where's she from?'

'She's from Dundee.'

'And she's your second kiss, eh?'

'I'm sorry.'

'There's no need to apologise,' I say. 'Your tantra yoga teacher has already explained everything to me.'

'Yoga's reputation has certainly grown everywhere,' Mahesh proclaims divertingly, 'but it's not because of teachers. It's because of the practitioners. As yogis get older, they usually look in better shape than most others of the same age. When people look into the eyes of someone who's practiced it most of their life, someone like Sita, that's where they can see its value.'

· · ·

WHEN I GET HOME, SITA HANDS ME A LETTER THAT HAS JUST ARRIVED, addressed to us both from the Peebles care home.

Inside is a typed message from the Kindare management, who are sad to inform us of the passing of Maisy Macdonald's older brother Tam. It goes on to say that he died peacefully at the age of ninety-five.

The envelope also contains a message from Maisy to Sita. I read it out loud, since handwritten Scots is still a challenge for Sita.

'Dear Mrs Sita... I just want tae thank you for being my friend. I think of you every day, every time I put my teeth in. It was old Tam's time to go. They took his teeth out for the last time at this morning's cremation and gave them to me. They said they would explode because they had metal bits in them. I've now got them in a cup on my mantle place next to his ashes. A cried a wee bit till they made me think of you. God bless you and yer wee boy and that nice man of yours. Love Maisy.'

Sita holds back tears.

'You made an impression on many old people that loved you at the care home.'

'Can you help me write a reply, please?'

'Yes, and she has just given you a wonderful reference for teaching yoga here,' I say. 'I can easily get more from Minister McRae about your classes in Peebles. You can be considered a qualified yoga teacher here, by popular demand.'

RAM IS ALMOST FIVE AND NOW HAS DEVELOPED THE COMPLETE EDINBURGH accent, thanks to nursery school. It's the way he forms sentences. I notice it one day when Sita and I pick him up. He stands waiting with his teacher Ms Macinlay, from the Isle of Skye. She's handing him over, praising his behaviour and language skills and as we walk away Ram says, 'Hi dad, when ah grow up... ah want tae be hur.'

Ram repeats what he's said in Nepali to Sita, but she nods that she already understood him in Scots. Ram's Nepali is much better than mine. When he's not happy with me, he'll slag me off to Sita in Nepali.

Along with his use of a *keelie* Scot's vocabulary, Ram has an adventurous streak that worries me. He has blind confidence in any physical challenge. There's no wall too tall to climb or too high to jump from. His enthusiasm for risks and his never-ending energy keeps me on my toes. At home he can be like a caged Temple monkey trying to get out. We regularly check the windows are closed, since he's now capable of escape down the back drainpipe into the gardens. Late at night, he becomes like a Buddhist monk, quiet and calm, mostly because he's exhausted. He'll walk sleepily from room to room, cuddle us and repeat whatever thoughts he has from his day at school.

'Ma teacher told me Jesus is the same colour as me and that he couldnae speak any English. Is that right?'

'Yes, that's right,' I confirm.

'She said all the other big-time holy men like Krishna, Buddha and Mohammed never spoke English either,' Ram adds.

'That's true,' Sita says.

'But Jesus is the one I see in ma class.'

I pause for thought at this.

'Does your teacher tell you that Jesus is in your class, Ram?' I ask, thinking Ms Macinlay might be secretly peddling strong religious beliefs.

'Yes.'

'And do you believe her?' Sita asks.

'Yes.'

'What makes you believe her?' I ask.

'Because I speak to him.'

'What do you mean?'

'He tries to speak in English to me.'

'Do you have to pray to Jesus?' I ask.

'No, our teacher just asks me to talk to Jesus.'

'And do you see him when you talk to him?' Sita asks.

'Yes.'

I suddenly realise what Ram is trying to tell us, but I let Sita continue her inquisition, knowing she will hear the funny side soon.

'What does he look like?' Sita asks.

'He looks like me, I see him in the playground and the dining hall.'

'Do you see him here at home?' Sita asks.

'No, mummy. He's never been here.'

Then Ram innocently delivers the punchline.

'Jesus is a boy from Spain, he's new in our class and he's trying to learn English.'

Sita takes a moment, before laughing.

'It's a popular name in Mexico too,' I say.

'Really?'

'Si.'

20

A few months after Mahesh begins his search for a yoga studio, he finally finds a large community hall in Stockbridge, not far from Ram's Nursery. We can rent the space for a couple of hours, one day a week. With some fliers printed and distributed by sympathetic shopkeepers in the area, news gets out and Sita teaches her first commercial yoga class in Scotland.

She keeps her introduction simple by talking about posture and practice rather than the philosophy of yoga. She makes sure everyone appreciates that yoga embraces a look at your whole life, on a scale few non-yogis really appreciate. She tells her class that yoga opens life up for appreciation. It can help physical confidence, conquer destructive habits, provide the sort of strength and stamina that people then use in any way they wish.

Sita insists people look and listen for results, not just listen to what she says. Those I meet from her class seem impressed. Just as I did, they fall immediately under her spell. Her demonstrations of hatha postures have always been extraordinary to witness.

Mahesh also solves the problem of how to charge people. He brings a small Bhaktapur hand-carved chest. It's the size of a shoebox with a lid that opens on hinges. At first, he leaves the honesty box at the main door.

Then someone suggests it's left more privately outside the changing rooms. This move works better and the chest is regularly filled to the brim with donations. Then, just when things seem to be taking off, Sita announces to her grateful flock that she is stopping classes. She encourages her students to continue practice on their own. I watch in disbelief, as twenty of her new devotees walk out the door confused after saying goodbye to Sita. She makes the point that people do not keep going back to their swimming teacher after they have learned to swim.

Sita tells me that all but two of her first class have learned enough of the basics for them to practice regularly on their own. Only then will they discover the real rewards of yoga. She says she doesn't want to hear talk about the rewards that the class gives them, they should begin to see what continuing the practice does. The reward to their lifestyle will come from understanding their lifestyle, rather than yoga being one of their many attachments in life.

After Sita makes this shock announcement, a few of her fawning fans plead that she continues. Sita holds firm. She is not a life coach, and real gurus never are. It brings a strange response from those who feel they need her class to practice yoga. Some approach me to talk sense into Sita, clearly fearing they have lost someone they were willing to keep close for guidance. I promise to inform them if Sita changes her mind.

Sita's actions become her Krishnamurti-moment, a repeat of the time when the famous Theosophical leader dissolved the Order of the Star in the East in which he was brought up and tutored to lead. Sita states she has no problems introducing yoga to newcomers, but the only place where advanced yoga exists is in the person practicing it on their own for long enough to change them for the better. It's simple for her. You have to participate in your own journey.

Thankfully, Sita's stance pays off. By the start of the second introductory ten-week course, it's fully booked. Sita is so good, people have begun to spread the word. She need only teach you ten weeks of yoga, and you'll learn something that lasts a lifetime.

Enrolment numbers grow and Sita becomes so in demand we introduce two evening classes for those who work in the day.

These new introductory evening classes are filled mostly with women. Many from the business or the education sector, some are in the medical profession or working in financial offices around the West End of Edinburgh. The yoga routines seem to be working for those in high-stress environments. There are also other teachers of yoga who plead for private lessons.

Sita notices that among the established yoga teachers in town, quite a few appear to be very hard on themselves whenever they suffer minor ailments or misfortune. They ask Sita why, why them, when they devote so much time to yoga to avoid such discomfort. Sita says she helps make sure their stress levels are not caused by their dependency on teaching yoga for a living. They have confused the reasons they are afflicted. Once they practice in addition to teaching, things change for them.

At our small Stockbridge community centre, Sita now has some eight classes per week, five in daytime and three at night, with twenty people in each class. She has become so popular that we arrange a long-term lease for the largest available room and call it The Yoga Studio.

In such a large empty space, with bare white walls, we decide some of dad's paintings are needed. They become talking points among students and one or two even sell for substantial amounts. Suddenly another source of income becomes available to us. Mahesh donates a concrete sculpture of Ganesh he's found at a garden centre, to keep the capitalist momentum going.

The ambiance in our yoga studio is Sita's creation. We find people donating stacks of blankets and yoga mats after their ten-week training, like children outgrowing their comfort rag. She has become very close to a small group of women socially who accept being cast out after ten lessons but refuse to let Sita go as a confidante and friend. They regularly arrange gatherings to meet up with her. She attends these sessions not to teach, she says, but to learn more about them and their lives. I sense this is just part two of her masterplan.

She rarely talks about what is exchanged, but one evening Sita open up with me.

'Some women pose a mystery,' she tells me, 'fruitlessly trying to use yoga on weekdays to help them recover from the excesses they indulge in at weekends. There are a few from other health clubs where they were battered into shape, only to find the demands of a heavy exercise regime almost abusive. They've told me they can't cope with the high levels of exertion required in cardio exercise, because they have to retain their energy for their binge night out. They've told me they need me in their lives, to keep them fit for piss-ups at the weekend.'

I tell Sita this could be quite a good marketing slogan. 'Binge-night training at The Yoga Studio.' Sita doesn't like the joke.

'There's nothing wrong with a fun night out,' she says, 'but eating and drinking like it's a Hindu festival every weekend, is just a fast route to reincarnation.'

'Speed up... into your next life... at The Yoga Studio,' I say, waving my hand as if it could be in lights above the studio.

SOON WE'LL TELL RAM THE FULL STORY ABOUT HIS PLACE OF BIRTH AND when he gets older maybe he'll wish to know more about his roots. On the other hand, he may want to open a betting shop in Pilrig.

In the meantime, I've began to mention Nepal more in his bedtime stories and Ram loves it.

'Tell that Nepal story again. Awe come on!' Ram repeats, singing it like a Hindu chant, 'Before aye go tae sleep! Before ah go...'

I tuck him in tightly and silence him with the sheer pressure of the bedsheets wrapped around him, from the neck down. This also proves a cure for him sucking his thumb. My mum is not keen on this practice, saying it's too much like bound feet, in China. Child services would not approve.

'Once upon a time...' I often start, 'there was a wise old holy man in Nepal, called the Moni Baba.' My bedtime stories then become ad-libbed. 'He once walked the length and breadth of the country in his bare feet. He kicked wisdom from under the stones and the dusty knowledge fell on people. Over hundreds of trails, down valleys and up tall mountains, for years the Baba shared his knowledge with village folk. Everywhere he visited, people were happier after they met him, than they were before he arrived. He was a special man because most people are not easy to please.'

'He kicked wisdom into people, that's cool.'

'No, he talked to them.'

'Bor-ing! Bor-ing,' Ram calls out at any mention of talking. He demands action, which I deliver – usually towards the end.

'His talking was like music to people's ears. He made up so many stories that people began to sing them.'

'Bor-ing! Bor-ing.'

'Then one day a miracle happened. The Moni Baba met a Living Goddess who had been cast out from her temple in Kathmandu.'

Ram settles down. This is his favourite part of this story.

'The Baba invites the Goddess to walk with him. He tells her silence is worth more than gold and talk can be like medicine and that one day she will meet a lost warrior.'

'Then the goddess meets the warrior?'

'No not yet, be patient. Once fully trained, the Goddess has to go out into the world, believing she does not need anyone to defend her. She fights off many land grabbers and bum grabbers,' I pinch Ram's bottom and he yells. 'And many other demons with her words, across the country.'

Ram's head nods gently to the side, we're nearly there.

'The gods then give the Goddess and the warrior a son to look after. They take this young boy to the land of many names, where he is protected for ever, and ever, and ever and ever, and ever.'

I say this hypnotically until he's nearly gone. Now, the moment for positive suggestion kicks in. It always seems worth a try.

'And the Goddess teaches yoga every day, so the boy will be able to play football and do his homework better, and swim better and...' I keep adding skills until Ram's eyes flicker shut and my job's done for the night.

I hear the bedroom door creak wider.

'Welcome home, Goddess,' I say.

She blows a kiss and leaves. This kiss blowing is something she's learned from movies. Once Ram is fully asleep, nothing can wake him, so I follow Sita into the kitchen and continue in my storytelling voice.

'Did you know, the Goddess finds so many things to do in the land of many names, her warrior husband has to put their boy to bed most nights.'

'Oh, and what is this warrior's name?'

'Big Jim.'

'Big Jim?'

'Yes.'

'Big Jim too often reminds the Goddess of these great sacrifices he makes for her.'

'He knows she is too smart to argue with, especially since he's taught her how to make fun of people.'

'And what fun can the Goddess expect tonight?'

'Big Jim doesn't know, but whenever he's alone with her, he seeks her wisdom...'

'And all his thoughts become concentrated in one place.'

'Exactly... as if a miracle has happened.'

'When the Goddess is weary from teaching all day, Big Jim is best to seek wisdom first thing in the morning.'

I put my arms around Sita's waist.

'Sex is not the healer you think it is, Lingum Jim, but sleep is. In tantra, sleep is the other thing that lets time pass, without you feeling responsible for it.'

'Om... to the Goddess who never stops giving good advice.'

21

As Ram prepares to leave his Stockbridge nursery, a joint school 'Show-and-Tell' gathering at his new primary school is planned.

On his own initiative, Ram puts forward the suggestion that his mother comes for 'show-and-tell'. The first we know about it is an invitation from the school headmistress thanking Sita for agreeing to participate as 'My mum the yogini'.

As the day approaches, Sita asks what exactly this is all about and what she's expected to do. I tell her that it is a new thing, possibly imported from the USA. It normally relates to showing objects to an audience and then discussing them.

'What sort of objects do they usually look at?'

'Something brought back from holiday, found on a walk or an item you hold precious, or which has been in your family a long time.'

'So... what am I?'

'Something I brought back from holiday.'

'Yes indeed... a surprise bargain you found in Nepal.'

'Well, Ram was kinda the bigger surprise.'

'How will he introduce me?'

'He's already described you to as a teacher of yoga and that's how you got the invite. You have the choice to go as Sita the mum and yogini or as Sita the Living Goddess. It's up to you.'

ON THE DAY, SITA DIGS OUT HER ONLY SARI, LEFT OVER FROM OUR wedding. It is made of cotton cloth with a bodice of red silk. I expect she'll stun the class with her appearance, as much as her speech.

When we reach the school, the assembly room is full of chattering children. Ms Macinlay silences the group with a hand clap, and she walks to the front of the stage. She introduces Sita as Ram's mother, a yoga teacher from the land with the highest mountains in the world.

She then invites Sita to join her on stage, along with three other class teachers. One introduces herself to the newcomers as Marcella, originally from Jamaica and now head of the new primary intake. Two part-time teachers also introduce themselves then walk down to the sides of the hall, like security guards.

Sita gives a Namaste sign to the children, then quickly walks down from the stage to stand in front of them. She asks the group to move all the chairs to the side and to sit down in a circle on the floor cross-legged.

There is an excited shuffle of chairs before all the children sit in this more intimate setting. Sita explains she is going to talk about yoga, but first she has some questions.

'Who likes eating?' Nearly all hands are raised.

'Who likes moving?' Again, the whole class responds.

'Who likes breathing?' The numbers decline and some children laugh.

'OK,' Sita says, 'let's stick to the two things everyone likes.'

'What do you think makes you eat?'

'My dad,' a boy shouts, and the others laugh.

'What happens if you don't eat?'

'We can't watch TV.'

'Or see friends.'

'No chocolate.'

'My brother gets my food.'

These answers are all shouted with enthusiasm until a small girl at the front says, 'You get hungry.'

'Yes,' Sita says. 'If you don't eat... you get hungry and if you are hungry, that's when you can't stop thinking about food.'

'Ah canny stop thinking aboot chocolate, Miss.'

Sita stands. 'I'm now going to show you the most important yoga posture in the world.'

I'm taken by surprise. I did not expect a demonstration. I see Ram look very excited.

Sita continues, 'Can everyone put your fists together?' She then turns to me and says, 'James, can you put your fists together too?'

'Look at your fists together,' she says. 'Always remember this is the size of your stomach.'

Sita then wanders around the group showing her two fists to the children. It reminds me of seeing her mingle with crowds around the Moni Baba in the hills of Nepal. She asks if they are now ready to see this important yoga posture. There is a shout of approval. She suggests they keep silent and watch everything she is about to do.

Sita stands in front of the class, bends forward and places both hands on her thighs. Then she lifts the front of her sari and reveals her midriff. She tucks the sari cloth under her chin, holding it against her chest. She exhales deeply and raises her stomach area up, holding it under her rib cage in Uddiyana posture. She holds this for a few moments, then she wiggles her stomach muscles from side to side.

A chorus of oohs and aahs come from the children. Sita's column of stomach muscles protrude like a tornado's spout, and she moves them smoothly from one side, to the other.

'This is a "know your tummy" yoga posture. Now, let's see, if you can all do the same – lift your stomach muscles and wiggle them around like I've shown you.'

Within a moment, all the children are standing. Boys immediately lift their shirts to show off their stomachs. Girls begin to do the same. I see a few open their school blouses. Some stand pushing down their skirts and baring their stomach. I look around in panic towards the teachers. A few boys have pushed their pants way too low as they press their chins against their chest trying to repeat Sita's demonstration. I suddenly see a danger in this childhood innocence – possibly an arrest warrant for Sita and I, for encouraging inappropriate behaviour.

The teachers quickly descend on the gathering, urging all students to put their school uniforms back on. A few boys have already begun teasing girls that they have seen their knickers and belly buttons. Ram is surrounded by girls and is showing them how easily he can move his Nauli muscles, just like his mum.

Teachers begin to herd the children like cats, back into their seated circle, tucking clothes back to respectability. The head mistress instructs everyone sit down and think up questions they might have for Sita.

Sita looks confused, suddenly out of her cultural depth.

Marcella comes over to us.

'I'm sorry,' I say, 'this has suddenly turned into a show-and-don't-tell.'

'What happens at de party stays in the party,' Marcela half sings.

A boy asks, 'Have you ever climbed Mount Everest, Miss?'

'No,' Sita returns to her comfort zone, 'but I have seen it many times from a distance.'

One girl asks, 'Do dinosaurs live in Nepal?'

'Not anymore.'

I talk to the support teachers while Sita is informed about Barney the dinosaur, who everyone loves on TV. They are all considerate towards Sita but one seems a little worried what the children might say to their parents when they get home.

Marcella turns to me and says, 'Ah wish I'd learned that posture when I was their age. Did you see them, they could all do it?' She thickens up her Sean Paul accent for effect. 'Dem pupils,' she says, 'never had no show-and-tell... like this before... wi a mother *wiggling her bod-ay!*'

22

O ne lazy Saturday while on duty in the yoga reception, I try to write some summaries for an article for the Nepal Heritage Society.

I'm approached by an elderly American tourist visiting Edinburgh who asks for a private session with Sita. She tells me her name is Jean Higgins and that on a recent visit to Nepal, she met an American yoga teacher called Swami Y. She tells me she mentioned she was heading to Scotland, and so Swami Y gave her the contact information for Sita.

Jean is accompanied by husband Bill. She introduces him as a businessman with no interest in yoga. He laughs, but clearly does not want to be here. Jean hands me a letter of introduction from Swami Y.

I tell Jean she can sit in reception and wait for Sita's class to finish. She takes Bill's hand to lower herself carefully on to our couch and squeezes it with a smile in thanks. Bill remains standing, upright, alert like a Texas Ranger on guard duty.

I read Swami's letter, which cuts straight to the chase. It indicates that Jean has been diagnosed with stage-four Cancer and is seeking help in understanding her options for the little time she has left to live. He mentions her husband is finding her travels and interest in yoga difficult to deal with. Swami suggests Sita might like to give Jean the Tibetan lessons on coping with death and dying. He says he's already suggested to Jean that Sita is well placed to help her. If Sita can speak to Jean, it may also in turn help her husband to cope.

The letter finishes with a brief update on developments at the new Moni Baba Centre, Kathmandu. I take this part of the letter, placing it in my jacket pocket to read again later.

When Sita's class finishes, I catch her alone and tell her about Jean Higgins. I show her Swami Y's letter and ask her if she wants to meet the woman now. I know Sita is very busy with existing classes and consultations, but I sense her curiosity.

'I can ask her to come back at another time,' I say.

'Let me meet her now and decide if it's possible.'

'If what's possible?'

'If I can help her or not.'

I smile. It's a reminder of Sita's capacity to read people in an instant. She only needs to meet someone and look them in the eye to see if there is any inkling of acceptance towards her. Without that, things take longer. If a person is willing enough to listen, she's off. If people are too wrapped up in their own talking, she believes it's more difficult.

Sita makes her living in possibly the most sustainable industry in the world apart from hairdressing. She keeps already healthy people on the right track through yoga classes, and there's a never-ending supply of customers.

She's incorporated special classes for people who, through no fault of their own, have been plagued by on-going health issues. Many are trying to correct the consequences of something that's happened to them. Sita tailors her classes until people understand how to sustain positivity on their own. When facing people with troubling thoughts, she regularly stresses her miracle cure of meditation. Balancing active mind and hearts with the peace in-between. Until a heartbeat stops, peace for so many comes from the taking control of thoughts.

These methods are so diametrically opposite to the way doctors, teachers, and carers operate. Our specialists are obliged to help everyone equally. They can't pick or choose which students or patients to show the most interest in before they help them. When they are successful it's because they obtain compliance on one issue only, and usually there is dispersion of medicine for a problem. It's not common for a doctor to pry into all the other personal details of someone's life.

Sita will decide in a split second, whether from looks or instinct, if she can help a person. If not, she will politely avoid trying.

I have watched her successfully counsel so many people now that I wish I could only translate this compassionate behaviour into practice in my own field.

We cannot wander the halls of a medical school, seeking the teacher we like most before attending their classes. Yet often at the end of the day it is the teacher we like most who has the greatest influence on our schooling. There is still an influential role for a guru, if they are accepted as such.

Sita agrees to counsel Jean Higgins and two weeks later, after her third lengthy consultation, I walk into the yoga studio to find them together. I realise instantly I'm interrupting a very serious conversation.

In an incense-filled room, Jean sits facing Sita on a floor mat. Bill sits on a chair in the corner, clearly uncomfortable. He's wearing his cowboy uniform, a suit with a thin lace necktie and a woggle with a steer's head on it.

Jean looks passionately interested in what's being said. Sita stops for a moment and gestures for me to sit beside Bill at the side of the studio.

Sita is inquiring about Jean's imagination; she is not talking about Jean's illness at all. It is Jean's imagining of what is about to come that will determine how her final days will unfold. I assume Sita believes the one thing Jean still has control over is her mind.

Sita asks Jean to recall the happiest moments she can remember in her life. Jean takes a moment then mentions memories of a few special events, some with her husband and some with her parents. They have no children, something she says she now thinks about often. The Texan disapprovingly eyes me up, presumably because I'm witnessing his wife's personal confessions and she might make uncomfortable revelations. I have the feeling if this were back home in the USA, this could've ended in a gun fight.

Sita tells Jean her regret over not having children is irrelevant and advises her to focus on the elements that made all these past occasions special. She suggests to Jean that these occasions can be reconstructed. There is no reason why opportunity – loving friends; meaningful communication; or a worthy project – cannot still manifest between now and the moment she passes away.

Sita even suggests that the most important and happiest days of Jean's life may still lie ahead of her, that there are no time limitations on the sensation of joy or accomplishment. All that is required is to move from the position of becoming preoccupied with mortality... to one that better understands what has been learned from life and how to live it to the full. That if life is still in her, she should let it retain her attention and use it in a constructive way.

In one dramatic move, Sita takes Jean's hands and asks her what she thinks people will say about her when she dies. She tells her not to speak, but to think and consider her answer carefully and keep it to herself. Then she asks her to imagine what she might be able to do now to change any negative perceptions people may have of her. Sita tells her that while she still has the intelligence, the energy and the resources to change people's perceptions of her, she can act on it.

Whatever Jean is now thinking brings her to tears and she breaks down in Sita's arms. Sita helps her up from the studio floor. Bill stands up and in the heat of the moment misjudges the reasons for his wife's breakdown. He launches into a verbal attack on Sita.

'Watch your tongue, young missy. I ain't sure what you said, but you've upset my wife and I'll take no more of it.'

'Hey, careful,' I semi-shout.

'I did not bring my wife here, to be made upset.'

'She's not upset, Sir.'

'Bill, stop it!' Jean says. 'I'm fine and you did not bring me here... I brought you here.'

Jean stands and hugs Sita and then takes her by the hand towards the reception area.

I'm left alone with Bill in the studio. He turns to me with slightly less aggression.

'That woman is a treasure to me. She has stood by me for over thirty-five years, not all of them easy. I've built a business. We have over three thousand people working in my company. I personally think you're all full of shit, sitting on your holy butts in a yoga studio. But for some reason my wife doesn't want to listen to me now, she wants to talk to people like your wife.'

'My wife is a treasure to me too.'

'That Sesame Street character Swami Y in Nepal, suggested she come here, but it was Jean who took his card with this address here in Scot-land,' He pronounces the country as if it's two words. 'If we were heading to Scot-land, he told us there was this woman Sita who could help my wife. So, I followed along. All I want to do is to protect my wife.' The Texan points his finger at me as if it's a gun. I am about to reply when Sita re-enters the room alone.

'Where's Jean?' The husband turns to Sita.

'She's just freshening up and will be out in a moment.' There's an awkward silence as I stand ready to physically defend Sita if need be. She takes on Bill herself.

'You came into this yoga studio and you don't seem to know why, Mr Higgins?'

'I certainly wouldn't be here if it wasn't for my wife.'

'Then tell me where you would rather be at this moment?' Sita sits on the floor in front of the Texan and I offer Bill a Tibetan cushion as an insult. He continues to stand.

'Anywhere but here, young lady. I don't think you people know anything about the real world,' he snaps at Sita.

I'm just about to launch a verbal attack, but Sita puts up her hand to stop me.

'You're right, Mr Higgins, I know very little about your real world. But I'm a good listener and I believe you might know more about your wife and her condition if you listened too.'

'How can listening help my wife?'

'Your wife believes your present lifestyle offers her little comfort at this time, and that something here does. It might help you if you understand what that something is. Your wife needs a kind of optional special support, not instructions or judgements on her choices.'

'I'm not ashamed of my lifestyle, it's what all you people want me to feel. Folks from your country have come in droves to the United States to escape their lifestyle and poverty.'

'You speak like a king to a beggar, Mr Higgins. Such *purthidekauni* (arrogance) has destroyed many a rich family. *Kasto ghanandi*,' Sita says, smiling, reassuring me she's still in control.

There is no response from the businessman. These are words and a situation he does not understand; from a woman and a world he knows so little about.

Jean returns and walks over to her husband and takes his arm. She then turns to Sita and thanks her for her counsel.

'I now know what I want to do with my remaining time,' she says, turning to her husband. 'She has helped me to find the strength to set a final path for myself.' She passes a small envelope to Sita and smiles.

Sita bows in a Namaste salute to Jean, then turns to Bill.

'I'm sorry, Mr Bill, it has been so disturbing for you. We talked only about what Jean still has a chance to achieve. She has, I believe, decided what that might be. I need not know. This is what you might call fair trade, no? If you are ever in need of a similar conversation, come and see me.'

As they leave, Jean looks at her husband with fondness. 'She's such a lovely girl, isn't she?'

Sita and I stand at the door, waving goodbye. Sita opens Jean's envelope to find it full of crisp one hundred US dollar bank notes. I see her look confused. It takes us some time to count out the five thousand dollars Jean left. A new record for our honesty box.

23

On a sunny April day, we decide to take Mahesh and Mandy down to mum's for the day. Mum has met Mahesh on several occasions at our flat, but he's never been to Peebles. It's nearly a year since we visited.

Mandy seems a delightful partner for Mahesh. Having won the young scientist award at her school in Dundee, she accelerated her education to work at university level, younger than most of her classmates. Mandy has very deep red hair that's brown until light hits it, when it explodes with colour. She has an attitude that Mahesh says scientifically authenticates her as a redhead. She informs us that it's common knowledge that dentists require twice as much anaesthesia to put redheads to sleep.

'It's something Mahesh can do easily by talking,' Mandy says with a smile.

'No, she told me it's a scientific fact that redheads fight against the loss of consciousness, more than any other hair colour,' Mahesh adds.

Mandy tells us that she grew up amid insults and compliments, but since university, compliments have become more common. Whenever she hears negative remarks, she loves being around Mahesh. 'He's like my own personal anaesthetic, he calms me down, and I don't feel as tempted to punch folk.'

Ram then takes both Mahesh and Mandy on the compulsory house and garden tour. By now Ram also knows many flower names. There's a clear difference between the names he's learned from my mum and those he's learned at school. Daffodils are what grow in Peebles, and it's 'dafis' that grow around his school in Stockbridge.

As we sit in mum's conservatory, she seems a little subdued. I assume because of Mahesh's presence; she turns the conversation to Nepal.

'Are Nepali mothers still very superstitious about their children, Mahesh?'

'What do you mean... *Ama* Munro?'

'Do they think some children bring good luck and others bad?'

'Yes, there's still a few people like that in remote villages.'

'And does a child's gender brings good or bad luck?'

'The gender brings power and income to a family more than luck.'

'Then, it's a power that's imagined, and surely superstition?'

'It's been researched in social sciences,' Mahesh replies.

'Because wealth is accumulated through gender, doesn't make it fair.'

'Let Mahesh enjoy Peebles, mum, not have to answer twenty questions,' I interrupt.

'I'm interested to hear how Nepali fathers treat their children nowadays.'

'What's the point, mum?' I ask. 'Mahesh is not a father.'

'It's OK, James. I'm not a father yet, but I have a father, so I can answer the question.'

'There you are, Mahesh has a father, that's more than you can say.' Mum looks at me with an irritated expression. 'The Avadhoot was never a father to you.'

Mahesh looks astonished at this revelation. His rhythm is interrupted. I'm amazed he manages to keep the conversation going, but he tries.

'Nepali fathers traditionally spent little time with young children. It was the same here, no?'

'Yes,' I say.

'I'm glad that Ram has Sita for a mother,' Mum says.

'And James for a father,' Mahesh adds.

'Yes. That too.'

'Well, thanks for that observation,' I say. 'Our son was baptised at the temple of Mothercare and since then we have showered him with blessings at the cathedral of Toys R Us.'

'You sound like Minister John.'

'How *is* the Minister and his band of minstrels doing?'

Mum pauses for a moment. 'I'm sorry James, I haven't told you and I don't think you know about Kenny?'

'What about Kenny?'

'It's not good.'

'What happened?'

'He took his own life ten days ago. The funeral is this weekend.'

'My god, why didn't you tell me?'

'I knew I would see you today and I didn't know how best to tell you.'

I look across to Sita. She looks stunned at the news. Mahesh and Mandy look confused at each other.

'Who's Kenny?' Mandy asks.

'He's a young man from here, who James met sometime back,' my mum says.

'What happened?' Mahesh asks.

'He walked into the ocean after taking drugs, apparently. Just like his dad. He drowned.'

'God... not just like his dad... like Jeff Buckley.'

'The police are positive no one else was involved. Who's Jeff Buckley?'

'Never mind, he's a musician Kenny looked up to. Where did they find him?'

'Across in Gullane. They found a large quantity of drugs in his system. Minister McRae said he would likely not have survived the overdose.'

'How is his mother?' Sita asks.

'The police say Kenny was spotted trying to find his mother at home before he stole his friend's motorbike and drove off to Gullane beach.

John McRae thinks his mother was lucky not to have been found by him. She had recently agreed to sanction him into a correctional facility.'

'For what?'

'Both Minister McRae and Fiona Dunbar's parents reported the boy was increasingly unstable and becoming violent.'

'John always seemed to have it in for that boy.'

'I had arguments with him about it all the time. These so-called support groups he runs. The parents are made to believe that if anyone leaves the church group, they'll immediately misbehave or turn criminal. For John, most of them are already in hell. I've told him he doesn't have the right to pass judgement on these youngsters. He's so quick to put himself forward as the community's judge and jury. If he'd done his work supporting Kenny, the lad might still be here.'

'What about Fiona?' Sita asks.

'I've not seen her since this happened. I heard she's very upset. She kept an interest in him all this time, until just recently. I hear she's going to perform at his funeral.'

THE NEXT DAY, MAHESH AND MANDY TAKE THE BUS BACK TO EDINBURGH on their own.

When we're alone, I ask mum, 'What were you thinking last night?'

'What do you mean?'

'Quizzing Mahesh around the table, in front of Mandy.'

'I'm sorry, I've been upset by the Kenny thing and didn't know how to tell you.'

'You mentioned the Avadhoot was my father, he's sure to quiz me on this later. Mahesh and Mandy believed my dad was dead.'

'You'll just have to make Mahesh swear on his Gurkha life he'll never tell anyone.'

'Tell what exactly?'

'The family shame.'

'It's too late for that. We'll be lucky if it's not all over campus by tomorrow.'

· · ·

THE ONE PLACE WHERE OUR COMMUNITY REALLY DOES WELCOME ALL sinners, is to put them in the ground. Minister McRae has organised a rare multi-denominational gathering for this occasion. There are twenty people in attendance, more than I expected. I recognise some from the youth group and one from the graveyard gang. Fiona brings along eight other young people from the choir to sing a tribute she's prepared.

Kenny's mother seems beside herself with grief. I've never met her, but I see from a distance she is being comforted by Fiona. Notably absent are Fiona's parents.

After a few words from Minister McRae, recognising the potential and the flaws of Kenny, the choir sings. As the room fills with the sound of voices in harmony, I watch Sita. She has experience of Tibetan chanting and I remember its repetitions can be mesmerising, but this is different. Sita begins to weep in the church, along with others. She has likely never heard a Christian choir sing before. The acoustics of the church seem to take the music straight to her heart. It's music designed to mourn the death of the son of God. In that extraordinary moment, Fiona and the choir's singing is sublime.

After the ceremony, Sita asks Minister McRae if the music had a name.

'It's Catholic,' he says, as if that answered her question.

'What does it mean?' she continues.

'It's a famous Psalm. I allowed it for this ceremony in our church,' he says, defensively Protestant, 'because Fiona told me that her and Kenny used to listen to the recorded version.'

'It was sung so beautifully. James tells me many such songs have been written to honour your spiritual leader, who was executed.'

'And born again.'

'Reincarnated, yes... like us all?'

'Not our Kenny, I hope,' says Minister John.

'I have never heard music like this before. Does this song have a name?'

'It was sung in the Sistine Chapel in Rome, way back in the seventeenth century. Years later I'm told the wee Mozart ran home after hearing it and wrote all the notes down from memory. It's called "Misery

Me" or something like that, in Latin, composed by Gregorio Allegri, I think. A good old-fashioned Pope song.'

'The choir was amazing,' I say.

'Fiona's been rehearsing it all week.'

'What went wrong?' I interrupt Minister McRae.

'With what?'

'With Kenny.'

'He drowned in his doubts.'

24

Outside the church, while everyone talks about the events surrounding Kenny's death, I can't stop thinking about my role in his slippage. I remember feeling I'd made a brief breakthrough, supporting the lad's interest in music, but when he left the church hall that night, he apparently met John McRae.

With the sole purpose of protecting his flock, McRae read the riot act to Kenny. He told him point-blank he would never be allowed back into the youth group if he continued to display such rage. Fiona's father told him in no uncertain terms that his relationship with his daughter must end. Minister McRae and Fiona's parents swore they would not allow such a special girl to be influenced or abused by a violent thug. Kenny was fifteen at the time his purgatory was imposed.

Mum tells me that Kenny just walked across to the graveyard group in defiance, after his telling off from Minister John. He then had the biggest laugh with his new best friends. Mad Kenny was welcomed with open arms, given a joint and slowly over the next year did what he presumably wanted to do all along, make close friends with people who didn't judge him. Like his father before him, he explored the local world of drugs.

Fiona reached out to Kenny several times. Being older than him by several months, she also felt responsible. She was angry at everyone's treatment of Kenny. She challenged her parents' attitude towards her friend. She said she even took some drugs with him early on to show she cared. Then, she says, Kenny began to hunt down suppliers and increased his sampling of what was available to buy. She says at first, she saw it no differently to how her father treats wine tasting. They were both similarly strong-willed people and liked to get drunk or in Kenny's case stoned. Her dad went regularly to wine-tasting parties. She says that's how Kenny treated drugs. It changed when he went beyond the taste and became dependant on sales. What these amateur experts described as good tasting, were the heavily addictive products Kenny began to trade.

Some of Kenny's new samples were instantly successful. He was always looking for what was the most potent for the least money he could scrounge. Things changed for the worse when he began to sample and trade in narcotics.

Mum tells me Fiona came round to see her one day, asking for me. They'd talked for a long time. Fiona believed it was her that started Kenny's problems, when she'd shared his music with me. That was the straw that broke the camel's back, because that betrayal caused Kenny's first major freak-out. She traced everything back to a mistake she thought she'd made. Mum tells me she assured her she wasn't to blame and that no one could have predicted the outcome that followed. Mum says she was also protective of me because I was doing new things in my life. She didn't want me to take any of the blame for exposing their relationship.

I protest and ask mum why she didn't tell me.

'I wanted to help Fiona get over this.'

'Really?'

'Yes, I placed the blame squarely onto Minister McRae's attitude. We've hardly spoken since.'

'What did you say to him?'

'I tore into him for not reading the situation properly, or from that poor lad's point of view.'

'Hallelujah for you.'

· · ·

Sita treats my sadness at Kenny's death by reminding me that nothing physical has happened to me.

'Physical knocks are easier to take,' I say. 'Such sad preventable news isn't.'

'Remember the yoga you have learned,' she says. 'The interior workings of your body are the same as yesterday. Protect the miracle that's involved in that.'

'I know.'

'All that's happened is a piece of information has been delivered to your mind. A mind that has an immune system of its own and is trying to recover control and as much normality as possible. Others will be suffering more and may need help from someone less bruised like you. Take comfort, you did not directly cause Kenny's death. Grief creates new trains of thought which slowly accommodate the bad news. Show confidence for the life you still lead.'

I drink in her words to create a new train of thought.

'Remember, we faced the same thing at the time of the Baba's death,' she says.

Some weeks after Kenny's funeral, Mandy offers to cook 'red' curry at our flat and invites my mum for dinner. Lentils, beetroot, and raspberry dessert are all part of Mandy's cuisine choice. After mum praises Mandy's cooking, Mandy tells her she has just finished reading my dad's book on yoga. Mum seems uncomfortable with this discussion, and turns the focus to Sita.

'How do you explain yoga... to a bunch of Scots?'

There is an awkward silence.

'Think of what the Avadhoot wrote,' Sita says.

'Mmm,' mother mimics the stance of Rodin's Thinker. 'You tell me, Sita, for I'm no fan of the Avadhoot.'

'OK,' Sita says.

'I also want to hear this,' I say

'I still think of many comparisons from Nepal.'

'That's OK... most around this table have experiences from Nepal.'

'Except me,' says Mandy. 'I have experienced a Nepali.'

'Well... people here will view the life of a porter in Nepal only in terms of the bags he's carried and the miles he's walked, rather than the rice he's enjoyed, the strength of his legs and the people he's met.'

'OK,' mum says.

'Let me think of something more Scottish for Mandy. The more things you want in life, the more you leave control over yourself to those who supply them. How does that sound?'

'You should write your own book,' mum says.

'I'm thinking of introducing a new class.'

'What kind of new class?' I ask, surprised.

'A tantra yoga class.'

'Why tantra?' mum asks.

'People here seem to talk about their sexual relationships all the time.'

'My god,' I say, suddenly realising the full consequences of this new train of thought. 'A tantra class!'

'Are you having a moment, James?' mum asks.

'We haven't discussed this, Sita.'

'I've spoken with a few of the young women in class and they are very keen.'

'Tantra? Yes please,' says mum, clapping her hands.

'If you are going to tell people about tantra it's OK. But I know you... you never just talk... you'll want to demonstrate too. Am I right? That's very risqué here, Sita.'

'Risqué... as in Rishikesh?'

'No, risqué, meaning rude or offensive.'

My mum laughs loudly and Mandy joins in.

'Sita, you are by far the best thing that's ever happened in my son's life.'

An extravaganza of outcomes are possible with tantra yoga. It's the cause of so much more than children. Our time on earth is blessed by the enjoyments we find in physical activity and our need for relationships. (Quote from the Tantra Times)

PART FIVE: BEYOND TANTRA

25

Because of Sita's friendships at the Yoga Studio, we now have an assortment of close friends with more invitations to dinners and functions than we can possibly accept. The Yoga Studio has become as much a part of our social life as it's become a lucrative business venture. Sita is adamant that she takes no salary, which means the studio running costs are supported by donations and a membership fee. It's financially complicated but we have an eccentric business plan, set up with help from friends. Membership of the Yoga Studio gives access to free classes; people trade ideas and artistic goods, and HMG taxes are all paid on time.

Sita doesn't care why people join her yoga class, whether for relaxation or recovery, but once they start, they should leave with an understanding of its long-term advantages. She refuses to teach yoga breathing to people who smoke, suggesting that such breathing would simply help them inhale smoke more thoroughly. She points out that thirty minutes of yoga a week does little to compensate for the bad habits and postures people hold for the rest of the week. She suggests people will get better results when their yoga integrates and enlightens them and is not viewed as an antidote to the rest of their lifestyle.

Sita's formative teenage years in Nepal were spent mixing with people who worked physically hard all day and had little to say about it. It was much the same here for people brought up in rural communities. Yet the demands from 'the City' have gradually influenced rural life here, to make life's challenges much more merged. Trades influence lifestyles as much as location because of the mental challenges to survive.

Since arriving here, Sita has discovered the over-analytical brain that is often its own worst enemy. Here, Sita faces people who want to talk about every aspect of their life, all the time. Recently we discovered she can earn as much in the honesty box for her private talking sessions as she does in her yoga classes. She tells me, the most popular topic for discussion is relationships, in all its forms. Friends, parents, bosses, employees and partners are both the source of love and of great stress. Sita seems to have a talent teaching people awareness of their choices. She emphasises this free choice, but stresses that freedom must be well-informed for choices to be of any value.

The other argument Sita hears regularly is one which I've taken interest in for my work. It's when people blame the industries they've built up and rely on. There's the food industry and the pharmaceutical industry, who rush to inform the public of their latest discoveries and products. Building new product on new product to put into the same ancient bodywork to keep it alive. The complexity of our body and simplicity of its upkeep is confused by what is now regarded as our complex upkeep of our simple body. It's now the food industry who are responsible for the weight gain of millions of people, not the individual choices people make. It's the pharmaceutical industry who are responsible for over abuse of drugs. Each week, Sita will hear her students blame governments; city councils; transport or health authorities for a whole series of problems that make their life miserable.

'When if, ever,' she asks me, 'will I learn all the names of all the thousands of agencies and authorities who are responsible for people's unhappiness here? Om, to have such a wide choice of people to blame besides God.'

I tell Sita this is likely why we invented politicians. 'If religion is understood as the cult of an individual's influence over the masses, then politics is the cult of opposing the power of the individual over the masses.'

'When people can settle for a balance in a sexual relationship, so many other forms of balance can fall into place in their lives too.'

'So that's why the masses need a tantra yoga class?'

'No... that's why the individual responds to tantra.'

As talk of Sita's planned new tantra classes spreads in Edinburgh, we receive unexpected news from Australia.

In that way which fate often distracts a train of thought, we get word from Mrs Baxter that her husband is ill after a severe stroke. She has made the choice to stay on in Australia, where their daughter is helping to care for her and her father there. His prognosis is not good, and the family feel the best thing to do is to sell their flat in Edinburgh. Mrs Baxter offers to give us first bid to buy the property before it goes on to the open market.

Trying to explain house-buying in Scotland to Sita proves a time-consuming challenge. The idea of making 'offers above' a seller asking price... is to Sita like going to a Nepali market and offering the seller of mangos the price he was dreaming of. Why give him more than he's asking for?

'The Baxters want to know what this mango is worth to everyone in the market, not just us,' I say.

Sita and I talk for hours about what we think the flat might be worth. We look at other flats of similar size in our neighbourhood and figure we'll never be able to afford a loan, or the long repayment schedule required. It's beyond our honesty-box earnings and my consultancy fees. It's the first time Sita is faced with making a serious financial commitment towards owning something and having to borrow to pay for it, possibly for the rest of her life. I know she wants to stay and live here, but a yogini's desires can be more fickle than financial.

As soon as my mum hears of Mrs Baxter's offer, she explains to Sita that because the owners are giving us first bid we must take advantage of this opportunity, before masses of additional bids come in from others.

Mum offers to guarantee a down payment for a mortgage should our bid be accepted. We estimate the lowest amount we think Mrs Baxter would accept, then contact her directly.

Mrs Baxter calls us back and is very friendly, confessing the flat has now become a bit of burden to them. She wants to sell it as soon as possible to pay for private healthcare for her husband. On the phone she tells me the price she was expecting. It's ten thousand pounds more than we offered. It is so close considering all the other zeros involved in this transaction, I tell her I will get back to her within the next few days with our final offer.

Our excitement that the house price is just within reach, is soon squashed by our bank's refusal to lend us more. I had no idea how many obstacles could be placed on obtaining loans. Mum decides to go the extra mile by selling her Mini. She tells us she can make do with the flower van until we get back on our feet financially.

Our offer on the house is accepted. A down payment is made and a mortgage, repayable over the next thirty years, is drawn up. Sita and I are bound together by love and property.

'SITA WAS DESCRIBING A VERY SPECIAL MOMENT IN HER LIFE,' MAHESH SAYS.

'What moment?' I ask

'When she had her big realisation about love.'

'Did she mention the Moni Baba or talk to you about conscious love?'

'No, but she mentioned a French acrobat she met.'

'That's what I was afraid of. Sita will make this tantra class a circus event.'

'Surely not. People here can be told... words can explain. People I've talked to are very interested in hearing Sita talk on tantra.'

'Yes, but Sita believes it's the spirit that moves people to talk, it's the spirit not the words that can be felt by others, that's how awareness spreads. Sita's aim is to unify people's spiritual confusion.'

'She may demonstrate a few things but only because she believes her English language skills may not be good enough to explain everything.'

'Yes, I know her argument... the language of love has limitations, but what your eyes see in a demonstration is universal.'

'Bravo!'

'What?'

'I'm being sarcastic, in Latin,' Mahesh says.

'Sita's choice here is questionable. You have to help me.'

'Why are you questioning her choice?'

'I'm simply questioning Sita... to see how much she understands.'

LATER, ALONE WITH SITA, I REALISE HOW MUCH SHE HAS PROGRESSED WITH her plans while we have both been distracted by house-buying. She believes both these things are happening at the same time for a reason. It's a further sign for her to expand her commercial worth and get rid of the debt we've now incurred through our mortgage.

'Are you absolutely sure you want to start this tantra class?'

'Why are you still asking me this?'

'Because normally you're not ambitious or predatory. I was in doubt when you stopped teaching pupils after ten weeks, but now I think it was a brilliant idea. I'm doubtful about tantra, so help me out here. I know you wish to keep your yoga students feeling they're normal and healthy without you. Your main contribution is in keeping already healthy people from habits that they might spend years regretting later.'

'What do you mean, predatory?'

'Hunting down new yoga students, seeking more vulnerable souls who have suffered. Making tantra yoga classes sound attractive for normal people to join in with.'

'The people I meet here, have a very different normal from me,' Sita replies. 'I find it a challenge to teach them all together in the same class. The Moni Baba believed yoga could never be taught in any class, only instruction on postures. I want to separate people into smaller groups because some are already interested in tantra yoga. I shall not hunt anyone down.'

'Surely most of your experiences with tantra come from your relationship with me?'

'Do you fear the secrets of our tantra will become public?'

'Perhaps I do.'

'It would take me far more than ten weeks to tell all.'

AS WE APPROACH THE END OF SITA'S UMPTEENTH TEN-WEEK INTRODUCTORY yoga session, we say goodbye to her new offspring as they float off like dandelion spore into the wind. Plans are then made for the next season to include tantra. Mahesh and Mandy go out for a walk along the Water of Leith to Dean Village, with Ram as their guide. I stay behind, having prepared the yoga schedule, to speak with Sita.

'I don't ever want to stop you doing anything. I really hope you've thought this one through. But as you say, choices should be informed choices.'

'In my conversations with younger people here, it's their perceptions of relationships that makes or breaks them.'

'And where specifically do you see a tantra classes helping with this?'

'Many women in class have already told me intimate secrets about their relationships. It's part of life, James, so it's part of yoga and I have to include it rather than ignore it.'

'If you begin teaching the joys of sex, I fear people here will take it wrong.'

'If you are inhibited by something, it is difficult to imagine what it feels like to be uninhibited by the same thing.'

'Are you teasing me?'

'It's not about teaching sex, it's the limitations of people's desire to bring them a sense of fulfilment. Like all the other Yygas, it can help people by suggesting what to control.'

'There is another risk of talking openly about tantra here, the risk of social stigma.'

'I'm sorry, I am ignorant of people's perception of tantra here. What do you mean?'

'Offering anything to do with love, or even comfort, or tantra to people here, you may be judged as capitalising on sex. I want to protect you.'

'You too were once protected and inhibited, until I taught you tantra.'

'That's not the same as you teaching strangers about intercourse in public.'

Sita remains stoic. 'It won't be the same teaching... it's just the same subject.'

'Then explain to me how you will do it, so I can tell you if it's legal or not.'

'Do you remember Cindy?'

'Yes!' I sense something sinister is about to be revealed.

'Well, she's been coming to my yoga classes for nine weeks now and I've talked with her a lot. She is a very friendly and funny person.'

Things fall into place. Cindy from the sauna has joined Sita's yoga class and now suddenly there is an interest in her teaching tantra. She's failed in luring Sita to her place, so she's become her friend, perhaps with a mind to finding more clients for her business, from ours.

'Wow,' I say. 'That's interesting.'

'I think you'll like her once you get to know her.'

'Yes. I'd certainly like to get to know her better.'

'And another thing.'

'Yes.'

'With Ram's bedtime stories... I think you should begin to tell them in a way that encourages sleep, not deep thought. For our son to accept challenges, he needs quality sleep.'

Me too, I think to myself, me too.

26

I submit to Sita's sermons and her glorious innocence. Perhaps as a result, our opposing minds on tantra trigger a mutual lust. As has happened many times, our intellectual exchange acts as an aphrodisiac.

She takes off her clothes and runs into the shower, shouting, 'How much should I charge for a private tantra lesson?'

I flop back onto our bed, bewildered.

As a fruity perfumed soap smell drifts into the room she appears, towelling herself dry. These prelude moments are a celebration. I love it most when I feel a desire in her.

Sita's tantra skills have already taught me well beyond the checklists for gratification. I've learned never to rate one's partner through a menu of positions or locations for satisfaction. Sita's yoga contains such a high degree of awareness that physical sensations can be generated from a distance or a single mindful touch.

When I finally reach the bed, Sita is stretched out with only a thin white sheet covering her. The sheet hides nothing of her shape. I am reminded of her white dress from Nepal, the way her shoulders appear. I kneel on the edge. She sits up and we kiss tenderly. We wrestle until I wave a white pillowcase in surrender.

It is lovemaking because love is created in these moments. It is not fucking because I feel no aggression in the act. It's an enjoyable, exhausting dance, not a fight. It's also a lot of fun and we return from this magnificent distraction with laughter afterwards. As control returns, we become silent, not for any divine reason, but because neither of us want to wake up Ram.

Next morning, I prepare some porridge for breakfast and take it into Sita. She is already stretching next to the bed, like a cat woken from a nap. She continues the conversation from last night as if it were a few moments ago.

'In my talks with women in the studio, some want to better understand their feelings related to sex. I understand you being cautious but I'm sure these women would enjoy a basic tantra class. Not just women but men too. I would like to involve everyone in the demonstrations.'

When the words men and demonstrations are mentioned, I decide to take a leaf from Sita's book and adopt silence as a method of negotiation. I'll let her imagine why I've gone quiet. It may have more influence on her than any argument I can presently make.

'There's something else I want to tell you.'

'What's that?'

'I didn't tell you before, because you said I should not discuss personal details about individuals in my classes.'

'I know you speak to them in confidence, and I don't need to know details.'

'Yet I teach people through the things we all have in common. Everyone has a mutual interest in love... it's a powerful common emotion.'

'You think people here want this tantra, but what if some want more? What if they begin to tell you they actually need something more?'

'Cindy has volunteered to help in the tantra classes. She says she can keep me straight with the locals.'

I hesitate, but silence has its limitations.

'OK. Let's arrange to meet up with Cindy together, before you make any formal arrangements to include her in your classes. Bring her here or let's meet up in town to discuss this further.'

MAHESH AND I SIT ON A BENCH IN PRINCES STREET GARDENS DRINKING chai, a few yards away from the bone-dry Ross Fountain. He has summoned me, saying he has news for me.

'Sita told me the full story of how your dad became the Avadhoot.'

'Well, she's known my dad for longer than I have.'

'She asked that I keep her conversations private, because she now regards me as a family member.'

'It's the Avadhoot's and my mum's choice to keep this secret, so we should all respect their wishes,' I suggest.

'She told me that James Munro senior is a wanted criminal in these lands.'

'What? She told you that dad's a wanted man?'

'Yes... because that's true, is it not... and a good reason to keep quiet about it.'

'But he's not wanted, he's just presumed dead.'

'Which is a lie, no?... and if he's found to be alive, he'll be wanted. Am I not understanding this properly?'

'As long as my dad remains the Avadhoot, he's not wanted.'

'Yes,' Mahesh agrees, 'now I'm part of your family I agree to keep this secret.'

Mahesh tells me he's decided to help my mum overcome her problems related to the Avadhoot and our family secret.

'In what way can you help?' I ask.

He tells me he has written to his father's friend in the Ministry of Foreign Affairs.

'Bahadur Singh is a friend to my father,' Mahesh says 'for many years and he is also a follower of the Moni Baba. I told him about you and Sita living here, and he was fascinated and wants to help.' Mahesh thinks the gods are all working together on this.

'How can Bahadur Singh help?'

'Don't worry, my knowledge of your secret I will only use to help the family.'

'And?'

'I've asked Singh what the possibilities are to issue the Avadhoot with an official Nepali passport. After all, he is a well-known holy man in our country.'

I nearly choke on my chai. 'My god, Mahesh! That's a big ask. What did he say?'

'That he would first have to prepare an application for citizenship. Your family name would not be linked in any way to this process.'

'Wow, and you think this is possible – that the Avadhoot can get a new official identity, not linked to his place of birth?'

'Yes, who knows or cares where or when a yogi is born? They grow up in our society as regularly as wildflowers. Quite a few from India have come to Nepal and stay on as citizens.'

'Has the Avadhoot been asked if this is what he wants?'

'No, not yet. I wanted to be sure it was all possible before anyone informed him.'

'It's best you keep this information from my mother at the moment.'

'OK. What's that British expression? Mum's the word.'

Mahesh says that if things are sorted, and my dad gets Nepali citizenship as the Avadhoot, he could then ask for a Nepali passport. Singh apparently sees no problems. Holymen travel across the borders of the subcontinent all the time, increasingly with passports. However, Mr Singh would like a favour in return.

'Singh wants you to write an article. A glowing view of Nepal's contribution to the world pantheon of yoga. The piece should include Nepal as the birthplace of the Buddha and the teachings of influential spiritual leaders like the Shivapuri Baba, the Koptar Baba, the Moni Baba and the Avadhoot.'

'What's it for?'

He's recently been appointed editor-in-chief for Nepal Heritage Society's magazine. He doesn't have a deadline, but the sooner the better.'

'And this is Singh's condition for issuing my dad with citizenship?'

'Not really a condition. A favour in return. He wants an outsider to describe the way gurus in the past have helped solve political challenges in ways that don't promote a violent rebellion. He says the timing is crucial. Our country is facing many political changes. Will you do it?'

'I'll try.'

'And will you be the one to contact the Avadhoot and ask him if he is interested in Nepali citizenship?'

I agree to both of Mahesh's requests. My sense is this might give dad an exit opportunity he does not have at present, and it seems the least I can do. I fear, however, what mum might think he'll do with freedom.

27

Sita arrives home from the yoga studio on her night off. Her work clothes must be washed almost every day. She piles one set into the washing machine, always saying the same short prayer. She shakes out her vests and tank top and folds them onto a large shelf in the hall cupboard.

Tonight, she has arranged for us to have dinner with Cindy at an Indian restaurant on Clerk Street. For the occasion she chooses to wear blue jeans with a silk sari blouse, with a Fair Isle cardigan on top.

I tease her on the way to the restaurant, asking what prayer she's reciting when she does the washing.

'Is it the chant of thanks for not having to beat your clothes with a stone on a riverbank?'

She assured me it's a genuine *Dhobi Ghat* chant that many low-caste women sing to pass the time.

'Washer women,' she tells me, 'often make up their own words to describe their husbands' faults.'

ON SUCH SPRING NIGHTS, EDINBURGH'S NEW TOWN GARDENS ACT LIKE A giant air freshener for the city. The smell of freshly cut grass is everywhere. We trek from Ainslie Place where the road is seldom used, where weeds and clover squeeze through gaps in the cobblestones. We stroll across Charlotte Square into the busiest corners for traffic in town. It's our nearest public-health risk with speeding cars and buses turning this corner like race car drivers onto Princes Street's west end.

I remind Sita that we visited this restaurant when we first arrived in town. At that time, she could not believe the price of a chapati. She questioned the bill, telling staff she could feed a household in Nepal for a month for the cost of their dhal and rice. Nowadays, she is likely to leave a tip.

Cindy is already seated at the table and appears to be halfway through a large glass of red wine. She now has white blonde hair and is wearing a smart black dress with black tights with no slashes across the thighs. Her bare shoulders look pale in contrast to her face, which is made up with some precision. Her red lips are shinier than a new fire-engine, and my alarm bells are already ringing.

My intention is not to insult Cindy or dismiss her motives for befriending Sita. If they are what I believe them to be, it's essential Sita discovers Cindy's ploy herself.

We order our food, and the conversation starts off well. Cindy shows a few signs of nervousness and talks about Edinburgh's troubles in bringing back the trams. She even uses the words *poor public consciousness* in describing the city council, as if she wants to impress.

The conversation continues over an excellent saag paneer, and I begin to feel as if I may have misjudged the situation entirely. There is more friendly banter than serious discussion and I can see how well Cindy and Sita get on. I start seeing Cindy not as someone who is trying to lure my wife into semi-prostitution, but as someone genuinely curious about Sita. I see the attraction they have for each other. Cindy may be vulnerable and Sita could be aiming to fix that. Perhaps I should never have been so protective or considered Sita gullible and doubted her.

Sita orders more Indian delicacies and Cindy indicates she'll try everything we recommend. Sita asks what Cindy would normally be eating at home. She tells us she never eats at home, especially at night, and if she did it would be pies from the freezer or a take-away burger.

The restaurant is full, and the tables are very close together. There is also Indian music playing slightly too loudly, so we all lean in closer when the conversation move onto tantra.

Sita turns to me. 'Cindy and I have been talking about this class for a while and we think I could start teaching a tantric class on a Friday evening.'

'There's a lot of interest, I mean a lot, from many of Sita's women,' adds Cindy.

'Why are you so keen?' I ask Cindy in a whispered voice.

Sita answers for Cindy. 'We decided it would be good to introduce two new classes together. One on tantra and the other an advanced Hatha class. For those beyond the beginner's stage, they'll see that all interests in life begin to merge and influence each other.'

'Ah wee bit of tantra for the masses canny hurt,' Cindy speaks louder, directly at me.

Sita continues. 'In discussions with those who have heard about tantra, they all want to know the techniques.'

'I thought we'd agreed that real tantra is impossible to teach in a classroom setting.'

'Yes. Until recently I've not really known how to teach tantra without having an actual lingam in the room to show women how to interact with it.'

'A what?' Cindy asks.

'A lingam is a penis,' Sita answers loudly.

Cindy bursts out laughing. 'I luv her, straight to the point,' she says, looking around to see the room's response.

'So, what's changed? What makes you believe you can teach it now?' I look from Sita to Cindy, who is sitting closer, still smiling.

'Cindy's offered help.'

I feel the tables turn. This is now a team set-up, to convince me this venture is on.

I flounder, searching for a better argument against the idea.

'Remember Ram's school,' I say. 'There are cultural taboos and laws against exposure of body parts here. Cindy will likely tell you more about that than I could.'

'Ouch,' Cindy says.

'People have more sensual experiences to explore than they think they have. It's harmless to do this. Less harmful than experimenting with substances to numb your mind. If I'm going to teach true tantra, I can't just talk about it, I must demonstrate it, in the same way I do with Hatha yoga.'

'Including that orgasm part,' Cindy adds, smiling.

My mind is racing at the thought that our yoga studio would suddenly become known as a place that offered sex classes. The scandal of Morningside ladies being taught the science of orgasm in Stockbridge would even make the *Evening News*.

'Our yoga studio has been successful so far because we have managed to attract the right sort of clientele.' As soon as I say this, I regret what I've said.

Cindy sits back with a look of disapproval on her face.

'The right sort of clientele?' she asks.

Sita whispers, 'who is wrong for yoga, Jamesji?'

'He's probably thinking of me, Sita, so tell him how we think this can work.' Cindy smiles at me.

'You can't do this, Sita.'

'Why not? People want it. Others teach it.'

'Yes, but they don't demonstrate sexual intercourse publicly in a class.'

'I won't demonstrate with people in class.'

'So how do you plan to teach?'

'I've been shown toys which women already use here, when they don't have a man.'

'I'm just her helpful advisor,' Cindy says.

Sita turns to Cindy. 'May I?'

'Aye sure, go ahead girl,' Cindy says.

Sita then bends forward into Cindy's handbag and pulls out a large pink-flesh-coloured dildo.

Cindy bursts out laughing. 'Sorry, ah didnae mean her to show it off unwrapped.' I quickly throw a soft chapati over the dildo before people can see it. Sita still holds it firmly. Cindy goes into hysterics and Sita also begins to laugh.

'This could make the perfect demonstration tool in a tantra class.'

'A lingam with batteries,' Cindy says.

Sita's face is close to mine. She's smiling, but I see she's serious. Staring into my eyes she switches the dildo on, and the chapati vibrates. That's when I lose it too. We all laugh till there's tears in our dhal.

Sita switches the tantra tool off.

'Keep it going lassie,' Cindy says, 'spin that chapati like a Chinese plate juggler.'

I can't control myself. Our commotion draws attention to our table. The restaurant owner's wife appears and enquires if everything is alright. We slowly regain control. Cindy tells her that it's Sita birthday and she's just been given an electric toothbrush.

'We were showing her how it works,' Cindy says. 'Today's technology, eh?'

'Happy Birthday...' says the owner. 'We must offer you an Indian sweet in celebration.'

'Thank you,' we three say in unison.

Sita returns the dildo to Cindy's purse.

'You both can't be serious.'

'Cindy knows a place that sells strap-on lingams.'

'No,' I say, stifling my laughter again. 'And what about men's classes?'

Cindy looks at me and mimes her hand moving.

'Lots of homework for men,' she says.

28

Later, when we are alone, Sita continues to press her case.

'I'll be able to show women how to control the parts of their body involved in their orgasm. Pure tantra as taught for thousands of years but explained in a modern style.'

'I assume Cindy knows lots of these people who need that sort of education, and that she'll bring them along.'

'Many seem unfulfilled and confused here. You must not mock it!' Sita says.

'But would many men come?' In my mind I immediately hear Cindy's comeback, calling me on the double entendre. I hear myself join in. Things are getting out of hand.

'It's sex, James... the one act every living creature on earth tries to perform. Surely you, more than most, can see that health is related to this act. It is something that yoga has something to say about... whereas religions are silent.'

CINDY IS MORE INTEGRATED INTO THE YOGA STUDIO THAN I FIRST THOUGHT. She has a habit of speaking to everyone, with an excess of physical touching. She'll grab an arm if anyone makes a comment or disturbingly touch my hair when she talks to me. In the time it takes to walk between studio and the changing room, Cindy is famous for undressing en route. Wearing only her leotard in class, she'll manoeuvre her arms out of the sleeves, exposing half her chest in the process, before reaching the private changing space. Her purpose, it would seem, is solely to attract attention. The hard-core yoga students seem indifferent, but a minority are mesmerized by her antics and talk about her all the time. In the presence of men in class, she is less subtle. There is even a noticeable flirtation when she talks to Sita.

Despite all this interaction, I've never seen her leave the studio with anyone and as far as I know she lives alone.

Sita doesn't talk about Cindy except to say she had a complicated upbringing. I try to learn more, saying I think Cindy seems a difficult person to please, that she rarely takes anything seriously and neither does she miss an opportunity to tease.

'When she teases people, she is very like you. And she and I have things in common, too.'

'What would they be?'

'Camping, for one. I told her I loved the outdoors. She told me there's nothing she likes more than camping it up.'

'I'll bet,' I say to Sita. 'There's another meaning for the word "camp" here.'

'What's that?'

'It's used to describe people who behave theatrically.'

Sita pauses for a moment. 'Exactly. Cindy's behaviour is entirely an act.'

FLIPPING THROUGH THE APPOINTMENT PAGES AT THE YOGA STUDIO ONE night, I see that Sita is on the schedule to give Cindy another private massage. As I turn and shout goodbye, Sita hears me and calls me in.

I open the door to the newly converted massage room, once a large walk-in cupboard with no windows, now the studio's Tantric Cave. Cindy is lying on her front, naked with a small white towel covering her backside. The lights are dimmed and Sita stands at the head of the massage table, working oil into Cindy's shoulders. Without stopping, she sweeps her fingers down Cindy's back. It strikes me as unprofessional for Sita to casually invite me in.

'I trust you're careful who you invite in,' I say.

'Anyone except the Leith police,' Cindy says.

'And you are OK with this, Cindy?'

'OK if it's you James, as long as you don't peek,' she says, her face pressed into the hole at the top of the massage table.

'What is it you need?' I ask Sita.

'Remember to take Ram for new shoes first thing tomorrow before school. His toes are bending in the old ones.'

'OK.'

'I can see your toes curl in your shoes from here, James,' Cindy says.

Sita slaps Cindy on the buttocks.

'Oh, that's new. Stick around James, it's getting interesting in here.'

'Neither of you ever miss an opportunity to tease,' Sita states. 'Is that a cultural thing?'

'I wouldn't know,' Cindy says.

Sita looks at me... and then the door.

29

After a few months of Sita teaching tantra yoga to her elite group of women, I notice after classes that there is an increase in banter compared to hatha classes. Exchanges between students seem less clinical. Whenever I encounter students leaving the class, they smirk back at me as if they know what I've been up to. I repeatedly suspect our personal life could be one of the topics of discussion in class.

Cindy continues to draw attention from male students as if she is in perpetual musk, whilst the honesty box is full and brimming over. It's like nothing before in our yoga crowd. All that's missing is the goldfish bowl for the car keys when they enter. There is an unmistakable overt sexuality I believe caused by brand tantra, and because of the popular acceptance in re-defining gender.

I tell Sita there are rumours that her new tantra classes are the place to go, not for enlightenment, but for an interesting relationship.

'One can often leads to the other.'

Businesswomen sign up alongside gentrified country ladies. Secretaries arrive along with hairdressers, young students and new mothers who find time to attend night classes. A few goths have turned up with black lips and leotards with holes. Some have cut the holes to show off tattoos. Many differing walks of life sign up and yet have one commonality – the look in their eyes when they first meet Sita. She has shown her gift at lifting people's barriers to converse and now she's dealing with their intimate relationships. Quite a few people have partnered up after joining and have become ambassadors for tantra's hook-up potential.

Gender preferences are completely lost on Sita. She doesn't care who pairs up. They must, however, appreciate the mutual love required to make a relationship work.

We are at risk of becoming more a dating venue than a yoga studio. After seeing her nearly exhausted after five classes in one day, I speak with Sita.

'I know you treat new students as one homogeneous group, like the way you told me that I saw all Nepalis, when we first met. All the same.'

'I see similar aspirations in people.'

'I'm worried you won't spot anyone enrolling in your class for negative purposes.'

'What do you mean, negative purposes?'

'Someone with malicious intent. In all things there's a percentage chance that someone with terrible perversions might show up and cause great hurt at the studio.'

'You mean spotting the pervert? That's what Cindy calls it.'

'I suppose so, yes.'

'Cindy says she'll keep me right on this. She says she's an expert at spotting the pervert.'

'Have you had any problems that I've not heard about?'

'No. I explain the difference between mastering sexual stimuli and being dangerously obsessed with sex.'

'OK.'

'That's where I think tantra can help.'

'I'm just trying to keep the studio's main intentions that of your own.'

'Cindy told me she believes every meeting between people presents an opportunity, not all of which results in sex.'

'And?'

'You both believe in the fun side of human sexuality. That anything can be turned into a suggestive meaning.'

'Well... surely anything can be made fun of at the right time, and sex is no exception.'

'So why do you say sex... instead of love?'

'Because I have a sense of humour?'

'Tantra helps people look beyond sex.'

'For life's intention? What do you think life's intention is?'

'Join the class and you'll discover it.'

'Seriously... are you now offering the meaning of life?'

'I want you right now!'

'Do you?'

'No, I'm only joking.'

'Ha ha ha, Sita Munro.'

'Help me develop a tantra class for men.'

'That is surely the cruellest blackmail.'

'Why do you think the lingam is worshiped so much in Nepal?'

'Because Hinduism recognises the role of testosterone more than Christian society does? I don't know.'

'No, because men turned it into a thing to worship. Men need tantra as much as women. God is not just a rock-hard cock.'

TWO OF THE YOUNGER CARIBBEAN MOTHERS WHO COME TO YOGA HAVE arranged a surprise Crop Over birthday party for Sita. They've brought food and a music box. Mum drops in while Ram and a few of his school friends are playing around waiting for the yoga session to finish. Quite a few mothers of Ram's friends have been coming to Sita's hatha yoga, so it is not unusual to find a gang of children waiting around after class.

As people exit the studio, everyone is invited to eat Caribbean finger food. A Trinidadian father has brought rum in a large plastic unbreakable bottle. It's then drunk as if it's a re-hydration fluid at a football game. People begin to dance, some with their kids. There are tracks from The Mighty Gabby and Kevin Lyttle with some Ini Kamoze and Craig David thrown in for Scottish mums. The children of a Bajan family arrive in Crop Over costumes and parade around with open shirts and bare midriffs. One boy has both gold and silver medallions swinging from his neck as big as saucers. When Ram joins in, wucking-it-up with his school friends, my mum seems surprisingly shocked.

Ram shouts, 'Yo Grandmuthur!'

'Where did Ram learn to speak like that?' mum says.

'His school friends. Don't jah worry none.'

'I heard him sing about a bitch a few weeks back.'

'Yes, he sings that song pretty reg-u-lar-ly these days.'

'But no woman should be called a bitch, especially by a six-year-old.'

'He was singing lyrics, mum. He'd never say it to anyone as an insult.'

'How do you know – why do you let him listen to such lyrics?'

'Can't have Ram being a muthafuckin outcast... he's gangsta!'

'Stop it. Don't you let the boy get away with it.'

'Away with what?'

'You know what I mean... there's always a rough crowd around. In your day it was Protestant and Catholics.'

'And which of those were the rough crowd?'

'Those that caused it to turn violent.'

Mum then suggests that Ram might be better off back in Nepal. As I hear this, I suddenly become furious.

'These kids are much less violent than the ones I knew. I could hardly deal with all that sectarian crap. Playground fighting was top of the school curriculum back then.'

Mum turns to leave. I know she has an appointment, and she must go, but I can't let her turn her back on me like this.

'Bye bitch,' I shout as she walks away.

She looks back and I put one hand on my crotch and the other in the air with my finger pointing. She smiles and shakes her head.

When I turn back to the party, Cindy is dancing with a Bajan father. They are moving as one, joined at the hips. His Bajan wife is eyeing Cindy as a combat sniper might.

Sita comes over and thanks me for arranging the impromptu party.

'I feel as if I'm attending my first real live tantra class.'

'What we have in common, bring us together.'

'Our love of tantra?'

'And... the love of cakes.'

Sita takes the remains of her birthday cake and puts it into the fridge. She tells me that the party was a wonderful surprise and how much everyone seemed to enjoy it. It was like a mini festival day in Nepal, she says.

I take Ram through to his bedroom. He's exhausted and instead of another story of Nepal, I open my guitar case and sing to him. It seems fitting that this instrument should at last be brought out of storage and introduced to my son.

I play Ram a reggae version of Evanescence, 'My Immortal', but it's as if he has red hair and is fighting the need to sleep. He finally gives in to a very slow acoustic version of 'Try Jah Love'.

30

'The dark cloud hanging over Cindy is slowly disappearing,' Sita says one night after a late tantra session. It's an unusual statement since Sita rarely discloses personal information, especially about the mysterious Miss Cindy.

'Explain, please.'

'I see positive changes.'

'After all my attempts to show you her negative side?'

'I sense the frustration in you. It's not helpful for you to hold on to that.'

'I seek only to protect.'

'Modern methods of protection and birth control was one of the most interesting discussions we had.'

'Very funny.'

'People talk openly about their experiences in bed.'

'Really?'

'Yes.'

'What do you do, compare experiences?'

'Sort of... we compare regularity.'

'And how do we compare with the majority?'

'I'd say we're average.'

'Well, the bar must be quite high if you are including the likes of Cindy.'

'Oh, we're way behind her.'

'The whole of mankind is likely behind her. There's a difference between an average based on normal and an average based on an addiction to sexual conquests.'

'Students are seeking a better experience during the act. Only some women want to have children. Most want a serious trusting relationship. There's been quite a few confessions recently.'

'Indeed.'

'Cindy says the only thing that men are now exclusively in charge of is finding out what gives them an erection. And that this increasingly does not involve very much physical contact with a woman.'

'Well, that's certainly one evolved way of looking at things.'

'I want to tell you about Cindy... because it turns out she's a special person.'

'Indeed.'

'She told me her real name is Margaret McKenzie. She was adopted and never knew her real father or mother. Her stepmother worked at a men's club that specialised in weekly stag nights. When she was a teenager, her mother also got her a job.'

'A job doing what?'

'I don't know, that's why I'm asking. I thought you would know what she meant. She said it was illegal – under the table.'

'I have no idea. Was she given the job secretly?'

'Maybe that's it.'

'If someone offers something under the table it's either an illegal opportunity or a stolen item.'

'Well. That was the start of Cindy's troubles. Her stepfather then got her into dancing with older women at the club and her mother divorced her step-father for his abusive behaviour towards them both.'

'That's terrible.'

'Her stepmother re-married one of the owners of the men's club. When Cindy was fifteen, she was offered a job at the massage parlour by her new stepfather. It's the only place she's ever worked and now she owns it.

'She says she's very thankful that we met and she's grateful for our friendship. Until she met me in the supermarket, she says every relationship ever offered to her came with conditions.'

'Well, I'm happy for her.'

'Her experiences have affected her view of men.'

After this conversation, I worry about Sita's cultural gullibility. She has an incredible ability to read people's motives and to anticipate when they want to help themselves. She may allocate a lot of time to Cindy in her current state, and I have unwavering confidence in her. She is not naïve, but Cindy, I suspect, is skilled in fake loyalties. We give each other a peck on the cheek, and I go to sleep fearing Cindy is more intimately involved in our lives than I'd thought.

MAHESH VISITS ME ALONE AT THE HOUSE WHILE SITA TEACHES HER classes. He wants to discuss the parts of Nepali culture that are under attack. It is a long discussion.

Our house phone thankfully interrupts us, and Sita tells me the postman has just delivered a package from my dad in Nepal.

'It's not April the first, is it?' I ask.

'No, I'm calling in case you want it immediately.'

It's so unusual for Sita to call me that I say, 'It's nice to talk to you on the phone.'

'You are not talking to me, we are communicating through a plastic device. I'll let you speak to Cindy. She is right here with the package.'

'Hold on... I'm with Mahesh...'

'*Namasti! Mahesh*,' Sita shouts loudly.

'*Namasti!*' Mahesh shouts back.

'I must go.'

'Hi there Jamesji,' Cindy purrs.

'Has Sita gone?'

'Yes... she has an enlightenment to deliver.'

'Which room is she in?'

'The mediation cupboard, formerly known as the Tantric Cave.'

'She says there's a package for me?'

'Yes. It's from your Nepal guru friend... "Ave-no-dhoots," or something like that. Would you like me to bring it to your house?'

'No, I'll come by the studio.'

'Whatever's easier for you. See you soon.'

I tell Mahesh that I have to leave and ask if he could watch Ram. I tell him I've received a package from Nepal from my dad. He suddenly looks guilty.

'Oh. I forgot to tell you.'

'What?'

'That my father wrote to me saying he'd met the Avadhoot at a function recently and spoke to him about us and the citizenship idea.'

'But I haven't yet asked him if he's interested.'

'I thought nothing would come of it so soon. It was just a brief meeting.'

'So what happened?'

'My father said he'd mentioned to the Avadhoot that we knew each other in Edinburgh. He said he spoke to your dad only briefly, but he did suggest, if he wished to obtain a passport, he could help him.'

'My god. How could you not tell me this?'

'Sorry, I've seriously had a lot on my mind recently and anything to do with the Avadhoot is all locked up in my mind's secret place.'

'But it's not a secret from me.'

Mahesh goes on the offensive. 'Well... you seemed moody and dissatisfied recently, James.'

'Sorry... I'm being stretched by this public health work, and the tantra classes. Things have changed a lot here in terms of responsibilities.'

Mahesh laughs uncomfortably, then says, 'I once heard Moni Baba speak of the power of work to heal.'

'That's all I need, more work to heal myself.'

'And you must remember to write for the Nepal Heritage society as part of the healing process, as promised?'

'Yes, that'll top up my dose of healing.'

'Write about Nepal as a guardian of a non-global culture – one of the many small countries still holding out.'

'But as long as we have a globe that we all live together on – we need a global culture of sorts.'

'The world is in danger from global thinkers who negatively stereotype local cultures.'

'At this moment in time, yes you are probably right, but it's what we all choose to contribute that will eventually be judged and accepted as part of a global culture.'

'Are you sure about that?'

'No, but it's worth thinking about.'

31

I recognize the thick Nepali paper the envelope is made from. It has taken six weeks to reach Edinburgh from Western Nepal. I open it to find a photograph of two men. A Nepali government official, complete with cap and pantaloons, posing next to a holy man dressed as a traditional Sanyassin.

I recognise the mischievous smile and a glint of suspicion in his eye. My dad Sri Avadhoot stands next to Nepal's Minister of Foreign Affairs. Behind them is a former Rana Palace converted into official government offices. Dad has also enclosed a manuscript with a note and a letter.

I glance through the manuscript. It's beautifully written by hand. It's entitled 'The X Gita' and the note describes it as the culmination of the Avadhoot's twenty years of work summarising traditional Hindu beliefs. It says it's compiled for young Hindus in response to a recent trend to politicise the gods in India. He highlights how ancient works of art are often now captioned with statements like 'Kali will kill the enemies who threaten her followers'. Never, it says, have non-Hindu believers been so threatened by this new religious interpretation. It's political propaganda, not the universal doctrine of Hinduism.

There is also a foreword written by a former Nepali Minister of Foreign Affairs, praising the Avadhoot's commitment to Hindu thinking for the modern world, and stressing Nepal's status as one of the only International Zones of Peace.

I turn my attention to the letter.

HELLO SON, SITA AND RAM,

Firstly, congratulations on the purchase of your new home in Edinburgh. I received this news recently in the outback, along with an interesting proposal. I do think of you all, a lot.

Since I began writing 'The X Gita', Kathmandu Valley is becoming more and more crowded. Farmland is disappearing rapidly. This country that I know you both love is changing very fast. Parts of it are under threat from insurrection. Life is becoming extremely hard for too many people in rural areas, and I feel local politicians can no longer ignore this level of poverty and hardship. There are a huge number of people from the hills trying to find jobs in the Kathmandu Valley.

I've spent the last two days visiting Swami Y, at the new Moni Baba Centre. I also gave some talks around the city. I was then invited to two official government functions and spoke to a few leaders who showed interested in 'The X Gita'. One suggested the Crown Prince might be interested in a copy, so I was later invited to attend a tree planting ceremony where the Crown Prince was scheduled to attend.

I've recently spoken to the Minister of Foreign Affairs. He told me about your friend Mahesh and his scheme of offering me Nepali citizenship. It sounds an interesting proposal. I believe many Sadhus who have lived here a while have gained citizenship.

I'm happy to remain here, for the time being, despite the Maoist influence spreading. The government control in some districts is very weak so there may be conflict on the horizon. It's good to know I may have options. Thank you for your help. Write to me soon and tell me your news.

Love to your mother.

Dad /Avadhoot

. . .

LATER, I READ OUT DAD'S DESCRIPTION OF HIS APPOINTMENT WITH THE Crown Prince after a Dhal Bhat dinner with Sita and Mahesh.

JAMSJI, FYI ONLY.

Many years ago, the Moni Baba first talked in Nagerkot, at the edge of this valley, about starting a project called the Valley Tree Garden Initiative. This has finally been set up and supported by the Nepal Boy Scouts. Last week the Crown Prince was scheduled to inaugurate it with some Embassy donors and officials, by planting the first trees.

I was invited to attend and arrived in an official vehicle ahead of the main dignitaries, carrying my copy of 'The X Gita' to give to the prince. Unfortunately, as we arrived a heavy rainstorm swept in, and things became chaotic.

The road was so wet that one of the lead vehicles became stuck and blocked passage for all others. Organizers were then afraid to let any more cars drive up for fear they could block the road for the royal entourage. All vehicles were made to park at the bottom of the hill and guests instructed to walk the hill. It was a trek up this swamp, the steepness of a ski-jump.

Luckily, I had an umbrella and managed to use it as walking stick while there was enough grip for the feet. Several diplomats and government officials with their wives were not so lucky. A few could not proceed higher and took their place at the roadside next to the boy scouts. In true Nepali custom, no discomfort was shown by anyone, as the rain lashed their fine clothes.

Only a few of us made it onto the hilltop, where a single tarpaulin had been erected to shelter the royal guests. It quickly became filled with water and began sagging, like the belly of a pregnant buffalo. A strong mist descended and was so thick no one could see the patch of garden we'd all come to inaugurate. As more dignitaries staggered in, it looked like the finish of a cross-country hill race.

Local farmers had been encouraged to attend and stood sensibly sheltered on the hillside, watching with their families. Once everyone was in place, the space for the royal vehicle to pass was still clear through the crowds. The final hundred yards was lined with the two columns of boy scouts and girl guides standing stoically.

As I stood at the top, I began to feel the mud harden around my ankles and realised it must be happening to others, too. One European woman cried out in panic and tried to crack the solidified mud around her ankles. As these cement boots formed on our feet, there was a sudden feeling of being trapped. Then a Western dignitary shouted 'leech', which sent additional fears through the foreigners. They began stamping rapidly, as if in a tribal dance, trying to rid the threat to their ankles.

An announcement blared from the single loudspeaker saying that the royal car was arriving. Some farm families pushed in closer.

Security officials identified a dangerously muddy spot on the last ten paces the Prince would have to walk. If he could make it through this patch, he'd reach the safety of large bed settee placed directly under the belly of the tarpaulin. A security guard pulled out his kukri knife to sacrifice a small number of saplings, possibly on their tenth year of growth, to be placed as steps over the mud.

A buzz of excitement rippled through the crowd, as the vehicle was heard approaching. A few Gurkha officers moved out from the trees, calling instructions into handsets. The line of scouts and guides began waving little paper Nepali flags and a small white Suzuki four-wheel jeep roared up the hill, splashing them all in mud. It halted just in front of the tarpaulin and as the car door opened, it was clear there was no Prince inside. It was, however, jam-packed with old men. The Minister of State tumbled out, along with the Minister of Foreign Affairs, a security officer and two others from Nepal TV. A film cameraman with his equipment, and sound man jumped out the back.

We soon heard an announcement from the Panchiat chief, stating that His Highness could unfortunately not attend. A sigh of disappointment came from the diplomatic community, who now looked impatient for all this to end.

With much pomp and ceremony, the Panchiat chief announced the speeches would all be read out in full, and the trees planted as scheduled. All this was to be filmed by Nepal TV and so would people please stick around. 'Stick' being the operative word. There was no further mention of the Crown Prince's absence.

Now to the moment the organizers had all been waiting for, as the guests were invited to plant a tree.

I want you to imagine the chaos such an instruction caused. For the next fifteen minutes, as another burst of monsoon rain lashed down on the hilltop, we were each given a one-metre tall tree and a hand spade. In such weather, it is hard to plant something on flat ground. On a forty-five degree slope, it proved impossible.

The New Zealand Ambassador was first to go. Possibly keen to get home, he slipped and disappeared along with two scout helpers, they took out a Nepali Minister on their way down. Whenever anyone lifted one leg, they were gone. Guests and their wives slid down the slope like bobsleigh contenders. One Minister slid so far that a Gurkha rescue party was dispatched to find him. Pantaloons, it seems, offer less resistance than trousers on mud slopes. A few people tried to grab onto each other but ended up taking down groups of bystanders. Some watched the tree they had just tried to plant being taken out by a human bowling ball.

I expect the Crown Prince yawned that morning, looked out of his window at the rain, called his assistant and asked him to request a few ministers to take his place. It's perhaps a small example of how detached the young royals are. They have privilege but no responsibility to exercise their duties these days.

I look up and notice the smiles and occasional laughter have disappeared from the faces of both Mahesh and Sita. They were with me until dad's last sentence.

I ask what's wrong and Mahesh shrugs and quickly recovers but Sita looks me squarely in the eyes.

'The Avadhoot speaks English differently to how he speaks Nepali,' she says. 'He sounds like an outsider. Politicians and religious leaders may be acceptable to poke fun at, but not the Nepal royal family.'

Even the Avadhoot can occasionally cross the cultural line.

IN PEEBLES, I TAKE A DEEP BREATH AND WALK TOWARDS MUM'S DINING-room cabinet. I bring out a bottle of Glen Jura whisky, offering it. It's a gesture she understands well, a well-known cultural sign that someone wants to share a problem.

'What I'm about to say may piss you off, so take your medicine in advance if you wish.'

'Really? I've been off these meds since before you were born.'

'I've been in contact with dad, and there are some new options opening up.'

'What's he up to now?' she speaks softly.

'Mahesh's father has introduced him to someone in the Ministry of Foreign Affairs, who happens to be a fan of the Moni Baba.'

'What are you two up to?'

'Don't worry, this is all above board.'

'Above board?! Exposing your dad to any authority, even in Nepal, is incredibly risky.'

'This minister only knows dad as the illusive sanyassin, Sri Narendra Avadhoot. He is willing to give dad citizenship and a passport.'

'What?!'

'Listen, I've checked things out. You don't need to worry. The insurance company that paid out the initial settlement money was acquired by a larger company years ago. There's little risk that dad's case will ever be opened or accessed again. I bet there are no records of criminal activity. This could be a fulfilment of your original plan for him to come back here.'

'If anyone here finds out your dad's alive, they could use that info to cause havoc.'

'You've been watching too much TV, mum. Listen to me, what does dad have to lose? Worst-case scenario, a prison cell here is a step up in luxury accommodation from what he's lived these past years. I think he's willing to take his chances with this.'

'But I'm not.'

'It's an opportunity to have the Avadhoot's identity made official and will give him more options in turbulent times.'

'I don't like this at all.'

'Mahesh has told me there's even interest at Edinburgh University in inviting a Sanyassin from Nepal to give a talk. All he'd need is a travel document for a temporary visit.'

'What makes you think his Holiness wants to come here?'

'At the moment, I don't think he does. But Nepal is not the same country it was when you were there.'

'If he comes back, I'm sure there are people who'll recognise him.'

'Trust me, they won't. He's a sanyasin down to his skin. And he's unlikely to want to stay.'

'If he starts spouting his yoga crap here and gets a following, he might want to continue.'

'I have to help give him this choice.'

'Beware, he's just an entertainer at heart.'

'I don't see dad as an entertainer.'

'You're a wicked schemer, James.'

'And where do you think I get that from?'

32

It's ages since Ram required bedtime stories to go to sleep, so currently I play guitar to help him doze off. He insists I make up lullabies from his favourite Caribbean, reggae and hip-hop songs.

I've also begun to prepare Dhal Bhat at least once a week since Sita has taken on her night yoga classes. Tonight, however, she's made a promise to make us both dinner. I sit waiting for her, exploring some new guitar riffs from Ram's CD collection, when there is a knock at the door.

I open to see Cindy standing there. She's wearing an Indian-style jacket, unusual for her, with jeans and boots. She's carrying a Marks and Spencer bag. She gestures to see if she's required to remove her boots.

'Sita got an emergency consultation at the studio. I'm here tae make you a meal. Where's the microwave?'

She walks past me into the room.

'You don't have to do this, Cindy.'

'I thought I'd help out and we can have a blether.'

'I'm fine, really.'

'What's a yogini's friend for, if she can't help out her guru's man?'

'What huv yi brought me?' I imitate her accent.

'That famous Scottish meal... Mac Aroni.'

She walks past me into the kitchen, stepping over my guitar case.

'Ah didnae ken yi played the guitar,' she says, thickening her already thick accent.

'I only recently started playing again.'

'Pans to the left o me, dishes to the right,' she sings like Gerry Rafferty.

'What sort of music do you like?' I ask, as she motions me to sit.

'This won't take long, three minutes to be precise,' she states, popping the macaroni delight into the microwave.

'I like Blue and Kylie.'

'I hate manufactured pop music.'

'What a musical snob.'

'All those simple chords and Hallmark lyrics.'

'It's good fur a dance, though.'

'I guess.'

'I bet you've never tried?'

'What?'

'Dancing, disco clubbing.'

'Disco, how old are you?'

Cindy bursts out laughing. 'That's classic, we've all had some boogie oogie-oogie experience?'

The microwave bell rings. Cindy opens the door, humming and wiggling to imagined music. She then serves up the steaming pasta in two plates and sits opposite me. She breaks off a piece of French bread, still smiling, still dancing with her shoulders.

'I didnae bring any wine, James. I dinae trust myself wi a drink in me nowadays.'

'Thank goodness.'

'About the wine, or the trusting?' She looks me in the eye.

'I trust you only because Sita does.'

'I do like a bit of hip-hop but I can't ever follow what them lads are saying. Better wi Robbie Williams.'

'People are just harvesting sounds from the past, these days.'

'Yeah, proper wee farmers they are, combine harvesting their music.'

'Do you ever stop trying to take the piss?'

'Come on James, we at least have the same taste in Asian women.'

I begin to regret Sita not being home.

'Wish I'd brought some wine now.'

Cindy falls quiet for a moment. I welcome the break. She is very difficult to read. Underneath she seems fragile, and I begin to see where her attraction towards Sita might come from. She is quite the project for Sita's therapy.

We eat the macaroni, since it cools quicker than it takes to heat it.

'Sita's told me stories aboot her growin up in Nepal. She's been helpful to me.' Is this Cindy turning serious? I wait for a punchline to find out.

'What do you mean?'

'She once spoke about reaching puberty in Nepal. She said that although some of us have very difficult upbringings, we all had the same physical bits, and often the same emotional landmarks over time with our age.'

'What do you think she meant by that?'

'Well, she then said something that helped me understand.'

'What?'

'That children can overcome more than any other age group...'

'What doesn't kill you, makes you stronger.'

'No, she didnae say that. Dinnae interrupt me.'

'What then?'

'We talked together about my situation.'

'I'm sorry, I don't mean to...'

'No... I don't mind telling you. '

'Why?'

'It'll help you overcome the negative fascination you have with me.'

I take the empty macaroni plates over to the sink to wash them before the sauce solidifies.

'Sita talked about emotional landmarks, an I guess she must have got that expression from you, naw?'

'No... from the Moni Baba.'

'Really, the auld joker she used to live wi?'

'Yes. He spoke a lot to people about their emotions, how they help you learn and move on.'

'Exactly, things like my first kiss with a real boyfriend.'

'That's a landmark, I suppose.'

'It happened in a graffiti-covered stairwell in hell-hole Muirhouse. I remember it fondly.'

'Really?'

'Yes, to the point where I can even experience the glow of that first kiss each time I see a dirty stairwell. Funny, eh? Other people just see the place as a shitty, smelly dungeon and it can still turn me on.'

'Weird indeed.'

'Sita told me no matter where people grow up, they have the choice of what memories to remain influenced by.'

'What memories influence you?'

'I was sexually abused as a child.'

Cindy says this so aggressively that I back off my questioning. We sit for a few moments eating from the single tub of ice cream she's brought as dessert.

'I didnae realize how much I had been abused until I reached puberty. I didnae see anything wrong with what had been happening to me until I discovered folk who were normal and then I begun to look at myself as a freak.'

'Sorry if this is uncomfortable to talk about.'

'It's fine. I brought it up. I'm telling you because Sita has helped me through this.'

I sense her aggression dissolving.

'Are you sure you're alright talking?'

'Ah widnae be doing it, if it wisnae alright.'

'Do you want a coffee or a tea?'

'You'll get the full story if you give me caffeine. Better make it a tea.'

'OK.'

'Most bairns are brought up on stories o Jack and Jill goin tae fetch water. I watched tapes showing how Jill sucked off Jack an all I remember is how much Jill seemed to enjoy it.'

'You watched porn?'

'No stupid, I dinnae watch it. I wis shown it while I was just a kid. It was all around ma hoose when I grew up. I had nae knowledge it wis wrong for me to watch it. My mum was a slut and gave sex for money in the same room. There were so many tapes, all with women who seemed to be really happy in a way, like I'd seen folk happy in the park cuddling their pets.'

'How weird.'

'Aye, weird indeed.'

'To think that adults could do such a thing to a child.'

'Both parents would often feel me up or slap me... all for my own good, they'd say.'

'Your father too?'

'Step father... he was responsible for fucking with my head.'

'What do you mean?'

'I wanted tae act like a loving daughter, like I'd seen women do on video tapes.'

'God!'

'He would touch me, like I was his pet.'

'What are you saying?'

'I responded like any animal to his attention.'

'What age were you?'

'It happened regularly until I was eight or nine.'

'What happened to make it stop?'

'Mixing with more normal folks at school.'

'Did your teachers know what happened?'

'No, but by secondary school I guess I was more sexually experienced than others. I was still a virgin but I'd beg to be fondled. Ma friends started treating me like a freak. Still, I considered myself better off than some kids who were seriously battered rotten by their parents.'

'Did you ever confront your folks?'

'Yes, I became very angry at my mum, keeping up this appearance of normality on the surface, while whoring it on the side. From the age of twelve I started to defy her and I had such hatred for my stepdad it damaged me even more. I hated them both until just a short while ago.'

'When along came Sita?'

'Exactly. I was one fucked-up girl.'

'What did she say to you?'

'She just pointed out how much the hatred was hurting me. Obvious, really. She told me her story and her background as the Kumari. Just to think this wee lassie was a living goddess, no less. She had an even weirder fucked-up life than mine... it made what I'd been through seem kinda tame.'

'What do you mean?'

'She told me about growing up, an being really famous in a city she could never put her foot into, literally. Then being cast out when she reached puberty and choosing to spend all her time in the hills with an old guru. How fuckin extreme is that? People here haven't a clue. She then told me all the things that parents do over there to children, out of sheer necessity. She'd seen mothers tie their young children to the pillars in their houses before going to work in the fields. They'd do it to keep the kids safe till they came back, from burning themselves on clay stoves or wandering off a cliff edge. Then as soon as kids could carry things, they'd be put to work in the fields. In some places up to six hours carrying heavy loads: firewood, water.'

'What did she tell you about being the Kumari?'

'Fuck me, what an experience that must've been. Being scared shit-less when she was first chosen. Having her skin scrubbed every day, sleeping with the heads of dead animals. Not to mention being taught tantra by her hundred-year-old guru, and some old white Sanyassin.'

Cindy throws out this last line as a casual afterthought.

'It made me feel watching *Debbie Does Dallas* was a safe childhood instructional film.'

'Did Sita tell you she had sex with the Moni Baba?'

'Well, no, she didn't mention names, but where di you think she learned all this tantra stuff? Did you teach her or did she teach you?'

I'm speechless.

'Anyway, don't distract me. This is my moment. Sita showed me that no matter what sort of hatred I felt for my parents, I also had the ability to do something about it.'

'What did you do?'

'I put a workman's nail-gun to my mother's head an then I slit my stepdad's throat. He bled out on the toilet.'

'Seriously?'

'I did fucking contemplate that at one time. That's how bad I was. I thought if I chibbed ma drunk dad when he was sitting drunk on the toilet, he'd just bleed oot, thinking it was a long pee.'

'Lucky you didn't.'

'I even had ma sob story all sorted for the jury. Abused child serves up justice.'

'What did you actually do?'

'I began to think if Sita can live through all her shit and be so cool, why can't I.'

'OK.'

'I grew up without knowing what was harmful. It took me a long time to realise there were plenty other survivors, who had recovered better than I from worse. You know, all that shit that's on the news each night.'

'What about your relationship with your mum now? Sita told me that someone had illicitly given her work.'

'What?'

'Sita said your mum got her job under the table.'

Cindy erupts into laughter.

'I must write this stuff down. It was my mum who was giving people a job under the table, at stag nights.' She howls louder with laughter. 'Glad I didn't tell Sita my mum got a job through the back door.'

I too lose it. Cindy and I bawl together, as if we're at a Billy Connolly concert.

'You are both such fucking wierdos,' Cindy says, 'but I gotta admit, I love you. You guys make me feel normal.'

Cindy stands up and lifts her blouse. She points to a neatly tattooed Sanskrit Om sign just below her belly button.

'I'm a convert,' she says. 'Gods are everywhere.'

. . .

When Sita finally arrives home, she witnesses a scene I don't think she expected. I am playing guitar and singing John Martyn's 'One World'. As she enters the room, Cindy stands up and begins to dance with her. She joins in using her traditional Nepali dance moves. They both frolic around, with Cindy looking like all she's missing is a fireman's pole.

When she leaves to go home, Cindy gives Sita a small kiss on each cheek. She also blows a kiss from the hallway to me, saying she'll only come back if I play her some ABBA songs.

'I hate ABBA,' I respond.

'Sita can help you wi that sort of hatred,' she shouts back.

33

In my field of work, unlike Sita's yoga class, any message directed at just one person's mind is a waste of time. Any communication job in the preventative health sector must reach enough people required to change the situation from bad to good. It might be a message that helps them individually, but it should also support health protection on an industrial scale.

Now having got myself up-to-date on the latest studies, I've managed to gain a broader work assignment from my old professor. He's tasked me to assess the current efforts in the UK charities sector at providing health advice within their fundraising adverts.

Professor Clark wants me to help him come up with an innovative plan to back up key public-health goals. One that will support the pressured and struggling National Health Service.

'Charities have a vital role to play,' he says, 'as long as they don't lie or exaggerate what they are offering. There are many signs that their adverts are guided by advertising agencies, not science. Everything they say to the public should be honest and tested to retain the trusted role they have in society. When they advertise a cure, whenever possible they should also be stressing the preventative measures.'

. . .

A FEW WEEKS AFTER MY EVENING WITH CINDY, SITA COMES TO SIT CLOSE to me. She speaks softly. 'I need your advice. I've had talks with two more women who want private tantra lessons.'

'Isn't that how you prefer things?'

'Yes, but lately I'm just as exhausted after a session with one person as I am with a class of twenty. The number of people now coming to the yoga studio is a concern I've not had to deal with before.'

I tell Sita I've been worried for some time. If statistics are to be believed, there's an increasing risk that someone in her class might have a stroke or a fall in a balancing posture.

'It's not only that, Sita, I'm also worried people might misinterpret what a private tantra session is.'

'Cindy told me she knows a lawyer who could help if we ever need it. She understands what she calls your orgasm of concern over tantra might be.'

'Sita, there are now people who come to your classes simply to get hooked up with others, not just to be taught tantra or get more out of their physical relationships.'

'People's interest may start with that, but that's not the main benefit, is it?'

'I feel we should be cautious because we are in dangerous territory here.'

'Cindy said she'd had a good talk with you. She is an example of what can be achieved. Did you know that she's only ever been in one serious relationship, which ended when it became a complete disaster because of sex? She has a history of abuse from her stepdad, and it's left her fearful to make love. She says for years she just wanted to "fuck" and be "fucked". She believed that's all she deserved. She is very mixed-up in her thinking.'

'That's her using the f-word for effect. That word has many uses here.'

'No, it's not just for effect, it's an attitude... and even if most people take that approach all their life, some should know there's a greater range of attitudes.'

'What about starting a children's yoga class?' I say.

'What do you mean?'

'You know Cindy's story, what she was surrounded with when she was a child. Let's dump the tantra classes as a cure for troubled older people and teach yoga as a prevention strategy for children. Think of what surrounded you too in Nepal. Think of Ram as he grows up here. He is already encouraged by young people trying to create their own roadmap for life and it's full of destinations that were once taboo. Now they have a checklist of sexual experiences to tick off instead of sex education. They could use some guidance.'

'So, you think my private tantra lessons are not helpful?'

'People are already talking at school about Ram's mum, the lady who teaches sex in her yoga class. It's not as if we don't have a choice or time to consider this. These children are fucked-up adults in the making. Don't let Ram have to deal with the need to be saved later.'

'I'm helping prepare Ram for the future,' Sita says quietly.

'You are and I will try to help you more, I promise.'

Whether this was Sita's skilful manipulation of a conversation, I may never know. Having me suggest something as if it were mine, that is really an outcome she desires.

OUR CELEBRITY WORLD IS FULL OF PEOPLE WHO HAVE RELATIVES WHO HAVE died of ordinary diseases. Many are currently suffering from a specific health condition themselves and will publicise their little heard of illness and raise money for research and care.

Alongside the health priorities for government, there are increasing numbers of independent charities who take on the more obscure ailments and begin funding to help them.

I discover a wave of new ailments that have been announced to the public recently. We have a rapidly growing list of dangers to fear, some of which can strike us down without warning. The list of acronyms for health menaces is growing as exponentially as the world's population.

Often these lesser-known health conditions affect so few people they are ignored by national campaigns or are given a token mention alongside the greater list of deadly ailments. There are signals too that large pharmaceutical companies have begun to make up names of ailments their drugs can alleviate. There is growing evidence of this issue, especially related to opioid addictions in the USA.

My professor believes this is an area of healthcare worth investigating. The collective efforts from individual charities dealing with recovery could become as successful as national campaigns on prevention. He suspects the charity sector is already contributing massively to our country's overall health awareness.

My brief is to look at when preventable illnesses information comes in most handy and what ailments people bring in most for treatment. I need to look closely at what and who delivers preventive messages.

Professor Clark has a reputation for being a radical. He has descended from his academic ivory tower more often than any other professor I know. He does this with the principle of sharing important health findings with the public, rather than holding on to them for his teaching career in health sciences. What seems his main challenge is to find what's needed to pry open the public's health consciousness and pop in the appropriate message, in a way that people will accept. I believe I will see it all more clearly when I understand what is possible to achieve.

One Monday morning, I wake up late and walk into the kitchen to see Mahesh standing there. He and Sita have pinned a large astrological chart to the cork board on the kitchen wall. Mahesh is carrying an old book written in Nepali. He tells me it's a book commonly referenced by gurus. He announces, 'A profound event will happen soon. No one knows what, but there are astrological signs showing it will take place here.'

'In this kitchen?'

'In this part of the world.'

Mahesh opens the book to show diagrams of planetary alignments and presents it to me.

I pull out a chair, joking that we may need somewhere comfortable so those spiritual beings can sit with us.

Mahesh laughs, more than the joke merits.

'The planets are predicting a new guru will suddenly make themself known today,' Sita says.

I suddenly realise who is missing from the kitchen. Ram is usually here, having breakfast before school. I look around and hear giggling from the broom cupboard.

'Oh my goodness,' I shout. 'I do feel a presence in this kitchen.'

Ram suddenly jumps out, shouting, 'Hunti gout!'

Sita and Mahesh look at me and laugh.

'Our family April fool,' Sita says.

Ram is still laughing as he tucks into his morning porridge. Mahesh takes me to the side, with a more serious look on his face.

'Jamesji, there is something I need to share with you.'

'What's that?'

'I found something in your dad's book.'

'Have you actually read my dad's yoga book?'

'Yes, I bought it.'

'What have you found?'

'Early in the book your dad writes, *My mind was filled with frustration and trickery. How can I argue with the Baba's suggestion that travel could help me to tame it?*'

'And?'

'Well, that seems like a life-changing moment for him.'

'My dad had many life-changing moments. One being his urge to commit fraud and another to leave his family.'

'But this perhaps is also an explanation. That in times of turmoil, your dad chose travel to tame wild thoughts.'

'What makes you say this?'

'Because he's coming back here to Scotland on a visit.'

'What?'

'The Avadhoot has accepted an invitation to give a very prestigious talk, an anniversary celebration of the first Ivan Illich talk to medical students in Edinburgh in the 1970s.'

Mahesh keeps talking nervously. 'It was Illich that first coined the phrase "Iatrogenic diseases", meaning all the illnesses we pick up from institutionalised medicine. After that talk in Edinburgh, Illich wrote the book *Medical Nemesis*.'

Mahesh keeps talking while I process what he's telling me. 'Illich was a popular rebel, highlighting cures which have more ill effects than a disease.'

'I know about Illich, Mahesh. But my dad? He's already agreed to come?'

'Yes.'

'When?'

'He arrives next week for ten days, on his new Nepali passport.'

'Oh my god... does Sita know this?'

'Yes. Since this morning. It was her idea I should tell you myself.'

'Does my mother know this?'

'No.'

'Why, Mahesh? Why would you arrange all this without telling me?'

'It was done at short notice. A note came round campus a few months ago asking student groups for suggestions on a speaker. I really thought they'd have someone lined up, but the professor organising the event asked me to help find someone international.'

'You contacted my dad before telling me.'

'I didn't want to involve you if he refused. I only heard yesterday from my father that the Avadhoot had accepted. He says he is looking forward to seeing you. He also told me that he attended that original Illich lecture. He's perfect to give this talk. He even sent a quote from that original Illich lecture. Listen... how relevant is this for today? *So many of life's changes are labelled medical problems and render people in effect as lifelong patients. Statistics show the shocking extent of post-operative side-effects and drug-induced illness in advanced industrial society.*'

'My god... I have to tell mum.'

'The gods are behind this, Jamesji. It may be their way of making things right once again for your family.'

Memories regularly clash in the mind, whenever time stops keeping them apart.

PART SIX: THE AVADHOOT VISITS SCOTLAND

34

Edinburgh airport is crowded with a fresh batch of returning holidaymakers. I lift Ram onto my shoulders so he can see people coming out of the arrivals gate. No easy task, these days. Whenever I put him down, he demands the elevation to see better. We finally settle on a vantage point where he stands in his socks on the back of a cushioned seat, while I hold his shoes.

'What does the Babaji look like?'

'Like an Indian Yogi... I hope.'

Mahesh and I explained it would only be for ten days, but mum's in a state of panic nonetheless. Plans are for him to give his talk on the sixth day after his arrival in a mix of Nepali and English, which Mahesh will translate as required.

My dad's warned me that part of his terms of citizenship was to promote Nepali culture overseas. The Nepali government believes the Avadhoot can give a favourable account of the current situation. No one is ever likely to find out James Munro senior is from Leith, or so we hope.

Sita has told Ram he'll meet a Baba she once knew in Nepal. She says he will remember Ram, because he carried him in the mountains when he was a baby. For my mum's sake, Ram has not yet been told this visiting Baba is his grandfather. Another withheld truth. Ram still doesn't know that I am not his biological father. In time, we all agree Ram will be enlightened.

I see dad before he sees me. He looks older, dressed in a saffron robe with a smart old-style tweed jacket on top. His hair is wild and his beard long, but he looks dignified, still slim and athletic. The outdoor life has baked his skin to a thick crust, his Caledonian origins well disguised. A few people take note of his presence, but it's unlikely anyone will peg him for a local.

I ask Ram if he recognises our visiting Baba. He points immediately to the man with a small cloth backpack, carrying a large architectural briefcase. Ram then runs in his stocking soles over to greet him. Dad's face changes from bewilderment to smiles as soon as he sees Ram and I.

'Is that fur me?' Ram shouts, staring at dad's leather briefcase.

'*Namaskar*,' I say.

Dad says nothing but returns the Namasti hand gesture, and pats Ram on the head. He steps forward and gives me a fatherly hug. He bends down and squats in front of Ram. He has the movement of a Nepali trail porter resting between hills stops. He's so swift to sit comfortably on his heels. He looks straight into Ram's eyes.

As Ram holds out his hand, the Avadhoot shakes it.

My dad speaks Nepali to Ram, telling him he's grown tall since they last met.

Ram understands him and replies '*Huncha,*' in Nepali.

'Where is your mother?' dad continues in Nepali.

'She wanted tae come... but she had tae go somewhere else,' Ram replies in English.

Dad stands and asks me in Nepali, 'Where is your mother?'

'I'll tell you on the bus,' I say.

I lift the Avadhoot's briefcase.

'Careful with that,' he whispers in English, a slight crack in his voice.

As we walk toward the bus stop, I see moisture in dad's eyes. I consider what he must be going through, returning here. The strange summation of a choice he made so long ago now brings him back to Edinburgh. His mind must be alive with faded memories, unleashed after thirty years of storage.

We step on a bus and Ram runs to his favourite seat at the back. I swing dad's briefcase onto the luggage rack.

'Is this your black tie and evening suit for the lecture?' I ask him.

'It contains two hundred and fifty A1 size, linen tankas.'

I whistle with an intake of breath in amazement. 'How did you get these through customs?'

'I told them they were visual aids for a lecture, and they didn't even check.'

'And are they for your lecture?'

'No, they're for you and Sita and your mother.'

'Wow. That's quite a gift.'

'Just paying for my keep.'

'That's generous of you. If we have any major sales, I'll be sure to erect a statue of you in Leith Docks.'

He finally laughs. 'Yes, that'd be popular,' he laughs more, 'put me in a lotus position facing Rank's flour mill.'

He hands me his backpack as we sit. It feels almost empty.

'Careful with that one, too – that's my evening Kurta, to wear for the talk.'

SITA'S SPECIAL DHAL BHAT IS LAID OUT FOR DAD'S ARRIVAL DINNER AND Mahesh brings along Mandy to meet the Avadhoot.

She seems impressed that my dad speaks entirely in Nepali to Sita and Mahesh and then breaks into the odd sentence in broad Scots to me.

Later, I take Mandy aside. 'Do you know what he's going to say?' I ask.

'No, but I'm hoping to have an English translation in advance so we can make it available to a wider audience. He speaks English well. He sounds like you,' she winks.

'I suppose.'

Mandy then asks dad if he wants to do anything special while he's here. She tells him it would be easy to arrange a short drive through the Highlands. I add the suggestion that we go out for a fish supper together before he returns. Sita mentions a yoga demonstration for the Kindare people in Peebles.

Dad suddenly looks tired. We agree he should have tomorrow off to recover from his journey. Mandy reminds us that on the afternoon of his talk he has been invited for tea to meet some of the students and faculty members.

Dad stands and excuses himself after finishing an enormous plate of plain rice. He congratulates Sita on her cooking. I don't understand much of what else he's saying in Nepali, they are talking so quickly. Dad seems impressed by the house and says we are lucky to have a home in such a regal part of Edinburgh.

When I show him to the spare room he moves toward the bed and sits on it, like someone rescued from a life raft at sea. He looks at me and says he's dreamed of this moment since we left him in Dhoti, Nepal.

He asks how my mum is. I tell him it's unlikely she'll attend the lecture but that I'm hoping she'll come and see him in private before he leaves to go back to Nepal.

'It may be the last time I ever see her.'

'I'll work on it,' I tell him.

'It's not your mum's fault.'

'She told me to tell you that whatever you do, don't become westernised again. And not to shave your beard off, otherwise some Leithy will spot you.' As I leave him to sleep, he drags the mattress off the bed onto the floor and lies on it.

'I don't need much comfort... but I do like a good mattress whenever I can get one.'

Back in the kitchen, Mahesh is excited.

'He's extraordinary, Jamesji.'

'How will you introduce him?' I ask

'I'll tell people he is our famous Sanyassin. That our earliest holy men were also healers and contacted regularly on matters of health by the tribe, or clan as you would say. They offered their services by winning hearts and minds with their stories.'

'Have you told him?'

'I didn't get the chance, but I thought you might. Mandy will get his speech in advance for clearance.'

'I'm sure he won't mind whatever you say about him.'

'There are a couple things the Heritage people would like him to state. Just that all cultures may be different, but people are basically the same.'

'How unique and scientific.'

'People won't be expecting a science talk from a Sadhu.'

Sita interrupts. 'Did you know, James, that yogis were the first to explore immunisation in the 7th century by taking small doses of snake venom to protect themselves from snake bites?'

'Is this a point the Avadhoot should add to his talk?' I ask her.

'No, but I do think he should state we have a cultural right to protect our own religious stories, even if they are now seen as fiction.'

35

Two days before dad's talk, I hire a car and drive him north alone, through the Highlands to Inverness. We've now exhausted talk about the risks of him putting himself in the spotlight, and mum's refusal to see him. He seems more relaxed.

We make a stop at the House of Bruar on the way up. Dad wanders among the tweed shooting jackets and leather boots, marvelling at the number of tourists. People from all over the world, shopping in a quiet Highland valley. He treats himself to a pair of corduroy trousers and some Brasher walking shoes. He also buys a small watercolour pad and paintbox. He tells me his last pair of corduroy trousers were cut in half twenty years ago and have been excellent for storing his rolled-up paintings in the legs.

We eat in the Bruar restaurant, fully stocked with local product. After a few awkward moments of silence, dad walks over to a bar-top tap and pours himself a glass of free water. He returns to the table and tells me the taste of the water is bringing back memories.

'Once, before you were born, I borrowed a friend's Hillman Imp to go camping with your mum. Somewhere up this road we found a sign saying fast food at the next turnoff. We turned off to find a lone caravan in a lay-by. It was just a beat-up temporary van with lots of old linoleum draped over the roof, held in place with stones. Patching leaks, I imagine. Smoke was pouring from an outdoor gas barbecue stove at the back. There was a large piece of wood wedged between two rocks and four deckchairs and portable table in front. The menu was written in chalk on a blackboard. I remember it had only two items. Egg rolls, or beans and chips. Your mum and I ordered eggs, beans and chips. The owner told us locals called him Lino on account of him having patched up his caravan roof with linoleum. Lino McCloud, it turned out, was a former gamekeeper who in summer set up his roadside café.

'He began making our fast food order by peeling potatoes. Actually he started by pouring the tatties out of a sack then peeled them, right in front of us. It took an hour and a half before we were served our fast food.'

'Was he the inspiration for your life plan?'

'I make fast food. On occasion I'll make Dhal Bhat in half an hour for travellers in Dhoti. There is nowhere else to eat for over a day's walk in any direction.'

'Exactly my point.'

Dad suddenly begins to laugh.

'I've just remembered more,' he says. 'Your mum and I came back to that lay-by years later and there was nothing there except for a wooden seat with a plaque written in memory of Lino McCloud. Some passing locals told us that he'd retired after his gas cylinder exploded. He wasn't hurt but his van was destroyed. He'd died a few years later, and was well liked and remembered by locals.' Dad begins to laugh more, then borders on hysteria.

'What's so funny? I ask.

'I've just remembered what someone stencilled on the bench.'

'What?'

'They'd neatly spray painted *Linoleum Blownapart.*'

'How do you store such vital information?'

'It's my curse and my gift.'

. . .

AFTER WE FINISH THE BRUER POACHED SALMON – THE BEST, DAD TELLS THE waiter, he's tasted in over thirty years – we take the road to Inverness. We approach from the eastern side of Loch Ness, from the hills above the southern end. This road winds its way down to the lochside and snakes along the beautiful eastern bank.

We overnight in a bed and breakfast with a view of Inverness Castle. The next day I ask dad if he would like to tackle a Munro or a smaller climb called the Cobbler on the way home. He seems game.

We drive south towards Glasgow, along the west of Loch Ness to Fort William. We eat under the shadow of Ben Nevis and are both in awe of the range of colours across the hills at this time of year. Dad says it's really something special about this place, which he took for granted all these years he lived here.

We park below a triple set of 3000-feet peaks. The clouds roll by overhead, as if on a fast-forward video. Shadows move under them like a strobe light. We start off, up the steep part of the trail, and I carry our backpack with rainwear, in case the strobes set off the sprinklers. Dad carries his small satchel containing his new watercolours and pad from the Bruar gift shop.

Up to that first knuckle, I struggle to keep up with dad. I pant like a spent greyhound. I notice dad has put on his new walking shoes without socks. He asks me how my relationship with Sita is going.

'Fine,' I say, breathing heavily.

Realising he's walking at Nepali pace, he turns and sits on a rock till I catch up. I sit beside him. I ask him how his relationship with Nepal is going, and he begins to tell me.

'Things are not so fine. There have been several attacks on police stations. Casualties among both the authorities and the Maoists rise each month. The rebels turn up unannounced and target government officials. The police and the army then hunt down the attackers and often isolate whole villages from outside contact. This tit-for-tat situation has become progressively more violent. The whole fabric of Nepal's rural life has been affected by it. News of one atrocity by the Maoists spreads, then news of a hard-hitting retaliation by the army follows. The timing of this armed struggle by Maoists has unfortunately coincided with a world-wide call for governments to unite in their fight against terrorism. Each time a village is accused of harbouring rebels, there are many innocent victims of the conflict. Relatives and sympathizers of these victims then join the rebels' cause, and a so-called terrorist is born.'

Dad tells me during the first attacks on police by the Maoists, he was horrified. He was shocked by the outdated philosophy they seemed to follow.

I ask if he's heard of any news from Barabasi.

'You mean you don't know?'

'Know what?'

We move under a Scots pine with hills stretching in each direction. I lean against rocks and try to stabilise my thoughts.

'I'm sorry, I thought you would have heard.'

As dad launches into Tilak's story, I'm transported back to the hills of Nepal.

'They were on an eight-hour trek to their nearest health post. Heavily pregnant, Maya was stopping regularly to ride out her contractions. Tilak was with her, prepared to deliver his baby at any stage on their journey. Apparently, they knew it was a boy. In Pokhara, they now have a scanner that can tell these things.

'Tilak was urging her to move faster to reach medical help for the birth. Maya was breathing heavy, and Tilak helped support her against a wall of loose rocks. Maya saw a group of young policemen coming up towards them, ready to pass on the trail up to the village. Then someone high in the hills stood and waved at them. Tilak suddenly pulled her away from the rocks, just before the blast, and stood between her and the bomb.

'From the village, they later said it sounded like a cough and a puff of smoke into the air above the vast Himalayan landscape. On the trail, it was strong enough to bring a small piece of the mountainside down in a landslide. Maya believes it was the first policeman who overtook them that triggered the explosion. They were thrown across the pathway, to where the land gave way. When she regained consciousness, soldiers had come to their rescue from the nearby village. Some shots were still being fired at rebels in the hills. Some had stayed to watch events unfold. Maya was pulled to safety and given attention by an army medic. Two policemen had been killed and two were badly injured. Tilak suffered injuries to his head, back and arms. His backpack, containing a thick blanket and metal dinner plates, likely saved his life. Both Tilak and Maya were carried by stretcher back down to the roadside by soldiers. A vehicle took them and the injured police to a military base in Pokhara. A caesarean was performed at the military hospital and their baby boy delivered safely. She says she was in and out of consciousness at first, but alert enough to tell the soldiers that Tilak was ex-Gurkha. Otherwise, they may just have taken them both up to the village health post.

'In the immediate aftermath of this explosion, villagers and the remaining police dug her out. She is certain Tilak was alerted to the explosion by a single rebel who stood and revealed himself, waving before the blast.

'A few days after this attack, the army stalked a group of suspected rebels back to the District Centre. Aware they were being followed, the rebels mined the path with another crude homemade pipe bomb. This time the army were aware the path had been mined, so lay in wait, not knowing where exactly the bomb was placed. Another group of civilians wandered through, and one was killed.

'Taking sides... in Nepal,' dad says, 'now seems compulsory. Good versus evil... it's always the story that proves most successful in recruiting converts. The traditional Nepali concept of "finding a middle way" has received no publicity at all, yet that's the part that makes their culture so great. This notion that in the end, people must see violence as the real enemy.

'Now both sides in Nepal have chosen the option that aggression against the other is the only way forward.'

Dad tells me the country is now receiving outside help to clamp down on the rebels. What he initially understood to be indifference by the majority of Nepalese, has suddenly become a polarizing situation.

The idea that your local bargaining power is substantially increased by the help you can get from elsewhere, is now the common perception. Any tangible help to districts is suspended until the politics of the local community is identified and labelled. In most cases the help offered from outside is money, and long before it filters down to those it's supposed to reach, it is syphoned off. A new flock of internationally aware politicians are ignoring local needs at their own peril. The constituents they represent will judge them in the end. Financial corruption, dad believes, is now the most severe threat to Nepal's stability.

36

Sandy Bottom's Fish and Chips is a small family business that has survived three generations with fry-ups in its original building off Fort Street. Sandy's grandsons now run the business, and all have the same ability to raise their voices above the sound of fish regularly hitting hot oil as they prepare suppers for take-away. The shop has been given a few coats of paint and new tiles but has the same glass frontage it's always had. The counter stands in the same spot along with a stack of newspapers into which the Bottoms wrap their fish and chips. A new computerized till sits next to the old silver bell-ringing, drawer-opening, classic. An antique that still shines with nostalgia.

After receiving our orders and leaving Sandy's, dad and I walk down towards Leith docks. Dad uses his power of pranayama to blow on his hot chips, so as not to burn his mouth. He keeps talking in breathy parables about the areas where he grew up. He spent the first twenty years of his life within this two miles square.

'What does a bag of brown sauced chips help you recall?'

'I could have stayed here and studied theology,' he says. 'I did consider it at one time, but the urge to travel was great too.'

'Still, you've earned some qualifications to preach. Anyone out there who wants to believe in God, you could be on their coaching bench.'

'Most people I grew up with around here had very little belief in God. He was just the big man upstairs who could see if you were bad and could keep an eye on you... even locked in your room. People I knew got away with so much bad, that they didn't believe anyone was watching them. They knew very little about their own family history, their parents and even less about their aunts and uncles, nothing at all of their ancestors. If you read history books, you are made to believe our culture was widespread. We had imported fruits and foods from sunny countries in the sixteenth century, but they never passed through the bowels of people in these streets even in the 1960s. Many didn't even know who their grandparents were because their parents never spoke of them. There were thousands of broken families, people who never knew or kept in touch with their children. They all lived in ignorance of this grand heritage they were apparently part of. All this time while history was being written, some of it even planned, most people were off the pages, just wild cards, on no specific path, making their own way hand to mouth. It's the wealthy who have management plans, even when it comes to organising the poor.

'Back then it was very easy to assess how good a parent had been in bringing up their children. You would just ask your mates – did you have a happy childhood? If they say yes, chances are their parents did a good job. If no, chances are they had shit parents.'

'And how did you assess your childhood?'

'Good.'

'Now ask me.'

Dad chews hard on a hot chip and bites his tongue. He waits a moment, till the heat disappears.

'James... you know...' dad sighs, 'it's not possible for you to know my mindset at the time...' he pauses, 'but you could accept my handling of the situation since we were reunited. I believe there's new feelings between us.'

'I accept we're on a path to reconciliation, but you still seem in denial of the hurt caused by your actions. Because you didn't mean to cause pain, doesn't mean it was not a painful blow.'

. . .

WE WALK THROUGH LEITH DOCKS. DAD SAYS THEY ARE ALMOST unrecognizable to him. The Royal Yacht Britannia sits on the site of his old shipyard. It's now flanked by a huge shopping complex. He asks me to take him inside, so we walk into the Ocean Terminal mall. Dad invites me into a large coffee area and finally settles into a seat facing the café windows. He tells me this is pretty much the position of his drawing board when he was an apprentice draughtsman. From the angle of views towards the Rank's flour mill and the remains of the old pier, he reckons this table is on the spot where he sat for six years. The height and angles match; this is place where his old drawing board stood and where dad first dreamt of travel.

'All the things I once placed value on, are now different.'

'And people?'

'Yes, they're different too, except for my attachment towards them.'

'Attachment?'

'Yes of course.'

'Isn't that radical for a sanyassin?'

'No, it's the realisation of a sanyassin. Do without. Learn to appreciate.'

'How did you get so involved in all this Indian guru stuff, sitting looking out over a shipyard?'

'I always held an interest in quotes or statements that were imbued with meaning. Then I found these Indian philosophy books that were just full of such statements. The Buddha has some of the best come-back lines ever.'

'But what made you want to do it yourself?'

'I found I could make up quotes. I could read a famous teaching and then think up the exact opposite meaning and write a well formed quote. I can now write this stuff until the cows come home. I'm never at a loss for words to propose an opposite that works.'

'So, this guru stuff is all an act. All made-up bullshit.'

'No, not at all. Bullshit, where does the word even come from? Being able to spot bullshit is the difference between being a helpful guru and a motivational speaker. Getting the timing right for a well placed quote is what guru-ness is all about. Speakers just rabbit on about the same stuff, all the time. A mind which is troubled by all sorts of beliefs can be greatly helped through persuasion to consider an alternative. Being a guru doesn't make you special or superior. It does, however, require knowledge of what to say at the right time, when it's needed.'

Dad stands without finishing his coffee or his train of thought. 'I only wanted to look out this window,' he says. 'We hold dear what we wish for, until it changes.'

'Om, guruji.'

'Let's go meet your art-gallery man.'

As we walk towards the gallery, dad says, 'I know you're critical of how I've acted in the past, but you must make your own way out of your discomfort.'

'I know.'

'Believe it or not, this trip is helping to change me. I never predicted I would ever come back, so it's helping rid me of the phantoms I still carry from here.'

As we walk into the gallery, Jim Miller is there to greet us, and suddenly on seeing him, dad begins to walk around on his own looking at paintings. He acts very strangely and when I approach him, he whispers, 'I've just seen a phantom,' then continues to talk to me in Nepali.

'So, this is the famous recluse artist... welcome. Does he speak any English?' Jim asks.

'No, he doesn't speak much.' I look at dad as he flips through some photographic books on sale.

'Tell him I'm a great admirer of his work.'

I jabber a mouthful of Nepali nonsense, and dad nods his head.

'He appreciates that,' I say.

Dad gives Jim a Namasti sign. Jim returns it.

Dad lifts a photography book containing arty images of the famous AI computer Big Blue.

'*Ke* Big Blue?' he asks me in Nepali, twisting his hand and wrist in the classic Indian question gesture.

I ask Jim what the book is about.

'Big Blue is the IBM computer they designed to play chess. It took on the World Champions. They feed old games from the past into these new machines. They can remember every move.'

Dad flips through the book and asks if the computer won.

'Yes.'

Dad then picks up a historic photographic book about the shipyards in Leith.

'You flip... you buy,' Jim jokes.

Dad looks up too quickly, exposing that he understands what Jim says.

'Take it. Keep it. A token of our business friendship. It's my roots in there.'

Jim explains that he used to work in Henry Robb's Shipyard. I look at dad but he doesn't flinch. He continues to look through all the photographs as if disinterested.

'I've got a few models of the ships we built back then through the back.'

'That's amazing,' I reply.

'Yes... ask the Avadhoot if he'd like to see some model ships. Those we once built here in Leith.'

Jim takes us through and asks me to explain to dad that this is the more secure part of his gallery and storage rooms. He parts the bead curtain with one wave of his hands.

'This curtain keeps everything in here secure and delinquent customers out.'

I hear dad muffle a laugh. Then he sees some of his tanka paintings hanging from the walls. He walks towards his paintings and stares at them. Possibly he has never seen them in a gallery setting and, like me, he is suitably impressed.

'Look here,' Jim shouts.

Over in a corner are several model ships in glass cases. A few dredgers, tugboats, a helicopter support ship and a paddle steamer. Each one is an exquisitely detailed miniature model.

'I got these in a sale when the Robb offices and yards closed. Small replicas of the ships we built here,' Jim says.

'It's certainly a small world,' I say, looking at dad as Jim laughs.

'Can you take a photo of the Avadhoot and me in front of his paintings, James?'

'He doesn't like getting his photos taken... he's a recluse, remember.'

'Oh yes, OK, sorry.'

Dad then nods his head in acceptance and stands in front of his tankas, gesturing for Jim to join him.

Jim goes to a desk drawer, pulls out his camera, and hands it to me. Dad puts his arm around Jim, and they both smile. I look through the lens. On one side is my slim and hairy dad, on the other is bald and clean-shaven Jim. Dad has his guru suit on, with a three-quarter-length loose shirt and tight pantaloons. Jim has on green moleskin trousers and a navy polo-neck. Former workmates, reunited by fate. I imagine them both in workers overalls, as in a postcard from the 1960s.

'Where's Babs today?' I ask, handing back the camera.

'She's just gone to the Co-op for some messages. She'll be back in a moment.'

I see dad's smile disappear and his eyes widen. He suddenly makes his impatience obvious and looks towards his wrist, tapping the bone where a watch should be. He bows a Namasti to Jim.

'Will you not stay for some tea?'

'Sorry, thanks Jim I'll be in touch.' I take the hint. 'The Avadhoot is giving a talk later. We have to go.'

'Babs would love to meet our most famous recluse. Can we come hear the talk?' he asks. 'Or meet up again?'

'Sorry, it's sold out... and the Avadhoot has several other engagements.' Our family capacity to lie kicks in, right on time.

'Oh well, all the best. Nice to meet you, Avadhoot.'

As we pace back though the bead curtain, Jim shouts, 'Ah just have to say Avadhoot... I don't have any doots about yeh anymore.'

. . .

'PERHAPS THE PHOTO WAS A MISTAKE. BUT I THOUGHT HE'S NEVER GOING to recognise me if he didn't in the flesh. He's Jimmy Miller. Worked as an apprentice in the pattern office of the shipyards when I was a journeyman. Had a fancy for your mother back in the sixties. They're about the same age. Last I heard of him, he'd joined the Merchant Navy. Your mother and Babs were pals, often rivals. Perhaps due to the fact I dated Babs before I met your mother!'

37

By the time we return home, dad has regained his composure. He asks Mahesh if he's ever heard of Big Blue in his artificial intelligence classes.

'It's a famous machine in my line of studies,' Mahesh confirms.

'How come I've never heard of this?'

'Because you live underground in a Himalayan man-cave,' I fire back.

THE ILLICH LECTURE, AS IT'S POPULARLY KNOWN AMONG STUDENTS, IS AN event that no longer has any professional connection to Ivan Illich. It's organised by a similar set of radical students to those in the 1970s who first challenged medical establishment policies. Students from many disciplines now attend and it is especially popular with members of the Medico Chirurgical Society. This year it has opened admission to students from other universities and professionals across a wide range of public-health disciplines. To my surprise, there are queues of young people, all speaking excitedly in several languages, waiting to enter the auditorium.

Dad's appearance is about as far from an old Leither as one can get.

He's dressed in his Nepali pantaloons and a kurta. He walks into the hall like an actor on a break from the film *Gandhi*. The room falls silent.

'Namskar. Thank you for your invitation to speak here this evening.'

Dad introduces himself by inserting whole phrases in the Nepali language. His gestures are also very Asian. These two languages spoken as one create a mesmerising atmosphere.

He praises the beauty of Edinburgh, as any newcomer might. He tells the audience he is one of the few Sannyasins who has a passion for the latest books on science, health and religion. He says he enjoys the latest research into the way our brains work, because it helps to confirm the strong links between the health of our mind and the health of our body.

There is no need for Mahesh to translate, though he is on hand throughout for this purpose. Dad appears as a scholarly man of international standing. He speaks with the authority of a guru, making it sound like his opinions originated in the Far East rather than the shipyards of Leith. He says the main goal of the evening will be to highlight two themes. One, the comparisons we make... the other, the ignorance we hold.

'I've not come to criticise modern medicine or to condemn the use of drugs. Nor have I come to praise God and religion. This series of lectures was begun by Ivan Illich, a man who spoke effectively on both these issues in the 1970s. Since then, research has brought issues of faith and faith in health closer together.

'Knowing we all contain the same component body parts we've carried for as long as human life has existed, it's no surprise we have learned a wealth of information about our health, stored it and passed it on. Yet every day a fresh mind in the form of a child comes into this world, ignorant of this information. Most of us move through life, happily ignorant of most health problems, until something goes wrong. We are then forced to examine ways of removing ignorance, and much of that process is done by making comparisons.

'Interestingly, the first few years of human life are totally dependent on being looked after... a situation that plants the seeds of faith. What those who surrounds us know and do is crucial to our survival. It was once the case that thousands of children died before their first birthday, many from what we now consider ignorance. Many more thousands died before their fifth birthday. It is hard today to fully appreciate this world of the past. Whenever you read a book about human history and all the things we have achieved, remember these two facts. Our children died in their tens of thousands and our knowledge is learned, not genetically transferred.

'In all parts of the world, a state of ignorance exists. Our collective knowledge may seem massive but it's often restricted, unshared or ignored by people just using what they were born with, to get through life. If you read any book written about my country Nepal before the year 1990, you may be captivated by descriptions of its natural beauty and its friendly peaceful people. The hospitality of those who live in Nepal's hills is legendary. What is ignored by these inspired foreign travellers is the child mortality rate that was among the highest in the world at that time. Children died in Nepal before their fifth birthday in numbers that today would be considered a slaughter caused by ignorance.'

Dad pauses for effect, before asking his audience a question.

'Can anyone in this audience tell me how many children here in Scotland died before their first birthday in the 1990s?'

Several hands fly into the air and dad choses a young woman sitting in the front row.

'I believe the IMR in the UK was and is about ten or eleven deaths for every one thousand live births.'

'Alright, let's say I believe you... and my belief is important to what comes next. Tell me, how do you know this information?'

'It's published in the UK's health statistics.'

'It's been researched and authenticated?'

'Yes.'

'And what are the consequences if I don't believe you?'

'None, the stats remain the same.'

'The stats remain the same, exactly. The truth is in the stats, whether people believe it or not.'

'Yes.'

'Do you know the infant mortality rate for Nepal?'

'No.'

'This is where comparisons are helpful. Comparisons are the most common route to knowledge for the human mind. Every traveller knows this. Whenever you arrive in a new place, the comparisons begin. It often takes up the entire conversation for a trip. How does the place rate compared to home, what about the food, the weather, the people? Look, people dress different, eat, speak and act different. Every holiday or break from routine is infested with comparisons. Think of all the stories you share that are based on one thing being better than another, or indeed being worse. Such conversations an opinion makes.

'In remote districts of Nepal, the mortality rate was over 350 deaths per thousand live births until the 1980s. From this information you can conclude that it was far more dangerous for children to be born in Nepal than in the UK. And, if you believe the global stats, it must be even safer for a child to be born in Japan, where the mortality rate is nine.

'Health stats that are gathered from last year when compared to this year, provide important information. But they can also teach differences when compared across countries.

'Here is where the words faith, truth and belief fit into our discussion. Statistics change if the conditions change and as this young lady says, not whether someone like me believes them or not. So how can I motivate my belief to change the conditions?

'I'm not talking about belief in God, I'm talking about understanding that changes have happened for the better in other places. It was only when people working in health in Nepal began to make comparisons on global statistics, that massive public action began to change things. No one wants their country to be the most dangerous place for a mother to give birth. No mother wants to lose a child. When someone views these stats in the UK they may feel proud and satisfied, but in Nepal these same stats were driving demands for change.

'As you all begin your careers in whatever field of health you choose, don't forget the importance of belief and the potential in comparing health conditions with other countries.

'Statistics can be helpful, but deceitful too. For example, the statistics that show that ill health is related to poverty. This statistic is useful for planners, until it is interpreted as meaning poor people cannot learn. Believe me, it does not take a lot of money to remain healthy, but it does take knowledge.'

The Avadhoot stops talking and walks over to a table, where he pours himself a full glass of water and takes three short sips and then one gulp.

'I'm amazed that in the countries where the water is so pure to drink, people have given up drinking it, especially children. For the past 50 years this glass of clean water has remained top of the UN's list of the most important health provision that any country can make for its citizens.

'Yet here a slaughter by ignorance is unfolding because people are more often encouraged to drink a sugary addictive substitute than water. What chance does a child here have of believing this water is good for them, when they see glamour and excitement attached to drinking carbonated sugar?'

Dad says this with obvious irony and returns to the front of the stage smiling. He then gargles another mouthful of water before spitting it out again into the glass.

'Here, in some homes, more water is spat out, than is swallowed. The nearest pure water gets to many a young mouth, is when children brush their teeth, then spit it out.

'If you have been brought up in the industrial cities of the West, you may be surprised at how the world's religions still shape the culture and health status of non-industrial countries and how dependant many people still are on a familiar belief system. There's arguably as many people dependant on religion as there are those dependant on drugs.

'Religion has played a historical role in organising our beliefs. These beliefs, however, have also found a new home in the sciences. I mention this because where we choose to place our belief is one of the few things still under our personal control.

'Consider this from Ivan Illich, from his early book written years before the scourge of opioids:

'*So many of life's changes are labelled medical problems and render people in effect as lifelong patients. Statistics show the shocking extent of post-operative side-effects and drug-induced illness in advanced industrial society.*

'For over fifty years, your National Health System has pioneered research at the sharp end of health care and through its success your people rely on it, your people believe in it.

'Fewer and fewer societies exist today without copying modern health interventions. I come from a country where medical help is still considered at a minimal level. There are less than one thousand doctors for 17 million people. Most who pass their fifth birthday live lives without seeing many doctors, free of medicine and treatments. How do they survive you may ask, or should I say you don't ask? It is a situation that is becoming rarer and so should become of interest to Western medicine.

'I once challenged a health official, who was proud we had so few road deaths in Nepal. This, of course, is due to the fact we have few roads. Yet even so, in Nepal we still manage to have road accidents. Hill people walk into to our cities and cross the road with what I call suicidal innocence. People here in the West try cocktails of drugs to cure themselves... with that same suicidal innocence. What we choose to research within society must be relevant and become useful to removing dangerous levels of ignorance.

'By far the largest number of threats we encounter in our lifetime are handled by our own personal immune system. This immune system is sustained by food and activity, not by drugs. It is in relatively rare and extreme conditions only that it can be assisted by drugs.

'Here, however, rather than wait five days for the common cold to pass, and for people to feel a sense of confidence in their own immune system, people choose to turn to drugs to feel better in three days. No longer is there confidence in one's self. Those who seem to remain healthy are often maligned as the lucky ones, yet this is also a sign of having good mental health. The multitude of different environments that we live in present different mental challenges. Here there is a definite increase in what is tagged as mental-health issues, which then produce physical health issues. We suffer most by being confused about where healing comes from.

'When the first lecture in this series took place, Mr Illich could not have predicted the personal abuse of and addiction to drugs designed and marketed to cure our ailments. These drugs cause real damage both mentally and physically when consumed by people who physically don't need them. The mind, it seems, can be at its most creative when justifying our addictions.

'Everyone needs to keep a sharp lookout for signs of mental fatigue. Constantly compare what consuming medicine might offer you, against a few simple changes to your personal behaviour. And if you take one memory from this lecture, let it be this: **What is of most danger to your health, is having a mind that wants to escape its thoughts.**

'Are there any questions?'

Someone from the back of the room in a wheelchair raises a hand.

'Some people are disabled from birth and need to take a cocktail of drugs to survive. What would you say to them about improving health?'

'People with life-threatening ailments know better than most how to focus their mind to take care of themselves. Where and how often they need to consume medicine becomes part of their survival consciousness. They understand how fine a balance is needed. What I'm suggesting is that those who are free from such necessary health precautions should place this same amount of mental effort into maintaining their healthy habits. Putting in effort now can help delay or avoid a more extreme commitment later.'

An older man chips in. 'You seem to suggest that with most sick people, it's their fault they are sick?'

'Absolutely not. People get sick through no fault of their own all the time. The more medicine is studied, the more we understand the causes of ill health. It's safe to say we now know more than at any other time. Yet we repeatedly get sick from illnesses we can avoid. All I'm suggesting is the cure for ignorance is as relevant as the cure for illness.

'If something is acknowledged as preventable in health, it is a communication problem more than a medical problem. Similarly, when someone is addicted and continues to create health problems for themselves, without a care for the consequences, it's more a mental-health issue than a physical health problem.'

The last question of the evening is asked by a long-haired young man, who noticeably slurs his speech. He's clearly drunk or high.

'Are you suggesting we all live life without risk or enjoyment?'

Dad pours himself another glass of water and lifts it in a cheers sign to the young man. The audience laughs.

'How many times have you all been out for a good drink only to listen to the person who has drunk most, talk about themselves all evening?

'No alcohol or drug is harmless. Even if it's for fun or experimentation, you are vulnerable. When you are told it gives you an unbelievable high, you should beware. This is the most dangerous persuasive lie in society today.

'As a seeker of good times, ask yourself where this attraction to drugs is coming from. It's very likely from people seeking you out. To join them, to meet their emotional or business needs. Such suppliers need your addiction for their own livelihood.

'Don't get me wrong, we all have addictions... but you should choose them wisely.

'As an addiction grows, enjoyment disappears. It can take away quality time you might have for other pursuits. Far more may be lost, than what's considered good for a brief time.

'Don't just listen to me. Look at the stats. There's an estimated 30 million registered recovering drug addicts in the US today – they should all be listened to when they talk about the dangers they faced.

'We can be made to believe a one-time drug intervention will work for illness, but please don't think such a drug exists to cure your unhappiness. Your health affects your mind, showing you that your mind is also connected to your health. It's a two-way union. That's the attraction of yoga to many people. Knowing that you can, on your own, scheme a recovery.'

Dad finishes by bowing forward, in a Namasti salute to his audience. I hear some students shout instructions to each other as they leave. A group are meeting for an after-talk drink in the Student Union bar. The persuasive lie continues its life cycle in student minds.

I see Sita talking to a group of young women who clearly know her from the yoga studio. They are joined by Mahesh and Mandy and engrossed in talk. I go in search of my dad backstage. I find him talking to the sound engineer who has recorded his talk. Dad requests a copy and I ask for one also for my own research notes.

After the engineer agrees, he walks off and dad turns to me.

'Do you want to go for a pint?'

'Yes, sure. That would do it. Blow your whole talk by being seen at a local bar afterwards, getting pissed.'

'But here's the thing, James, it would be OK for me to do it, because such drinking is not a habit with me. It would be a once every thirty years experience. Hardly destructive.'

'How would it look, though?'

'OK. Let's go hame and have a hot chocolate. That's my favourite sin, anyway.'

38

The morning after dad's talk, I drive us all to the nursing home in Peebles. I tell dad that if he decides to stay in Scotland, this is where we'll likely put him.

Sita has convinced dad to come see a sample of the landscape work mum's done at the home and she's asked if he could give some of the residents a yoga lesson, secretly hoping mum'll drop by and see him.

We are escorted up the driveway by the mobility scooter gang, as though it's a State visit. Dad is welcomed by the management and Sita's told Maisy is very excited at her visit.

I see dad stand alone at the entrance, looking towards the surrounding hills of Peebles. In front of him are the terraced lawns mum and Sita created. He walks towards the lily pond and places his hand on the waterspout, washing his face and taking a drink as if he's on a Nepali hill stop. He doesn't realise the sheep piss that's likely washed down into the pond. It's just recycled dirty water, not a fresh stream. He says the place has the look of a Rana palace garden. He seems in a daze. I haven't told him mum's still refusing to meet him.

Maisy tells Sita she was distraught at her brother's passing. She whispers, 'In this place you canny concentrate long on yer sadness.

Some get over it by getting angry at oor handlers. But no me – an that's thanks tae you, pet.'

Sita now fully understands Maisy without needing translation. She questions her why people get so angry at the staff.

'They've put millions of pounds into upgrading this nursing home and do yi know what the improvements are in my room?'

'No,' Sita says.

'Draught excluders, hen! A man came to ma door and told me he'd make sure we'd awe save on energy bills by having draught excluders fixed tae the windaes and doors. He said it wid keep in the heat and was awe part o the improvements.'

Sita looks at my dad and they both laugh, but Maisy's not finished yet.

'Now, whit's a draught, onyway?' She turns to me. 'It's feckin fresh air, isn't it James? They're plannin tae stop us getting fresh air in tae the rooms. A've lived here all these years withoot excluders an now they want tae seal me in... cut off awe ma oxygen.'

'So what did you do?' Sita asks.

'Ah chased the man away.'

'Keep practicing that prana,' dad says.

'Ah havne got a piana... what's he talking aboot?' Maisy looks at me.

Sita invites dad to follow her to the yoga studio to give the residents a short demonstration of postures for old bones. The room is full of the elderly inmates, some bulging out of their lycra. Their multi-coloured leotards seem to have folds in odd places. Seams don't look strong enough to support any movement at all. Some look moulded out of children's putty into odd shapes and sizes. Without talking, dad gives a spontaneous display of flexibility and strength which is impressive for his age. He is older than some of the residents in the home but even the young staff members are impressed by his range of movements.

When dad finishes, he tells them he's going to leave them with a yoga mantra they can all chant together. He looks at me and I remember the first time I saw him in the hills of Nepal. I suddenly fear he is going to have them all chanting, 'Hitler has only got one ball.'

Within seconds he has them all in a conga-line singing 'Show me the way to go home.' They all sing it loud and in perfect unison and dad joins in.

When we leave the room, some are still singing, waving their arms in the air, geriatric Hare Krishnas. It has become an instant hit mantra for them, and they lose themselves in words and their memories.

'That worked well,' I say to dad as we leave.

'It's one of the most favourite chants in Nepali down in the Terrai,' he says.

Before we get in the car, Maisy waves Sita over and whispers something in her ear.

'What did Maisy say?' I ask, as we drive off.

'She said... that auld yogi looks a lot like the young James.'

'She's a yogini, that one,' dad says.

TWO NIGHTS BEFORE HIS DEPARTURE DAD TELLS ME HE'D LIKE TO HAVE A walk around Edinburgh alone, before he leaves. I tell him he can borrow some of my clothes if he wants to remain less conspicuous. Surprisingly, he agrees. He ties his hair in a ponytail and walks out of the flat, looking like a seventies rock star on vacation.

Six hours later, at ten o'clock that night, Sita and I both become concerned that he hasn't come back.

'It's unlikely he'd get lost?' Sita asks.

'Yes, no way he's lost. I hope he's not done a runner.'

'What do you mean?'

'Gone into hiding somewhere in Scotland.'

'Why would he do that?'

'All he'd have to do is shave and cut his hair and he'd fit straight back in to some Highland village here.'

'But why?'

'I don't know, but he's unpredictable isn't he?'

'Only to you.'

'I'll never figure why he ran off to the hills in Nepal.'

'That was his calling. I don't think there's any doubt he wants to go back. Do you think something might have happened to him, like an accident? Should we call the police?'

'No, not that, not yet.'

'James, he's not had to look sideways for oncoming traffic for almost thirty years.'

'I know. But let's wait.'

By eleven o'clock, Sita and I are still wide awake, sharing scenarios. He's lost his sense of time. He's met someone he knows. He's been in an accident. He's been arrested or scarpered to the hills again. He wouldn't have gone to see mum without an invite... would he?

Just before midnight, dad finally arrives back at the flat. He has a cut on his forehead, and a plaster crudely applied to his cheek. He smells of alcohol. As soon as Sita sees him, she seems relieved, as am I. She tells me she's feeling tired and a bit queasy. She suggests she'll hear dad's story later and will now leave us to go sleep.

'You'll have lots to discuss with your dad. Just let me know if he's fully reverted to his former life. We can discuss the karmic consequences of that in the morning.'

Sita gives dad a Namasti sign, palms closed, but with her eyes raised to the heavens, then leaves us alone.

'Have you been out on a piss-up?' I ask, shocked at his appearance.

'Just a little bit, at the end of the evening,' he says. 'I spent most of my time in a bookshop.'

'What have you been up to? Did a pile of books fall on your head?'

'I've not been in shops for nearly thirty years. It was all so commercial, confusing and tempting.'

'The shops closed hours ago. Where have you been?'

'Some nice people took me for a medicinal drink... after I was attacked.'

'Attacked... where were you attacked?'

'I was walking back here, along Rose Street, when I saw three young yobs shaking a signpost out of the ground, for no reason.'

'And?'

'Basically, I told them they were being destructive.'

'And?'

'I forgot myself, and where I was. One of them stepped forward, right up to my face, and started cursing, shouting I was a street bum and to mind my own business. I pushed him back and he head butted me. I saw another in the corner of my eye coming at me with a punch. With great yogic agility, I avoided the punch and drop-kicked him in the goolies.'

'You what?'

'It was self-defence... I gave him a Davie Mackay... between the legs.'

'Then what?'

'I ran.'

'And?'

'All the time I ran, thinking *I can't get questioned by the police*. The youngsters chased me along Rose Street. A crowd were standing outside a pub and I shouted for help. Three men stepped in between me and the yobs. They were big rugby lads and they just blocked their way, telling them to piss off. My attackers turned back to pick up their friend. They were shouting at everyone.'

'Shouting what?'

'That I'd attacked them, or something like... yer lucky these poofs helped you, you auld fuckin hippy. Then they started shouting at their friend. You got suckered by a pensioner, eidjit. My three saviours told me my head was bleeding and took me into the pub to get me cleaned up. We started talking and they offered me a drink.'

'So, you set aside your temperance vows and accepted?'

'I was grateful. I bought them a round and then time disappeared till now. Told them I used to work in the Leith shipyards. They wanted to hear all about the docks in the 1960s. Dug out memories I forgot I had.'

'What were you thinking?'

'I've had such vivid flashbacks all day. Memories poured back while I talked to those lads. I just blethered them bored and they listened. I thanked them for saving me from hospital.'

'Or jail?'

'Yes. Funny... my main ambition on leaving school, was to stay out of prison.'

'And you're still working at it.'

39

At the yoga studio, dad's farewell gathering turns into a dance party. The studio is filled with people come to see a last yoga demonstration by the now famous Avadhoot. Cindy has been the main organiser of this event.

The Caribbean contingent bring the snacks and music. They lead the way with Soca music between food and asanas.

I tell dad that Sita's classes are successful and continuing indefinitely despite her unorthodox approach. His tankas are selling at impressive prices, and it looks like the studio is finally providing a reliable income for us as a family.

Two Caribbean yoga mothers begin wucking their way through the song, 'What happens in the Party, stays in the party'. Then they play 'I am a Bachelor,' which they tell me is a special request for the Avadhoot from Cindy.

Out of the corner of my eye, I see mum arrive. The studio is filled with revellers. Mahesh is on the dance floor with Mandy. Ram is dancing with Lotisha. Sita is having a deep conversation with Cindy. I then see my dad recognise my mum.

What happens next is not what I expect. There is no explosion of loathing, there is not even an embarrassed walk-out. There is just a tender shared smile.

I look to see if anyone else is clocking this event. After all, this could be the moment the family lie is blown wide open. I can't let this be a dramatic ending to our personal Bollywood movie, where all is revealed and forgiven in a family dance scene. I realise it's up to me to save them from themselves, so just as they walk towards each other, seemingly to embrace, I tackle them both into the adjoining office. I close the door behind me.

They look at me, then each other, and hug affectionately.

'So, what will you do now?' mum asks dad.

'I go back to Nepal tomorrow. I'm only here on a tourist visa.'

'That's what you've been all your life.'

'A tourist on earth.'

'Yes... going back to live on your own?'

'I'm not alone there.'

'Good.'

'I feel ignored here.'

'That's unfair.' Mum smiles. 'It's good to see you.'

'And you.'

'What do you think of our son?'

'I'm proud.'

'Me too.'

'He could use a bit of getting used to that pride, from you.'

'That's unfair.'

'Well, it's something we two must try harder at doing.'

'Keeping in touch?'

'Yes.'

TOWARDS THE END OF THE EVENING, I HEAR THE ROLLING STONES BEING played loudly. And as 'Honky Tonk Woman' is shout-sung by a lot of older people, I walk through to where I've left mum and dad alone. I find them dancing together. They are not just dancing; they are lost in the dance. Dad and his flexible knees are bending, twisting and grinding to the guitar riffs. Mum is prancing around, arms in the air, like a hippie at Woodstock. A few people from the main studio see me through the open door and suddenly a circle is formed around mum and dad. People are clapping and laughing. Quite a few look at me, then at my mum and dad, possibly wondering how quickly a love bond can be formed.

THE NEXT DAY, I TAKE MY DAD TO THE AIRPORT ON MY OWN. HE SEEMS happy and appears relieved to be travelling home. I ask if he's enjoyed the trip.

'It's been good.'

'Any highlights?'

'To catch up with the wife, see Edinburgh and do a ton of shopping,' he says sarcastically, waving a cloth bag with hardly anything in it.

'It's been wonderful to see you, Sita and Ram.'

'But especially mum?'

'Yes. We love each other in our own way. We are just very different.'

'These different bits are inside me too. They both fight and feel for each other as much as you both have.'

'Well, that's not really us inside you, it's more likely last night's curry. You have a rich choice of options for your future, James. I hope you age with the contentment I feel, as much as the ambition your mother has instilled.'

'Are those books in your bag?' I ask.

'Yes, I bought them on my parole day. I'm already halfway through one, and I love it.'

'What is it?'

Dad reaches into his bag and pulls out two books, one the Jimmy Miller photo book of the shipyards and one the novel *Trainspotting*.

'You're reading *Trainspotting*?'

'Yes, there's nothing like a laugh in the native tongue.'

'If you ever come back, you'll likely find an Edinburgh *Trainspotting* theme park.'

'Ha! You've read it?'

'Yes, it's popular in Peebles.'

'The theme park would have to contain a walkthrough living room full of broken syringes... and a joyride down the toilet before you reach the gift shop.'

'... where people queue to buy fake-blood-splattered t-shirts.'

'And fake broken noses to pretend they've been head butted.'

'Better to pretend than experience the real thing.'

'Enlightenment has so many glorious distractions.'

We laugh and hug before I watch dad walk off... with his cloth bag slung around his neck like a Tibetan khata scarf.

WHEN I RETURN HOME, SITA APPROACHES ME AND HUGS ME WITH UNUSUAL strength.

'Did the Avadhoot catch his plane?'

'Yes, I don't think I've ever met anyone more resistant to change in their lifestyle and more open to change in their thinking.'

'He has routines that keep his mind steady. He needs them to deal with change. I have some news of change for you, however.'

'What's that?'

'Are you prepared for another change in your life?'

'That depends, do I have a choice?

'Not at this stage.'

'What is it... another type of yoga class you want to teach?'

Time often takes a holiday. It sends you postcards of old memories and wishes you were there again. It omits to mention that things are never quite the same.

PART SEVEN: RUNNING THE RADICAL ROADS

40

During the height of popularity for her tantra classes, Sita told me she learned as much as she taught from the women who attended. She discovered we had laws on reproductive rights and that protection was available to modern women to prevent pregnancy. Her fertility until then was always something she believed she could control through awareness and yogic senses. This emancipation she saw in other women, she felt she'd already experienced through tantra yoga.

In the last few months, however, I've sensed a change in her. I witnessed her being less cautious about times in the month that we tantra'd. I knew we risked pregnancy and she did not seem to mind. I began to joke about her losing control. I spoke about having a huge family, like in the old days here or in Nepal, with five or six children. I told her I would accept it if a big family came along by chance. She assured me that chance did not have a chance, so we should decide.

Little did Sita know that our one-child family would suddenly have twin Buddha baby girls to worship.

. . .

Sita was understandably delinquent about health check-ups. This was not an illness, it was a pregnancy. Despite me voicing concerns when she seemed to grow excessively large, she simply took more rest, rather than consult a doctor. We spoke at length about her preference to give birth at home. Sita said she would be happier bringing our son into the world on our laundry room floor, than in a sterile hospital environment. She had never visited a hospital here. She'd never had the need to.

I secretly approached a nurse and a former midwife who had both attended Sita's yoga classes. As they began to take an interest in Sita's condition, they too became concerned. The midwife suggested it could be twins. Sita's yogic senses did not stretch to realising dual occupancy.

Two months before her due date, I found Sita in distress in our bathroom. I called an ambulance and within an hour she was rushed to hospital.

Sita gave birth at Edinburgh's Royal Infirmary in a sterile room, surrounded by medical experts. Doctors and nurses dressed in space-suit protection were so concerned, I was asked to leave. I did not witness the birth. Nor did Sita, having been rendered unconscious for the first time in her life. It was in complete contrast to the delivery of Ram, born healthy on the floor of a dusty room in Kathmandu.

I was told how lucky Sita was to survive the immediate circumstances of the twins' births. After the first was born, the second twin was left breach and only saved by medical intervention. If we'd been in Kathmandu, Sita and our second twin would have certainly been in great danger.

As soon as she regained consciousness, Sita was introduced to the first twin, who she named Maya, and insisted on breastfeeding. The second twin still needed some attention, but Sita insisted she was brought to her immediately. Hospital staff were reluctant, but Sita insisted. She was not going to let this moment with our second twin, Meena, be lost. I watched on through a glass door as a series of 'who knows best' exchanges were made between hospital staff.

Sita insisted she would get out of bed and find Meena unless they brought the second twin to her immediately. Finally, a smaller and frailer version of the first twin was brought in to Sita, crying her lungs out. Sita fitted the second twin onto her other breast and lay back in relief, like an exhausted astronaut after a successful docking into the space station. The room went silent as the twins suckled, and staff stood around with their masks on and an incubator trolley at the ready.

With two hungry mouths to feed, I was struck by the pressure on Sita to give up breastfeeding for her own sake and impressed by her insistence that it was her choice to keep it up. She was informed that the logistics of moving the twins around and the energy which would be sapped from her body would make her recovery much slower.

Sita informed everyone at the hospital that as grateful as she was for their help, she had different references and comparisons to them. She knew that she alone was a source of so much more than just paying close attention to the children. Despite the challenges, she knew the long-term value of her breastfeeding the twins.

There may not be any other alternatives in Nepal, where mothers will often breastfeed children until they are three or four. But the practice of breastfeeding was also one of the main reasons children there survived so many of the other childhood health dangers later in life. I knew that in Nepal Sita might have died without medical assistance, but at this stage she would easily have found another lactating mum to hand one of the twins to, while she was building up her milk supply. The option has long disappeared in the UK.

For the first time I began to understand why so many new mothers here choose to opt for formula feeding and why fathers encouraged their wives to give up breastfeeding so quickly. Their logic is based on convenience and that there's no point in any baby having an exhausted and stressed-out mother. A mother's health is paramount and necessary for the family unit. This is basically the same principle Sita follows. What is different is the knowledge set that informs Sita's choice

Here am I with knowledge from both camps of thinking, one being Public Health research, the other supporting a woman's right to choose in everything regarding their own reproductive health. I feel support for Sita's choice is crucial since the health and wellbeing of my wife and twins are at stake.

I study more to make sure she is making the right choice. I look into the science that informs mothers to breastfeed, rather that the persuasive lies of adverts that encourage new mothers to use formula. The World Health Organisation has documented the situation for years. It has been a battleground in the law courts with formula companies, some of whom have been accused of aggressive marketing techniques in poorer countries which actually cause infant deaths. Mothers from poor families were given a packet of free formula at their child's birth, forcing them to continue buying formula, only to dilute it with dirty water, endangering their children. All this while at the same time being robbed of crucial bonding with their child, which can prevent their ability to breastfeed at all, even if most of them can.

Sita's mindset may seem like it's from the Middle Ages to many women here, but as she explains to her yoga students, our bodies still work with the same components as they did in the Middle Ages. Sita thinks it's the mental-health moments surrounding childbirth, when women are most vulnerable and insecure, that can be exploited. She convinces a few other mothers to continue with their breastfeeding in the recovery ward. She knows some will never listen, but she also believes some are giving up too easily under outside pressure. The few medical professionals employed to encourage breastfeeding are fighting a losing battle against society's glamorous definition of what breasts are for. Most mothers who choose formula speak of their belief that 'no harm is done' and that formula offers relief from worry.

From the studies I dig out, the far most convincing argument for breastfeeding is the fact that you can never overfeed your baby with breastmilk... and with formula you must be extra careful with measuring amounts. You risk far more when you let the child decide when it's full or not, if feeding formula. Much of early childhood obesity is now linked to overfeeding formula to young children. If this start in life is not fully understood, the infant can face a greater number of health issues later, not of their own making.

The knowledge is there, compiled by women. Stacked high in the poor areas of the world is research showing the value and convenience for mothers to breastfeed their children, but it's slowly disappearing as industrial lifestyles are copied. It's being ignored here because our industrial lifestyle conflicts with nature's timeline. Mothers who want to return to their previous normality quicker risk later worries and problems without realising it. Sita appreciates the choices offered here and that there is no choice for most Nepali mothers. With more options, comes the need for more knowledge to make choices. Mothers have been persuaded to put their faith in the health system, more than themselves. Yet that same system is now trying very hard to hand some responsibility back.

FOR THE NEXT FEW YEARS, THE FOG OF CHILDCARE TAKES OVER, WHILE I also try to make a living wage in Public Health. Sita manages to construct a support network of yogi friendships, much like the communities she left behind in Nepal. She now has genuine friends willing to help her in every aspect of childcare, many of whom are new mothers themselves.

Maya, the older twin by four minutes, is now beginning to talk and never lets Meena forget their age difference. Maya is definitely the big sister. They are not identical twins, but they are very similar in looks. Maya has a slight fleck of grey in her left eye which helps me identify her. I still find it impossible to tell them apart if their clothes match or if they are asleep. Sita says it's their body movements that are different. Meena is fearless, Maya is more cautious. So I have begun to understand their body language despite their increasingly frequent plots to change places.

Most of my work until now has involved creating three large lists for my professor. First, I compiled the known threats to public health faced in the UK, through everyday work and behaviour. Then I made another list of things that are stifling or preventing important health information from reaching the public. My third list contained the names of all the people I needed to consult.

In the beginning, there was weeks of travel around the country. Much as we like to believe we are a homogenous community in Britain, we are not. Like all industrial countries, our work dictates much of the good and bad health we experience. Our health has been linked to our income, but it is also important to view the job. Work impacts us differently in city centres than it does in villages or rural areas.

The list of things standing in the way of dispersing knowledge, despite our increased standards of education, seems to be endless. There are far more distractions, more outright oppositions, more politicising and tailoring of information to suit specific interests, than I ever imagined. The spread of ailments from generation to generation still exists, but newly created unhealthy social conditions are everywhere. As I delve into communication problems, I find there is an establishment view of the situation and there is also a group of radicals on the fringes. I decide to give the radicals my attention.

The first consultant I interview is a behavioural psychologist called Murdock, who sums up his radical views quite succinctly.

'The *people's* solution to avoiding mental stress – is to tell themselves not to give a shit as often as possible. Our bars and social gathering places are full of people saying this in almost every leisure-time conversation. "Honestly... I've got to the point where I don't give a shit!" It's become the espresso version of a placebo for stress.'

'To be fair,' I tell him, 'the bars and places we frequent after work **are** the places to chant such a message. You should not, for example, chant this to yourself while driving a car.'

Murdock responds, 'Wherever modern life forces us to think responsibly, there's a stall nearby selling a drink or drugs or in some places a god to help us chill out. And all of life's risks are now clumped together and peddled to young people for that time in their life when they're told they should live life to the full. All this freedom is translated as carefree indulgence and unfortunately figures are showing an increase in casualties. No one keeps tabs on those who actually believe they are having the time of their life. It's assumed that when they get older the young will judge this for themselves. It's presumed there's an age when people do figure out they have responsibility, to themselves. But we only count casualties.'

An ex trade-union boss who now consults on workplace health conditions, gives me a further angle to consider.

'People will put themselves in harm's way for a salary as much as for any cause. At least until faced with the consequences. Finding a job that supports you can be easier if you are willing to take the risks that others don't. At the point where things go wrong, people here rely on the health system or legislation to help.

'An increasing number of young people put themselves into harm's way during their recreational time. There was once a social divide among young people who chose trades and those who went for higher education, but today they face equal dangers. If you take away the consequences of young men being sent as the fodder for wars, we have suicides and life-changing consequences because of behaviour as well as dangers from work. Finding a subtle way to reverse this trend is a major challenge for employers as well as health authorities.'

If it's your job to make sense of preventative health information, as it has become mine, you might see where these discoveries are leading me. In public health you must suggest ways to reduce the incidence of preventable ailments by showing people, at the right time, what they can do about it. When, however, is the right time?

In another influential interview with a radical scientist, she shares her studies of our brain's workings. It appears that the more people are told they face life-threatening conditions the more they can go into a panic that affects their mental health, which can in turn bring on illness. She informs me that even the most important messages in the media can be dismissed as subliminal manipulation by some people.

If you add poverty into this mix, you can predict the stories of despair that forces people to rush towards a health system that can barely cope.

As I begin to share some strategic ideas with my professor, he suggests we find ways to widen our audiences and diversify messages as much as possible. When I ask how, he suggests using the media and the authorities together. The battle will never be won on the advertising pages: it will be won on the editorial pages. We need to attract journalists to join the cause.

To move from the comfort of academia into mass media is the very definition of radical.

I propose writing a communication strategy first, to see if we can find funding to implement it.

'Write me a sentence and I'll try to get funding,' Professor Clark says.

'What should the sentence contain?' I ask.

'Set out a new goal where business and industry are not just held accountable by the media for their economic health, but for their social consequences and for public health.'

I write a paragraph.

In industrial communities, a major threat to public health originates from the collective side-effects of what are legitimate businesses. These businesses and industries employ millions of people to keep up their growth and profits. This group of employees and their daily work schedule are arguably far more dangerous to us than any germs or infections we currently use health funding to control. While we regularly tackle threats to personal health, we are also committing matricide on mother nature, through the mismanagement of our own business activities.

I finish by suggesting that *we can tackle this through new alliances and by working together.* This last sentence is the most used line for every problem in the world. Humans working together can solve everything. We say it and read it all the time... and it is the reason we already have such large industries with people working together for a perceived common good.

After sending the fuller strategy to London, I get a reply almost immediately. There is an extension to my contract. The funding is approved.

THE WORDS 'IF WE ALL WORK TOGETHER' ARE PERCEIVED DIFFERENTLY BY A pragmatist and an evangelist. In fact, they are interpreted differently by everyone who has the letters 'ist' at the end of their persuasion. Race, gender, nationality can all be set aside without a problem. It's the persuasion of the 'ist' that causes different outcomes.

Professor Clark agrees to writes some priorities for me. He tells me to include some catchy new slogans like Healthspan instead of Lifespan.

I'm told to be pragmatic and include what big pharma has done in terms of plans for vaccines and show how much promise they have for prevention. Also, I am to try to reveal some false perceptions of dangers from tried and tested medicines, that some people have experienced. We need more creative ways to reduce the legitimate fears some people have over drugs and vaccines, while also stopping their over-use.

Reading Professors Clark's priorities is the first time I seriously consider taking a drug cocktail for recreational use. The scale of the job is far beyond my original assignment and pay grade.

Professor Clark's assumption is that because information is pouring into our lives at a rate unimaginable a decade ago, information management should finally be recognised as a critical element in Health Behaviour and Prevention campaigns. The environmental side-effects of a global lifestyle that more and more people aspire to, is not sustainable. People are already predicting that the levels of growth of our largest industries will eventually endanger us all and cause irreversible damage to our ecosystems. Yet typically we react differently on hearing this news. Too much positivity causes negativity and vice-versa.

Last comes Professor Clark's insistence that I involve the media. What changed days. Health academia finally courting publicity.

AFTER COMPILING OUR RESEARCH, WE PUBLISH IN A PAID-FOR EDUCATIONAL supplement in a popular newspaper. The beautifully illustrated cartoons suggest different ways of viewing good news and bad news. The current definition that economic growth in all industries is paramount should change. What we thought would seem obvious, that the growth of harmful industries should be seen as bad news and that a decline in harmful industries should be celebrated, was not obvious. There was an overwhelming opposition to the supplement.

Hundreds of letters from the public objecting to yet another form of control over the people's free will, made the front pages. The right and left wings of political ideologists flap in unison. We all apparently have the human right to kill ourselves any way we wish, even if we do this of our own ignorance and others die in the process.

Especially critical are those in the News and Information trades, who rebel at the notion that anyone else should tell people what is news, and what isn't. Everyone in **our** country is educated enough to make their own choices. No one is ready to commit to economic suicide or follow draconian measures under the banner of better health for all. Most people currently earning a living have got to the top the hard way. They've made their life plans and do not want to consider anything that remotely threatens it. They are clearly the vocal majority and they overwhelm us.

In one of Professor Clark's only public interviews, he says, 'Good intelligence is now useless to humanity, because of the scale required to get people to agree.' The subsequent press fallout makes him a celebrity for failure. He apparently is not aware of the will of the people. No one likes news of a spectacular media botch-up more than the press itself.

The most positive coverage I find is from the *Edinburgh Evening News* which on page five asks, 'Has Health Education lost focus? Local researcher from Leith behind new health study takes a break.'

AFTER A MONTH'S BREAK, MAHESH ENCOURAGES ME TO TURN MY misfortune into success. This botch-up is now a qualification, for I am someone who has spectacularly failed. The world, Mahesh says, is full of experts who once overdosed on the subject they now preached abstinence about.

According to Mahesh I now have experience in two fields, from being qualified in preventive health to becoming a spokesperson for recovery from failure. Over the next months, I give several such talks. Sita suggests I avoid doing any more in case I have a breakdown.

'How to become ill from promoting public health,' I tell her, could become my autobiography.

Professor Clark is now retired. At first, he told me he felt like running back to his ivory tower and never going public again with any sort of information. He said he'd felt safe in academia all his life. No one questioned his ideas publicly. Any useful discovery could be used in lectures or kept in the library as harmless intelligence. The more you keep to yourself, the more valued your career. If you go public, unless it solves an existential threat, it will be chopped up and chewed for breakfast by critics and the media. Even if the threat you spotlight is existential, the algorithms will still line up people in denial.

There were few journalists at Professor Clark's final press conference, but there was a group of young radicals. He had managed to create a message that resonated with the young. He suggested that in the same way a few people can cause havoc in society, our saving grace usually originates from new leaders, knowledgeable enough to self-correct our behaviour. 'We may not be able to do this together,' he said, before disappearing into retirement, 'but you know who you are.'

SITA'S RELATIONSHIP WITH OUR TWINS CHANGES DRAMATICALLY WHEN THEY reach their fourth birthday. This is the age when Sita was taken from her mother and made a Kumari in the Kathmandu Valley.

She begins to act more possessive of the twins and is more reflective of her own childhood. She tells me one night that she can remember the event.

'I remember the tests, along with all other girls shortlisted. The priests examining everyone for perfect skin, looking at hair and teeth. I see this so differently now as a mother looking at our girls, and I can't imagine offering them up to such a childhood.

'At the time, I wanted to be chosen. My mind had been set to the challenge by the priests, telling me what an honour it would be. They never described the restrictions I would face were I chosen.'

'How did they choose?'

'Each girl was seated among the decapitated heads of sacrificed animals, with judges watching our reactions.'

'Surely things must have changed by now?'

'Many people are suggesting change. But it's not enough to just add reading and writing to the Kumari's existing duties. She'll still spend all her time in the upper levels of that Kumari house. Each day she'll be painted exquisitely by trained courtesans. This is all done so she can peep shyly from an upper window towards the crowds of people entering the courtyard, hoping to glance at her face and photograph her.

Can you imagine what this will become like with the increasing numbers of tourists? Can you imagine any schoolgirl here going through this? All that time on your own – with no freedom. Every new Kumari will become the face of tourism in Nepal, with more cameras on her than ever before, and the world won't know what she's going through.'

'You should write a book about this.'

'There are nine Kumaris in the Kathmandu Valley. Some more have now defied the curse and married. Perhaps you should get together with the other husbands and write a book. Thapa will connect you.'

'Exactly... The Cursed Nine. There's a book title.'

'I think you have managed to survive the death curse of marrying a Kumari, but maybe the curse was transferred to your work.'

'Only a former living goddess would say that.'

ANOTHER TRAGIC STORY SURROUNDING MY RESEARCH WRITING IS THAT I managed to publicly embarrass a small-scale cancer charity, almost into bankruptcy.

Research showed that almost eighty per cent of what they earned went into keeping their charity staff employed and less than twelve per cent into any practical effort to fight cancer. I flagged it as an example of false advertising. I felt so guilty when the charity lost support that I anonymously signed up to run marathons and fundraise for them.

I now see the exposed cancer charity was a soft target. They may not be as efficient at helping cure cancer as they claim, but their work is contributing to increased public health by providing an incentive for people to run and stay healthy.

I increase my yoga practice during this time, but I really miss the feeling of utter physical exhaustion from my days in Nepal. Back then, I was giddy and content from exertion. The mellow recovery from a hill-walk with a cup of tea, or my healing drug, the sound of a good piece of music. All these simple things, powerful enough to change a mindset.

This is where Ram steps in and suggests we run a few races together. First, we run five and ten kilometre routes from our house, then move up to a half marathon. For Ram, this is quite an accomplishment. His favourite run is Sita's favourite walk, around the Radical Road in central Edinburgh. The route carries new meaning for me.

It's definitely an extreme way of getting back my Nepali fitness. So much energy is expelled in the build-up to a marathon, that you have very little time to feel fit.

Ram's routine, however, changes my opinion of what we call extreme. He can now run an average of 30 miles per week. And in in the world of marathon running, he points out this is not at all extreme.

My limit is quite tame. But Ram introduces me to running magazines he's read at school. They advertise races where people run for hundreds of miles in the space of a few days, basically until they drop. People have extraordinary differences in their energy outputs. My yogic eyes were first opened to this sort of extreme fitness by Nepali village folk. Here, Ram points to the outer limits of human endurance.

Sita tells us that making games out of physical fitness is all that's left for people here to use everything we were born with at once. We don't use our physical attributes to survive anymore, yet it's the only thing we don't have to learn how to use. It just comes as natural and here it's mostly ignored. I stand, or rather collapse, in awe of all these extreme fitness groups.

After three years of running with Ram, six miles now seems easy, and my longer runs on a Sunday are enjoyable quality times my son. Together we keep in shape. The vision of stretching out flat on my back is something I hold in mind until the last step. Sometimes I end my runs at the yoga studio and lie on my back, contemplating bliss on a hard wooden floor. I remember this exhaustion from Nepal, and find this type of recovery is as soothing as anything people crave.

If I finish my runs at home, I recover in our bath. I sit there watching the water fill up, looking at my fish-eyed reflection in the chrome tap, feeling grateful.

41

The Yoga Studio is now successfully managed by Ms C McDonald, affectionately known as Cindy. She has the collective support from a core group of enthusiastic yoginis. Almost every profession in Edinburgh is represented or within referral distance.

Sita still teaches but has a reduced number of classes. Her skills at placing a self-corrective thought into a person's mind at the right time has never faltered. While most students earn a living wage and some raise a family, all are encouraged to learn from their own efforts whatever their current lifestyle is. It is not all about yoga, but Sita stresses that nothing stops people from enjoying life more than their own mind.

The intravenous drip of funding from dad's art sales keeps the family economically healthy. Quite a few of dad's extremely large paintings have sold. Two now grace the lobby of one of Edinburgh's largest insurance companies. An irony not lost on dad.

Meantime he still lives and works in the remote western hills of Nepal. He has promised more of the smaller abstract tanka paintings, telling me his latest efforts have Maoist sympathisers incorporated in them. I tell him that this may not be a good selling point, especially for the international market.

In a recent call, he says he's weathering the ever-present political storms in Nepal, but fears the worst is still to come. He says the centuries-old feudal system is collapsing in district after district. He is not against the changes but disheartened by the methods used to accomplish them. Sporadic violence and backlashes are ever more brutal.

Mahesh and Mandy are now married and live permanently in Scotland. After finishing their studies, Mahesh is working in the development of Artificial Intelligence whilst Mandy works is assessing the social consequences. We are regularly invited to dinner, which is often a ringside seat to hear them spar over feminist philosophy and AI.

Mandy thinks AI is a man's thing, being used to disguise the male's relentless pursuit of power. It's merely man's latest tool to conquer, and it's based on a male obsession with control, nothing to do with intelligence itself.

Mahesh argues that the artificial aspect of Intelligence is genderless because everyone has contributed to its development and application. Intelligence, he stresses, is merely the effort to keep life going, and everything created by AI has that objective.

'A good man,' Mahesh says, 'witnesses creation in all its forms, with empathy for the process.'

'Exactly,' Mandy says. 'Men are detached, and that's the reason they are so often cold blooded. Women are a more complete manufacturer of life. They construct human life within them; they don't just throw out a seed and watch it grow with curiosity. It's about time women are given more choices before AI chooses some new future role for them.'

When I ask Sita if she believes Mandy and Mahesh have begun to show symptoms of FOOLS, she tells me no. Their relationship could be under strain for many different reasons. It's not FOOLS as we know it, but it takes time for people to cope with any desire that's unfulfilled.

'What unfulfilled desire have I missed seeing in them?'

'They have been trying hard to have children. Also, they are academics in different fields so are always looking for reasons to support their own opinions. When someone contradicts them with evidence, they can still find an excuse to dismiss rather than update their opinion.'

Sita thinks their intellectual boxing matches are part of their recovery process. 'We can only encourage them to find new routes for their togetherness, even if it becomes different to what they each expected.'

ONE NIGHT, SITA TELLS ME THAT CINDY HAS DECIDED TO LEAVE EDINBURGH and go travelling.

'Where will she go?'

'To visit Nepal. She'll take time off to visit Swamy Y, whom she has heard a lot about.'

This to me sounds like the news of the century, so a week before Cindy departs, Sita invites her for a farewell dinner.

Cindy seems happy but fragile. While Sita cooks a farewell Dhal Bhat, I ask her how she is coping with the planned departure.

'I'm trying to not think about being away from you all here, but then some wee fragment of thought connecting us all pops intae ma heed telling me a have tae do this.'

Sita's interested to see if I'm willing to take over some of Cindy's duties at the yoga studio. She's invited some other students to dinner to dish out Cindy's responsibilities to them too.

'I've been walking a lot through Princes Street gardens lately,' Cindy tells us all. 'Past awe these statues where Sita and I would first talk. We shared a lot of gossip in those days, didn't we hen? I can't claim any credit for your lassie's smartness,' she says, looking at me, 'but I did help her increase her Scots vocabulary. She'd read me out all the English words carved in stone on the auld statues, and I'd correct her. She'd practice lots of words on me for language lessons. I remember we used to view all these memorials as a form of art.'

'She's never mentioned that.' I look towards Sita.

'We have a few secrets, Sita and I,' Cindy says. 'She'd ask me what words like Valour, Bravery, Heroism meant, and I'd try to explain. It made me think. I mean, I grew up thinking *valour* was somebody who would park a posh car for you. I told Sita that most lads from poorer families in those days never got to travel unless they sign up for the military. An she said it was the same in Nepal.

'Sita once asked me what *sacrifice* meant here. This was shortly after I heard the story of Mahesh and his pheasant. I suggested it didn't have the same meaning as it might in the Nepali. She'd seen it used here on a monument. *Their sacrifice will never be forgotten.*

'When I told her all these monuments were to people who died in wars, that they were memorials commemorating all the Scottish blood spilled for some cause, she told me there was no such thing as Scots blood... there was only blood. That Gurkhas were killed along with Scots in conflicts across the world. She said this type of sacrifice was one of Nepal's most famous exports to India and Brunei as well as the United Nations and Nepal itself. She hoped it was not something to celebrate but something to learn from. I'll miss the wee soul.'

Sita finally walks in with a tray of rice and lentil curry announcing it as an introductory treat, not a farewell treat.

'In Nepal, Cindy, this will be your staple diet.'

SITA CONTINUES TO LIVE WITH A DIFFERENT LEVEL OF UNDERSTANDING TO my own, despite her acclimatisation here. I'm amazed at how she has moved on from our first years. Those early days of talking in Walter Scott-ish. Now, if she tells me not to be so bothered by *wretches*, she is saying it as a joke. One sign of her assimilation into the culture here, is her well-timed comeback.

Sita also says she loves me more often than before. She usually expresses this sentiment after I've done something wrong or failed to do it. I understand her words as affectionate, despite being stimulated by my bad behaviour, as much as her love.

She'll often add a sentence like *I love you, no matter what you've done.* Or *I love you whatever you look like* or my favourite *I love you, no matter what people say about you.* I accept these statements because I know I have been her work-in-progress since we met. And her work is not yet finished.

By far Sita's proudest accomplishments is the confidence she senses in our children. Despite our dual work schedule, Maya and Meena have flourished as much as Ram. These young humans have been showered with conscious love all their lives. A full-on six years have had such a positive result, that the application can now be measured. If we compare ourselves to most families we know, I'd say we have managed to deal with whatever's happened to us, without much mumbled suffering. Those who experience this sort of freedom on life's radical road, also never know what troubles they have bypassed, or what lies just round the corner.

RAM HAS JUST RECENTLY ENROLLED AT A NEW SECONDARY SCHOOL. HE IS A tolerant and supportive big brother. We are currently in the process of talking about his new friendships, and I detect a familiar anxiety.

I try to help Ram deal with this move from the wee school to the big school by telling him of my own experiences when I was his age.

It is a comparison he doesn't accept. He doesn't sense the hostile sectarian differences within the same religion that used to exist. He doesn't accept that they could possibly have contained the same level of hurt. He tells me his challenge is from new classmates who have shown an awkward interest in his unusual ethnic background.

I feel for him. He's managing the task of growing up in a society where people's first response is always to his differences. He's cruised past the stage of being labelled the 'broon bairn,' at nursery school. Later he's dealt with more racially charged encounters at primary school. By mastering the Scots vernacular, he has managed to dilute prejudice. He's forged many strong friendships with his former classmates. It is now difficult for me to watch him go back to square one with this familiarisation process. Why should someone who has known nothing other than Scotland as his surroundings, his community and his reference point all his life... have to walk into a new school and hear a classmate immediately ask, 'Which country are you from?' Human curiosity at its most basic but also a primary educational system that fails to provide children with any preparation for diversity in secondary school.

Ram respects it takes time to find a new set of friends and by now he knows what to look for. His friends all seem to bond on different aspects of the arts. Whether it's the international appeal of music, I don't know, but he's shown a recent interest in learning guitar.

With his two sisters, he'll now climb into a bed and tell them stories. He'll make a dent in the pillows and talk about the Himalaya, punching valleys and folding covers into terraced hills as if he can see these in his mind. He'll ask me to tell them all more stories of Nepal and I begin with my usual simplification of rural hill lifestyles. Ram's managed to retain his childish enthusiasm to listen.

One day Ram comes home with a cut on his forehead and a note from his schoolteacher. She writes that the cut and bruise on his face came from another boy whom Ram had been arguing with. It seems the boy took a dislike to Ram and shouted something, then clubbed him with a book. A few of Ram's friends then pounced on this boy and beat him up. The boy's nose had been bloodied and his clothes torn by Ram's friend Lotisha. The school had therefore put them all on suspension.

I called Ram's teacher, who assured me that things in the classroom were overall good with Ram. She told me not to worry, that it was temporary suspension and 'a statistical certainty' that boys of his kind would be involved in some sort of minor scuffle at this stage in his school life.

When I asked what she meant by 'boys of his kind', she responded without thinking. It was children from mixed marriages.

I took a deep breath. What hope is there for Ram's future with 'this kind' of teacher? I then asked if she could give me a fuller description of what happened.

'It's just... we have trouble, every year with...' she hesitates. 'It was not Ram who was injured most, it was...'

'The white boy, who started it?' I interrupt.

'No... I was going to say the group who ganged up on this boy. If they had reported it, instead of taking matters into their own hands, the school could easily have dealt with it all appropriately. We pride ourselves in the diversity of pupils at our school and I assure you we will not tolerate mob violence.'

'Let me talk to the other parents and I'll get back to you.' I bring the conversation to an end, before saying anything I might regret.

I then call Lotisha's mother to find out what she has heard from the school.

'What was the argument about?' I ask.

'Oh, some rap song that is popular among older children.'

'Do you know what caused it to turn violent?'

'This one boy, who is known to be bit of a bully,' she hesitated, 'well someone shouted in the playground that he'd called Ram the N word. Lotisha and her friends stepped in to protect Ram.'

'Goodness... well, thank Lotishi from me.'

'There's more... you should know the full story. I later heard from the bully's mum that the N word her son called Ram... was not what Lotisha assumed it was.'

'What was it?'

'He apparently shouted, "Hey you, you fuckin Nepali!" Then someone in the group shouted, as a joke – he's called Ram the N word. That's when the mob violence occurred.'

'You think Ram's friends overreacted?'

'No, and Lotisha doesn't think so either. She told me this boy was intent on insulting Ram. I agree with my daughter... it was childish, but it had hurtful intent. Lotisha ripped a bully's shirt off. I'm proud of her.'

'It's sad this still goes on.'

'It's kids finding their way with words.'

'You don't think it's part of the prejudice in our culture here?'

'Well, that is a question, James. There are words from rap songs, if repeated in your thick Scottish accent, loose their Caribbean rhyming charm. Ram's pronunciation of the rs in 'mother' and 'fucker' ... which he called this boy, gave them a far more aggressive tone.'

'And he's learned the consequences.'

'And that bully too. Him using "Nepali" as a cus word, no way man.'

'The devil's in the intent?'

'Aye – me know.'

Time can age the meaning of many a philosopher's quotes.

PART EIGHT: SIX WEEKS AFTER THE ROYAL MASSACRE

42

It seems an eternity between my phone call with Sita and her letter arriving. Although I am positive about her forthcoming return, I've developed a fear of messages in envelopes. News that is suspended in time, travelling in a sealed envelope while the world around it changes without influencing its content. My heart races as I open the letter. Could the world have changed the meaning of what I'm about to read?

Dear James,

This letter may be a disappointment for you and your expectations of me. The meeting of spiritual leaders was an excuse to come here for another reason. Despite your enthusiasm and support for me, I don't really have any power to influence the predominantly male clique who control spiritual events here. I don't represent a particular group of people, nor do I have any say in organisational matters of religion or state here. Nepal has changed so much since we left, and its leaders at this moment seem very confused.

You know, more than most, how hard it is to introduce new ideas into bureaucracies. I've discovered that here I'm just the freak celebrity Cindy once called me.

I did not mention my doubts to you before I left. You might have suggested I didn't come.

Leaders in the Kathmandu Valley are in the process of choosing a new Kumari, a four-year-old girl, as a living goddess. Our Newa tradition will impact her life. She will be younger than our twins and I want to try in some small way to influence the way these girls are treated.

I've spoken to a few people, to suggest the outgoing Kumari receive a normal education and not be cast aside as I and others were. Some are willing to introduce transformations to these old traditions. I thought by telling the human consequences of the Kumari tradition from my personal experiences, I could promote this change.

At the meeting of spiritual leaders, I talked to them informally, to find out who may be willing to help. I hoped perhaps to get an audience with the new King. He has the most powerful voice to be heard on this matter. Unfortunately, this has not been possible.

Swamy Y, Cindy and I have instead collected names of concerned local business leaders in Patan and Kathmandu. Some have agreed to help modify the old traditions, one goddess at a time.

I miss you all and will return to Edinburgh very soon. I will first go to Barabase to see Tilak and Maya. Once I have my return date set, I'll call you. Until then I won't be in touch for a little while.

Yours always with conscious love,
Sita Munro

I'M RELIEVED TO READ SITA'S LETTER. THERE'S A REFERENCE TO CONSCIOUS love, and none of the tell-tale signs of FOOLS. I talk with Ram and the twins, saying their mother will soon be back. In order to prepare the house for Sita's return, I take the girls once more to my mum's.

We have kept the twins out of nursery since news of the royal massacre broke. Their school has been helpful and understand that as a family we are in mourning. Also, because both are still pretty bald, from their recent hair cutting experience.

In truth, during Sita's absence our bedroom has become my secret sanctuary. It's the place I feel most comfortable feeling sorry for myself.

As a result, I now see the place has become filled with spiritual junk. I've unconsciously surrounded myself with things from Nepal. I've tried to preserve Sita's presence in the building. I've dug out old treasures and hung more of dad's tanka paintings on the wall. Our flat now resembles a shrine room at Bodhnath instead of our home. I even slept on Sita's side of the bed, wrapping myself and my fears in her side of the downy.

I meet Ram at his school and his teacher approaches me as I wait. She's learnt her lesson since Ram's playground punch-up, at least in how she speaks to me. She says Ram's been laughing and playing with all his friends as usual during the weeks Sita has been away.

She tells me that this is a good sign, but a few days back he'd stood up during Comprehension... read out an emotional passage from a novel and burst into tears. He'd then turned to the class, wiped his eyes and said, 'That's been me, awe week.'

His teacher says his friends were very supportive and although she was a little worried about him on that day, now he seems fine again.

I feel proud of Ram. We go for a few runs together around town. I have conversations with him about separation from his mum. I also talk to him, for reassurances in myself. Ram asks me if my yoga helped me get through this time of uncertainty. I tell him it could have been my lack of yoga that caused me to feel uncertain.

'Yes, it's difficult when you feel your happiness is in the hands of others, dad.

I CALL THE SUMMIT HOTEL WHERE I KNOW MY DAD IS STAYING WHILE IN Kathmandu.

'Hello, is the Avadhoot still staying with you?'

'Yes, Sir.'

'Can you put me through to his room?'

'Certainly, Sir, hold on.'

'Hello.'

'Hello.' I hear a female voice answer.

'Sita. Is that you?'

'Yes... James... how did you know I was here?'

'I didn't. I was calling my dad to find out where you were.'

'How is everyone?'

'We are all fine.'

'You were right.'

'About what?'

'You once said that money would eventually become more central to people's lives in Nepal than spirituality. I've had to borrow from your dad and kip with him in his room. People in Barabase emptied my pockets faster than the Scottish tax people.'

'Goodness. What's happening in Kathmandu?'

'I returned from Barabase a day ago, because yesterday there was a follow-up meeting of spiritual leaders. It was a much better gathering, less people and less formal and more positive suggestions. I gave the Moni Baba's perspective on invasive religious rituals and the challenges for yoginis.'

'How did that go?'

'There are still some clan tensions among the religions represented here. Even within our Hindu and Buddhist communities, people appear less devoted and more business worried. Young holy men see the Baba's perspective as a challenge to their salaries and existence. I stated my surprise at their negativity. At one point I called some of the delegates "blinder than the Baba". I would never have used that phrase without your influence on me.'

'Good on you, lassie.'

'I told them they were ignoring new modern-day responsibilities as religious leaders. I challenged them to bridge this gap between what they regard as their spiritual domain and the people's lives. People now have many more opportunities. If they as leaders do not change, I said, there were Maoists in the hills who would change things for them and make them irrelevant to the people.'

'Do they think you are a Maoist?'

'No, but they think the Avadhoot is. He was the only one who clapped after I talked. My talk was the shortest in all the conference. Some older leaders spoke for two hours. The Avadhoot spoke last, he was good. All I want now is return to Edinburgh.'

'Well, then. When are you coming home?'

'Soon.'

'Do you have a date yet?'

'The Avadhoot is helping me.'

'Good... so when?'

'Ask him yourself... he's here. We're sharing quite a luxury suite.'

Dad then comes onto the phone. I hear both Sita and him laughing. They exchange something in Nepali that I can't hear properly.

'Hello, dad.'

'Hello son.'

'What were you laughing about?'

'I told Sita we should call you back and charge the conference priests who are paying this hotel bill. I said you'd appreciate saving expensive phone bills.'

'Why is that so funny?'

'You've no idea how funny that can sound, especially to Sita. She always laughs hardest at ideas of thrift and the ridiculous.'

'I heard you talked at the conference after everyone else spoke.'

'Yes, they got their priorities right. I was the last in a long day. I spoke my concerns over all the missed opportunities to unite people at the main conference. I'll send you the full speech if you want it.'

'No thanks. I've already had a failed career, translating your ideas for modern society.'

'You had a minor setback, that's all. You underestimated how much people still mix up miracles with placebo to sell alternative medicine. It's our differences that are defined by all these unbelievable stories, not our unity.'

'Om put a cork on it. Buy my wife a ticket home, dad.'

'Yes... I'll let you talk to her again, since this is your money. Love you, son.'

'Love you more.'

'Hello, yes, your dad was very brave to speak about everyone playing into the hands of the Maoists. They are increasingly seeing this government as the enemy. No official feels safe anymore.'

'Ram and our daughters miss you very much.'

'And I miss Ram and my daughters and you... very much. I'm trying for a ticket home next weekend. Maya and Tilak are here in Kathmandu so I want to introduce them to Cindy. She's pregnant.'

'My god! Who – Cindy or Maya?'

'Cindy.'

'No way. That's remarkable... is she in a relationship?'

'Yes, she's very close to Swami Y.'

'Is he the father?'

'I suspect he is, because she's begun to call him Swami Why.'

'That's hysterical. Is she still helping with efforts for the ex-Kumaris?'

'Yes, and she's doing very well. She's met many educated young women here, who are very aware and active on this issue.'

'Do you think she'll stay much longer?'

'Yes. She has a passion for the cause. She was with me when two spiritual leaders told me that I should be grateful to have been a Kumari. Cindy let them have it.'

'What do you mean?'

'She spoke in such broad Scots, I laughed when translating her for the priests. She said their beliefs were off-kilter.'

'Send Cindy to see the King. That's where the real change is needed.'

'I suspect those left in the royal family will be contemplating a lot of changes of their own.'

'Let this new King's middle eye be opened.'

'I miss you.'

'You are so full of secrets, Sita Kumari.'

'And you always end conversations... as the jester. Love you, James.'

FIVE DAYS LATER RAM, MAYA, MEENA AND I GO TO MEET SITA AT THE airport. I drive mother's flower van because I have plans to go and pick up some new bunk beds for the twins at IKEA tomorrow.

We wait long after the wave of passengers from the flight pass us. Ram occupies the twins while I check Sita's status at the airline desk. She appears as a no-show on the passenger list.

There is no explanation from the airlines, and they tell me they have no record of the passengers on her earlier flight to Doha from Kathmandu. I would have to contact Air Nepal direct to see if she left Kathmandu.

I inform my disappointed children there is a likelihood their mum missed her connection. That we should all go home, and I'll call the airlines later and find out when the next flight comes in.

On the drive back, I begin to feel a sense of dread.

Our phone is ringing as we enter the house, I run and lift it to hear my mum's voice. I tell her that Sita must have missed her connection.

'Has she sent any message to you?'

'No... but surely that's a good sign? She would have contacted me if something had gone wrong.'

'She's not here. Something is wrong.'

'What are you saying?'

'I hope nothing's happened to her. I had a...'

'Stop it. We would have heard from dad if something had happened.'

'He's the expert on silence, James.'

'I'm going to call Air Nepal and see if Sita got on the flight to Doha from Kathmandu.'

'OK, let me know as soon as you hear something.'

Ram takes the girls out the back and supervises them on their new favourite toy, a trampoline. This purchase has helped in occupying the family and opened me to a newfound relationship with the megastore IKEA.

I call the Kathmandu hotel and am told dad checked out several days ago. I ask if Sita is there but they have no record of a Sita, only the daughter of the Avadhoot, who left with him.

Before I descend into a panic and try to find further answers from the airlines, the phone rings again. It is Sita.

'Where are you?'

'I'm in Pokhara.'

'Why are you in Pokhara?'

'Listen, James... I have a limited time to call you on this line. I've waited in a queue for this airport phone booth and there are people behind getting impatient, our flight is about to go.'

'Where are you going?'

'Silghari in Dhoti.'

'Are you going with my dad?'

'I'm sorry I couldn't get a message to you earlier, but I have news for you.'

I hear a crack in Sita's voice and clench my teeth. I stretch my arm out involuntarily, and stare at the black plastic receiver. The earpiece of doom.

'Last night your father died.' I hear Sita's distant voice speak.

'What?' I shout, far too loudly into the phone.

'He collapsed walking around the stupa at Boudhanath. He was on his way to the airport. He asked me to meet him before he left for Dhoti. It was so near the place we were married. He died in my arms. I'm so sorry.'

'What did he die of?'

'I will explain later. You know our customs. As soon as it happened, people prepared the Avadhoot for immediate cremation. I helped and I didn't want anyone else to tell you. I missed my flight this morning. I've been guessing what time you would return to our flat from the airport.'

'Yes, we all went to meet you.'

'I'm so sorry, James. I will tell you all about it when I arrive back next week on the same flight, but it was something that your dad said to me before he died that's made me come straight here to Pokhara.'

'What did he say, Sita?'

'We were walking around the stupa when he collapsed.' She talks as if she's reliving the scene. 'It was that busy sunset time. Monks came running out with a wheelcart to take your dad to the nearby clinic. He was having trouble breathing and I tried to calm him down. It seemed he was panicking to say something, because after he spoke he became still and smiled. It was a very peaceful passing, James.'

'What did he say?'

'His last words were, "Sita if this is my time... save my paintings for James and Helen." That's why I'm now on my way to Dhoti to reach the

Avadhoot's home. I felt I had to come before news of his passing reaches there.'

I feel my throat swell and I begin to breathe deeply and slowly.

I ESCAPE FOR A LITTLE PRIVACY TO OUR BEDROOM. ONLY A FEW WEEKS AGO, these walls witnessed the depth of our family despair over the royal deaths and a few hours ago echoed my angst over Sita. Now they are being redecorated with memories of dad. I suggest that I hold myself together before telling mum. But that's not how it works. I find I can't manufacture control as a coping mechanism for grief. It's grief that steps in, as a coping mechanism of it own.

When I tell the twins, like most young children, the girls seem part bulletproof to bad news. The first thing they ask is whether they will have to shave their heads again. Ram takes the news more emotionally. We hug for a long time, reinforcing each other's resolve.

Mum's in her garden when I call. I give her the facts, telling her the reason why Sita has not arrived back. James Munro senior has died. She asks rather callously if Sita saw the body, as if dad might be pulling another disappearing act. I tell her I don't yet know all the details, but she should accept the Avadhoot has ascended.

I sit on our bed thinking I need to put in some housework to get the this room back into a recognisable state for Sita's return. I find clumps of hair, blown by indifference into crevices after our initial family *Mundan*. And there is plenty un-swept incense ash all over the fireplace shrine. As I begin to tidy up I see my dad's Hatha yoga book, placed as it always is on the bookshelf. That's when I lose my shit. The eulogy page in dad's book is sticking out the top. All these years ago, I used it as a place marker... after his first death.

I DON'T SLEEP MUCH THAT EVENING AND IN THE MORNING JUST WHEN MY hair is back to normal, I shave it off once more. Ram chooses to be more Scots about the Avadhoot's passing. He keeps his hair and asks me if the Avadhoot's paintings will now increase in value.

After collecting and unloading new bunk beds from IKEA, I take mum's van back to her. I know that as soon as mum sees me bald, she will be affected, no matter how stoic she's been on our call. The Hindu tradition of *Mundan* takes away any need for words. People can see you are in bereavement.

As I approach her, we hug and I cry. Then mum cries too and for a moment I sense her suffering from this complex distant relationship she's had with dad.

She offers tea and tells me it was dad who encouraged her to use that first separation from him to seek ways to love herself more. She says this brought her to loving him in a different way and she'll always feel grateful for knowing and loving him.

Then mum suddenly shocks me by suggesting that we have a memorial service in Peebles for my dad.

'Why would you suggest this... after all these years of keeping his existence a secret, that you want to give him a memorial service?'

'Not your dad, James Munro,' she says, 'the Avadhoot. A gathering for everyone here who met him and know him as the Avadhoot. I want to give the man a send-off in his native land. Don't you worry, I'll arrange everything.'

43

Six days later, Sita calls from Kathmandu. After exchanging assurances that we are both coping, we talk at length. Two significant deaths have affected our family within two months and I feel a slight sense of desperation without Sita at home.

She tells me that she's managed to pack up dad's house within a day. She hired eight porters to help, and they took two days to walk to the Avadhoot's home and two days to walk back out of the hills. Each porter carried 35 kilos of paintings and Tibetan rugs from dad's underground bunker. She said she found a biscuit tin full of American hundred dollar notes in his studio. She packed up his entire collection of painting and rugs at the airport near Silghari. And from there she's managed to send them along with a few prized books on Hinduism to Scotland as airfreight.

'And what will become of the famous Sanyassin's house?'

'I did think of cremating it, but I decided to give it a sky burial. I've left it for nature to reclaim. Meantime the metal doors are bolted and the Avadhoot's woven bed and slippers are as he left them.'

Sita asks me how Ram and the girls are.

'They want two puppies – one each. They say they deserve it for being good while mummy is away.'

'Why puppies?'

'I've been letting them watch more TV than normal and every child on TV has a puppy. Apparently, I don't make food as nice as you, so I said they could have something special when you return. They've had to suffer in all sorts of ways, they tell me, because I don't let them do things that you allow.'

'I guess so.'

'I now hold the record for inappropriate things I allow them to lick, wear, or throw around.'

'They are likely affected by all these events. Or perhaps they sense how these events have changed us.'

'They've made a safe space under their bed, where the mad prince won't shoot them.'

'How did Ram take the news of the Avadhoot?'

'He's looking after me like any single parent might. He's even invited me out to a lunch party with some of his new school friends.'

'That's nice... that's a breakthrough for him.'

'Also, my mum is proposing we have a memorial service in Peebles for the Avadhoot once you're back.'

'That's a wonderful idea.'

'Why do you say that?'

'It's part of your custom, is it not? Also, your mum deserves it.'

'In what way?'

'She is now truly a single mum.'

'I guess so.'

'When we started the yoga studio, she was particularly helpful to me about single mums. I had no experience with women who bring up children on their own, in Nepal.'

'But you were a single child.'

'No, I was a child singled-out – made unique from my family. There's a difference. Your mum spoke about the many challenges of bringing you up when you first returned to Scotland.'

'It's still too weird for me to think all these years of me growing up here, while dad was alive out there in Nepal.'

'And weirder that I've actually spent more of my life knowing him than you. How karmic is that coincidence, that I should be there at his passing?'

'Tell me what you know about his last moments.'

'You are so like him, James. I thought that when he visited us in Edinburgh, but more so since I came back here. Maybe it's knowing him that attracted me to you.'

'In what way?'

'Well, one thing is you both voice hate at the expression that nothing is impossible. I've heard you both scorn this positive figure of speech whenever people say it or write it. You believe it is not truthful to suggest such things as a universal principle. In both your minds, much in life is indeed impossible, and the more we accept this, the less delusional our life is.'

'I faced just such reality today. It is clearly impossible for me to put up an IKEA bunk bed on my own.'

'Exactly, you both helped me to understand that encouragement alone is useless when assembling bunk beds.'

'I can't wait till you come home.'

'Yes you can.'

'Well, likely possible.'

'I'm going to see Swamy Y and Cindy before I leave. I'll see you very soon.'

'By the way, mum thinks you should give the eulogy.'

I MEET UP WITH RAM AND HIS FRIENDS AT A FAST FOOD RESTAURANT IN THE city centre. They sit at a large table near a play area for younger children. It's in a corner surrounded by bunting and about fifteen of Ram's new friends are gathered. I'm the only adult and Ram introduces me as his father. They all look surprised at this announcement, and I guess it's the unfamiliar concept of interracial families. Ram greets me with what looks like a three-pint carton of coke and a bucket of popcorn. We sit opposite each other and share in the noisy feast.

A young girl at the table next to us is trying to make her friends laugh by repeating the phrase. 'It was so funny... It really was so funny.'

She is laughing hysterically, trying make these words sound funny in themselves. Her audience, however, need more. 'Brian,' she adds, 'his fall it was daft. Did anyone see it?' The more she talks the less her friends find it funny, but they smile out of courtesy. As some begin to look away and talk to each other, she adds an extra really. 'It really, really was so funny... it really was. He fell sideways – but he wasn't hurt.'

Ram looks over the table at me. He senses I'm smiling not at this young lady's story, but at her attempts to make it funny by saying it was funny. He leans over and says, 'You need to be less judgmental.'

'It's the coke,' I say, smiling at him.

'It's a trait and I've inherited it from you. I'm now trying very hard to correct it in myself.'

I smile. 'Just stop drinking coke.'

'How are you coping, dad?'

It seems Ram is currently in a mature mood, so I respond in kind.

'At one point I felt that being a father to my son and being a son to my father was all too challenging for me. I found I was like a confused middle child.'

'What, like Mena in our family?'

'No, not exactly. She's not middle, she's two thirds a second child.'

I realise we are approaching a time when I will have to tell Ram that I'm not his biological father. I justify my silence as protection for the boy. Now never seems the right time. His friends would view him differently at a sensitive friendship time. I suspect my procrastinations over this are as firmly in place as my mother's were in telling me about dad.

I raise my container of coke with both hands, and smile at him. I remember how similar my own thoughts were at his age. I too wanted to correct habits I believed I'd inherited from my parents. I decide I'll tell him the whole story soon. No more secrets. It's a perverted form of empathy to keep such secrets. That protective shroud a parent develops at their child's birth is hard to throw off. At what age will Ram ever be truly ready to hear who his biological father was?

· · ·

SITA LOOKS RADIANT WHEN SHE SEES US ALL. THE GIRLS RUN TOWARDS HER, striking her simultaneously like twin bowling balls. Ram marches over and hugs his mother tightly. We kiss briefly twice. Me her, and then her me, for longer. We head to the flower van, and I notice Sita is carrying a small Thimi pottery jar, the type many tourists buy in Bhaktapur.

'Have you been souvenir shopping at the market?'

'It's the Avadhoot's ashes.'

On the drive home, I ask where dad's funeral was conducted. Sita tells me it was held with great ceremony in Kathmandu and that thousands of people turned up.

'The Minister gave a speech and the priests chanted. Some of the monks from Boudhanath came also. The news of his passing spread quickly across the valley. Swami Y helped with the arrangements. Even the Moni Baba's followers came in numbers. His ashes were collected, and Cindy and I shuffled a few tea glasses full into this container.'

'I didn't think that was a tradition.'

'It's not, but I thought of Maisy's mantlepiece and and thought your mum might like it.'

Meena interrupts and tells Sita that daddy has cleaned up the mad prince's ashes from the fireplace.

Maya says they have waited so long for Sita to come home, and they have behaved so can they now get a puppy dog? Meena says they have waited so long can they have a bigger dog?

I whisper to Sita how proud I am of her. She smiles, then turns her attention to Ram and talks to him in Nepali all the way back into town until we park outside the house.

I keep my emotions bottled in for the children, until we reach the door. Ram sees a few friends playing in the gardens and asks if he can join them. The girls run off too, into the house. As the door closes behind us, Sita stops and takes my hands. 'I prepared his body for cremation, James. He had a tattoo above his heart with the words *Wee James and Helen* and an Om sign.'

I kiss my wife and we hug, tears running down my face.

· · ·

SITA TELLS ME HER DISCOVERIES FROM NEPAL. IF THERE IS JET LAG, THE time difference is obviously in her favour. She seems wide awake. I believe she is talking fast and continuously to help me avoid talking or thinking about dad. Here in the same space we were a few months, our roles are reversed.

'How's Cindy?'

'Good. She told me when she first arrived in Nepal, she loved the place for two weeks. Then she freaked out. Two weeks is the longest she's ever had a holiday. Things all turned smelly and dusty with pollution before monsoon. She said she nearly came back after her 'trades fortnight', whatever that means. She has now built an interesting network of friends through Swamy Y. She lives with him in Bhaktapur. There's a young Kumari being chosen there too. I overheard Cindy arguing with an older priest about it. She said it was OK to preserve traditions but "No tae keep ony future Kumaris locked up in a mud brick room".

'Swami Y is also well informed on the legal side of the issue. it It is now law in Nepal that every child's upbringing is protected by the Convention on Children's Rights. I'm confident things will change.'

'Bravo.'

'James, I know it's your dad that you want to hear about, more than my travel stories.'

I swallow at the mention of dad. 'In your own time,' I say.

'The Avadhoot knew he was going to die. He didn't say anything to me but when he was here in Scotland, apparently he went for a BUPA health check, the day we thought he was missing.'

'The day of his street fight?'

'Yes. He kept it secret, but he told Cindy and Swamy Y in Kathmandu. It was one of the reasons she decided to stay in Nepal. She said it was a quiet way of paying back all that we have done for her. At the BUPA clinic they found substantial damage to your dad's lungs, related to exposure to industrial levels of asbestos. They were confused as to how a man who lived in Asia all his life and was otherwise in such good health, could exhibit this condition. Your dad told Cindy he was exposed to lots of asbestos in the shipyards in Leith as a draughtsman.

He spent years of his apprenticeship in the rusty interior of ships while they were being constructed. Your dad had practiced Pranayama all his life, trying to compensate for this exposure.'

'I had no idea.'

'He regularly went to see doctors in Nepal about his breathing. We believe certain signs of this illness were ignored, because of his overall good health. Anyone seeing swollen fingertips may have put it down to his many hours painting tankas. His swollen toes gave him the look of an average barefooted porter in Nepal. Swami Y believes the Avadhoot died from pleural disease, but we will never really know.

'He'd perfected everything else in his body and had control for the moment that his lungs might finally give up. It all made sense when I heard this. He passed away like a true yogi, peacefully accepting his ascension. He faced the sunset under Boudhanath Stupa and took his last breath. When I reached his house in Dhoti it was almost as if he knew the end was coming and had packed things in readiness for his passing.'

Another secret – to keep or tell?

THE NEXT MORNING, SITA WALKS TOWARDS THE PILE OF MAIL THAT I'VE stacked for her, and like a water diviner she lifts out one.

'Did you not notice where this letter is postmarked?'

'No it's just arrived yesterday and I was up early dealing with some very excited twins. Where's it from?'

Sita opens the letter in front of me. Scanning it quickly she tells me it's from Bill Higgins and contains a leaflet on the opening of the new Jean Higgins School of Yoga Studies in Austin, Texas.

Sita hands me the leaflet which shows a state-of-the-art yoga studio offering classes in a wide range of disciplines. In one highlighted box I see a mention that the centre is non-for-profit and has an honesty box in which people can leave donations to sponsor lessons for people in deprived areas.

Bill's letter says that his wife Jean died peacefully some eight months after visiting Scotland and that she had spent those last months full of enthusiasm for the creation of a new yoga facility in Texas. Bill continued with her plans until the project was completed to her design.

Sita reads, 'It is no Taj Mahal but this was something that I know Jean was most proud of creating and this is primarily due to your advice to her.'

Bill says he was instructed by Jean to enclose a donation for the Edinburgh Yoga Studio as a sister enterprise.

Sita unfolds a cheque for twenty thousand dollars, with a handwritten note saying, 'I hope you'll use some of this to visit us one day.'

44

Eulogy for Sri Avadhoot, written and read by Sita Munro
11:00 AM August 10th, 2001. Peebles, Scotland

'NAMASKAR AND THANK YOU ALL FOR COMING.'

Sita is wearing her white mourning dress from Nepal, with a tweed jacket and laced brown boots. She bows slightly to the audience with her palms pressed together.

At the back of the church, Mahesh returns the namaste sign with his hands. Others follow his example, while the Reverend McRae stands with his arms crossed.

'We are gathered at this memorial Puja to celebrate the life of a unique Nepali Sanyassin known to us as the Avadhoot. He was a follower of the legendary Moni Baba and was also the man who helped to bring James and I together.

'I'd like first to begin by reading a quote from the Avahdoot's guru, the Moni Baba...

'*You either have or have not a relationship with God in your mind. The important thing to appreciate is that it's in your mind where this relationship exists. If you do not believe in or are uncertain about God... that uncertainty will inhabit your thoughts. If you have invested a great deal of belief in God, the results of this faith will also manifest in your mind.*

'I first met the Avadhoot in Nepal, when I was a teenage girl. He was making jokes to farmers in the hills. He told them they had to rise at first light to work in their fields, before followers of the Moni Baba woke up to do their yoga breathing. Otherwise, he said the Baba's followers would practice pranayama and take all the oxygen out the air.

'Both the Avadhoot and the Moni Baba were guided by the idea of conscious love. The Avadhoot was a storyteller and an artist and he took these ancient human skills very seriously. Conscious love cannot be measured, but those who attended the Avadhoot's talk in Edinburgh will remember his references to the predictive brain. In the Avadhoot's opinion, the nearest thing to a research-based description of love comes from using the healing qualities of the word as much as the practice of conscious love for a healthy mind.

'Love – the word itself is perhaps the most used healing word in the world. Given its equivalent translation from all languages, we find the mere mention can resuscitate a troubled mind, soothe a person's anxiety, and gives a sense of wellbeing like no other word can. It is a mental-health potion that all cultures share.

'The Avadhoot also taught me about a world which at the time I had never seen. He had a talent for seeing the gaps in other people's knowledge and he never missed an opportunity to fill these gaps with suggestions. He was special because his search for truth was guided by people's reactions and observations. He changed advice if facts offered a different truth. He suggested that we make faith-based decisions every day in our minds, whether we are religious or not. Many people here today will remember the Avadhoot's prescriptions for health, that certain habits are as curative as drugs.

'In his art, the Avadhoot took the traditional skills of a tanka painter to a new level of communication. Not only did he paint religious deities, but he also included the entertainment deities we worship, the modern characters that influence us. Those who have visited The Yoga Studio will have seen the abstract tanka work of the Avadhoot. James believes that if were given a donation for all the times we've had to answer the question why super heroes are flying in the clouds beside groups of Bhodisatvas in his paintings, we would be rich. Why were they there... because they are influencing our children's minds. They are simply a new social focus for worship.

'I see that Mr and Mrs Miller are here at this gathering today. You both may be interested to know we have a large number of the Avadhoot's latest paintings, which represent the last of his work.

'James has written here in pencil saying in brackets – *commercial break.*'

'For the second time in the past two months, James and I have been reminded of the fragility of human life. Amongst all the news we face every day, our hearts respond differently at specific moments. People like the Avadhoot are mourned by many thousands in Nepal when they pass on, because they have helped us restore our resilience to continue life. Facing life without such people is life's hardest lesson. They are as a father to us.

'I'd like to end this Puja with a musical tribute. This music is something that James and I have already found solace in.

'Fiona, the choir master of this church will now lead the choir to sing a harmony called "Misery Me". It's something I believe was adapted by the popular Scottish composer Mozart.

'And here is the last word from James in pencil. "Before you leave, please be aware there is a donation box at the church entrance, to help buy schoolbooks and to build latrines for schoolgirls in Nepal – the Avadhoot's spiritual resting place."

'Om Shanti Shanti.'

After the choir sing, there is long sustained applause, led by Mahesh and Mandy and the forty or so people in attendance. I see my mum with her head in her hands at the back of the hall with the Reverend's arms around her. A group of Scottish monks from Samye Ling chant outside as people leave the church. As they finish, mum approaches them and introduces the Rinpoche to Minister McRae.

Out of the side of my eye, I spot Babs Miller from Leith talking to Jim and pointing at mum. As the Millers begin to walk towards mum, I step in and interrupt them.

'Good to see you both. What did you think of the service? Do you think you might be interested in looking at the Avadhoot's last work?'

'Excuse me... but is that your mother over there talking to the monks?'

'Yes.'

'So, Helen Munro is her married name? I think I knew her as Helen Lindsay at school in Leith. Is that her maiden name?'

'Yes.'

'I knew she looked familiar. I said to Bob, I think that's Helen Lindsay. What a coincidence. Fancy that. We were very sorry to hear your dad died.'

'You knew?'

'Yes, all those years ago. We heard the news. It was so tragic, after you all went off to India or someplace. Bob knew your dad from the shipyards. I dated him a few times.' She laughs. 'Wasn't my type.'

'Nice service,' says Bob, winking at me. 'We have to go. We'll be in touch about the Avadhoot's paintings.'

ABOUT THE AUTHOR

George McBean spent 36 years working for UNICEF in different parts of the world. From 1982–89 he was stationed in Nepal as Chief of Communication. This fictional story is the second novel influenced by the author's knowledge of the country and his personal interest in public health and yoga. He worked latterly as Head of Graphics and Animation at UNICEF HQ New York. A visual biography of his work was featured in a Retrospective Exhibit at the Oxford Human Rights Festival 2015.

See www.georgemcbean.com for more about George, his writings and illustrations.

facebook.com/IdleGeorge

instagram.com/george.mcbean

ACKNOWLEDGMENTS

I would like to thank those who have supported me in creating this latest book, *Radical Roads*. This book is dedicated to my daughter Ainslie who is now a mother of two daughters, and motivated me to include references to the many preventable health challenges women face in the western systems of Public Health.

To the people at the Scottish Arts Club who have encouraged me to take this story further. To all members of the SAC Writers' Group who read the draft story and gave me feedback. Especially George Wilson, Linda Grieg, Glenys Mclaren, John McLoed, Hilary Munro among others. To friends and readers Callum Campbell, Sangharsha Bhatharai Lindsay, Lou Turnstall and Eleonore Dambre. To Claire Wingfield for her editing and guidance.

Lastly, I'd like to thank my prize-winning novelist wife Sara Cameron McBean, whose writing skills far exceed my own and whose encouragement and conscious love inspire me to try.

Printed in Great Britain
by Amazon

10459983R00192